John Bowen ░░░░░░░░░░░░░░░░░░░░░░ ord. His novels ░░░ ░░░░ ░░░░░░░░ and his stage plays performed in the United States and Europe as well as Britain. He has written award-winning television drama as well as film scripts and radio plays for the stage, taught in a drama school and worked as a drama producer for television.

David Cook was born in Preston, Lancashire and trained as an actor at RADA. He has appeared on TV and in films as well as on stage in the West End. He began writing in 1969 and has won several prestigious prizes for his novels and television plays. His novel, *Missing Persons*, in which Hetty Wainthropp first saw the light of day, is also available from Headline.

Hetty Wainthropp – Woman of the Year is the second set of stories from the highly successful television series, *Hetty Wainthropp Investigates*, which John Bowen and David Cook co-wrote. The first set of stories, also called *Hetty Wainthropp Investigates*, is available from Headline.

Also by John Bowen and David Cook

Hetty Wainthropp Investigates

Also by John Bowen

The Truth Will Not Help Us
After the Rain
The Centre of the Green
Storyboard
The Birdcage
A World Elsewhere
Squeak
The MacGuffin
The Girls
Fighting Back
The Precious Gift
No Retreat

Also by David Cook

Albert's Memorial
Happy Endings
Walter
Winter Doves
Sunrising
Crying Out Loud
Second Best
Missing Persons

Hetty Wainthropp – Woman of the Year

Adapted from
the television series

John Bowen and David Cook

HEADLINE

First published in 1996
by HEADLINE BOOK PUBLISHING

10 9 8 7 6 5 4 3 2 1

ISBN 0 7472 5564 4

Typeset by CBS, Felixstowe, Suffolk

Printed and bound in Great Britain by
Cox & Wyman Ltd, Reading, Berks

HEADLINE BOOK PUBLISHING
A division of Hodder Headline PLC
338 Euston Road
London NW1 3BH

Contents

Poison Pen	1
Runaways	47
The Astral Plane	101
Lost Chords	147
Woman of the Year	199

Poison Pen

£15,000! It was a fortune.

'It's nothing of the kind,' said Robert, who took a serious view of his responsibilities as the Agency's accountant. 'Start thinking like that, and it'll be all gone in no time flat. That fifteen thousand goes into the building society to top up my much depleted redundancy. It'll put us back on our feet, which is something to be thankful for, but just remember there's still two years before the Old Age Pension.'

The Wainthropp Detective Agency had been founded by Mrs Hetty Wainthropp who had discovered a natural talent at the age of sixty and followed her star. Her Junior Partner – plucked from a supermarket check-out – was Geoffrey Shawcross (18). The Agency's accountant, consultant and occasional leg-man was her husband Robert (63). Together they had struggled from one financial crisis to another, one day in search of a missing budgie, the next tracking down a young man whose fingers kept arriving through the post, individually wrapped, at his parents' hotel in Tuscany. Now they had finally hit the jackpot by unmasking an elderly arsonist who had set fire to three houses in the Mid Lancs Area.

This brilliant piece of detection had earned the Agency a reward of £15,000 put up by the insurance companies concerned. The cheque, which was on a piece of cardboard much too large to be handed in at the till of any bank, had been presented to Hetty in the Banqueting Room of a posh hotel in Bolton in the presence of the press and public. There had been champagne with little sausages on sticks which fell off when one dipped them in the sauce provided and tiny triangular sandwiches containing bits of left-over smoked salmon. Photographs had been taken. There had been interviews with local radio and TV. It had all been extremely enjoyable and had made an excellent impression on their neighbours in the village. But success brought its own disadvantages.

Letters and phone-calls. Offers of work. They had longed for work these last few months, and now there was too much. They sat at the kitchen table, which was covered with newspapers. Their local paper, the *Record*, had splashed the presentation ceremony over its front page. A photo of Hetty – one arm round Robert's shoulder, the other round Geoff's and the cardboard cheque propped up between them – went across three columns with the headline

LOCAL DETECTIVES UNCOVER ARSONIST

AND WIN £15,000

The national newspapers had been more restrained, and confined their coverage to inside pages, but there were photos and headlines just the same.

The *Mirror*

SUPERGRAN SLEUTH

FOILS FIRE-RAISER

The *Guardian*

GRANNY KNOWS BEST

The *Telegraph*

Local Initiative in Arson Case

The *Sun*

WHO'S A CLEVER GIRL, THEN?

There were ten letters already that morning, and phone calls.

Robert said, 'You shouldn't have let them print our address in the newspaper.'

'They didn't exactly ask permission.'

They were going to have to choose their cases. They had never had to do so before but had taken whatever was offered. They had no experience of choice.

Geoff had opened one of the letters on the table. 'This one's not a case: it's from an *Avengers* fan. He only wants a photo of you in black leather. That should be easy to satisfy.'

'Where do we get the black leather?'

'Oxfam shop.'

Robert said, 'All we've got to do is take the jobs which are the least work for the most pay.'

'How like a man!'

'I am the accountant. And we are a business.'

'I didn't go into this to make money.' They were both looking at her. Money – or at least the absence of it – had been the Agency's major concern for almost as long as they had been in business.

'Not just to make money,' Hetty said. 'I did it for . . .' and discovered that she couldn't finish the sentence.

'For the interest,' Geoff said. 'You like puzzles, Mrs Wainthropp. So do I.'

'She likes tidying people up.'

'I don't like mess. People whose lives have got into a mess – they ask for help. It's right to help.'

'If you take a proper fee for it.' Robert rooted amongst the letters to find one he had already opened. 'There's one here – deckle-edged notepaper with the address embossed – a man of means who can afford to pay.'

'I never expected to have to choose. Reject people. It's not my nature.'

There was the sound of the second post dropping through the letter box onto the lino in the hall. Robert went to collect it. Geoff said, 'Life is choice, Mrs Wainthropp.'

There were four letters. One could be easily recognised and discarded as being an announcement that the Wainthropp household, almost uniquely amongst those of the Darwen/Blackburn/Bolton area, had come through all the preliminary stages of a Prize Draw and had only to order a profusely illustrated copy of *Pond Life of Guadeloupe* to qualify for the final. Beneath it was a cheap envelope with the name and address of the Agency roughly printed in capital letters. It looked odd, even threatening. Robert began to open it as he returned to the kitchen.

'Funny one here!'

He handed the letter to Hetty, who opened it and began to read.

It was on a single sheet of lined paper, printed in rough capitals like those on the envelope:

4

THIS IS A POISON PEN LETTER
IT COULD BE ABUSIVE . . . OBSCENE
IT COULD ACCUSE YOU OF CRIMES
YOU COULDN'T PROVE YOU DIDN'T COMMIT
IT COULD THREATEN TO KILL YOU
IN VERY NASTY WAYS
OR HURT YOUR CHILDREN

Robert said, 'That's sick.' There was a ring at the front door. 'Damn!' He went quickly to answer. The doorbell rang again. 'All right, I'm coming!' He opened the door. There was a woman, middle-aged, soberly but smartly dressed, standing outside.

'Wainthropp Detective Agency?'

'No callers at the house.'

Hetty was at the open door to the kitchen. She still had the letter in her hand. The woman said, 'You got my letter, I see.'

Hetty said, 'You'd better come in.'

The village school in Shepton Fell stands next to the church. At the end of the morning break the children were rushing about in the playground, partly to keep themselves warm on a wintery day, but mainly because rushing about was what the playground was for. Three teachers in heavy overcoats, all women, watched the children and thought, If only it will start to rain, we can all go indoors.

The headmaster, John Winterton, was also watching the children from the window of his office. The children were not conscious of his watching: the three teachers were. Inside the office the telephone rang and he answered. The teachers heard it ring. Mrs Bell, the oldest of the three, said to Miss Ratley, who looked after the littlies, 'I think we know who that'll be,' and

5

Miss Ratley said, 'You can't help feeling sorry.'

John Winterton was flushed and although, in these days of education cuts, his office was by no means overheated, he was sweating. He said to the caller at the other end, 'There's no truth in it, Mrs Bransby, none at all: I hardly need to tell you that. Obscene lies! Filth! Just like all the others.'

Mrs Bransby had received a letter – roughly drawn capitals on cheap lined paper. But this letter had been photocopied and a distribution list, which included the local police and the local paper, had been printed at the bottom. It lay open in front of her by the telephone. 'I don't know what to think, Mr Winterton. Copies seem to have been sent everywhere; it's very embarrassing. I can't talk to Tommy about it: they have trained social workers for that kind of thing. All he says is, "Everyone knows I'm his favourite." Meanwhile it seems better to keep him out of school.'

John Winterton put down the telephone. He closed his eyes to stop the room spinning. But it continued to spin.

The name of the middle-aged woman was Miss Helga Alloway from the village of Shepton Fell, north of Ackersley. For two years the village had been plagued by poison pen letters – obscene abuse, accusations, death threats sent out like scatter-shot, almost it seemed at random, usually to individuals but sometimes copies of specific accusations would be broadcast to everyone of influence in the village as well as some outside. Nobody knew who the Poison Pen was and the police seemed to be unable to act. Then Miss Alloway had read in the *Record* about the unmasking of The Butcher of Burnley arsonist and had decided to approach the Wainthropp Detective Agency.

'But why should *you* pay for an investigation?'

'Because I'm the prime suspect.' They looked at her. Geoff

put down the pen with which he was making notes. She seemed singularly unruffled by what she was admitting and happy to explain. 'Repressed middle-aged spinster living alone, watching the village from my first floor window. Classic case!'

'What are you repressing?'

'Disappointment mainly. A wasted life. Of course most people do feel they've wasted their lives when they reach my age.'

'I don't. And I'm older than you by at least ten years,' said Hetty.

'You're lucky. I was an accountant, good at my job, but the firm was taken over and I was made redundant. Then I discovered that there were lots of accountants as good as I was, most of them men and most of them younger. I lost heart.'

Robert knew the feeling. 'Right,' he said.

'Wrong,' said Hetty.

'Maybe. Anyway my parents were old. I came back to the village to look after them. They died and left me reasonably comfortable if you're worried about your fee.'

Robert said, 'How much were you thinking?'

'Six hundred. Three hundred down, the rest when the job's done.'

It seemed to Geoff that it would do no harm and might do good to upgrade Robert in front of this dauntingly self-possessed woman. 'Mr Wainthropp's an accountant,' he said and was alarmed to get a glare from Robert in return.

'Oh, really?'

'Store-keeper,' said Robert. 'I've no qualifications. They made me redundant too where I used to work. Called it early retirement but it came to the same. I do the accounts for the Agency. They've not been very complicated up to now.'

Hetty said, 'You're serious about being the prime suspect?'

'Oh, yes. I was attacked last week, verbally at any rate and very much in public. Mrs Harrow. Youngish couple – yuppies – two children: they bought a house in the village and he commuted to Preston. Poison Pen picked on her, must have harried her privately for a while, then suddenly everybody knew what she got up to in the afternoons. They've moved out, the whole family and a spaniel puppy, into a small flat somewhere near his job. Removal van outside the house, the Harrows start to pile into the car, then suddenly she leaps out into the middle of the road in the rain, looking up at my window, waving her arms and screaming threats. And now *that*'s all round the village too. You'd probably better talk to her. I'll give you the address.'

'How do you know the address?'

'Mrs Garbet at the post office forwards their mail.'

'Have you had any of these poison pen letters yourself?'

'A few. Some sexual. Some actually accusing me of writing the letters, but those could have been from anyone.'

Robert said, 'Six hundred! And no knowing how long it'll take. With all the publicity, we have had other cases offered – that table's littered, as you can see. When you consider what we're in a position to charge—'

Hetty said, 'We'll accept the case. It's not a question of money: it's a question of need. There'll be expenses on top, but we're not extravagant. I don't see why the police can't help. You'd think they'd be able to do something.'

So Hetty went first to talk to Detective Chief Inspector Adams, who had become almost a friend since their falling out over a piece of evidence which had found its way onto her shoe and been temporarily withheld during the arson case.

'Just don't tell me it's a low priority.'

'Worse! It's an impossible job.'

'Local postmark.'

'Means they were posted anywhere in the Ackersley area.'

'Fingerprints.'

'Lots on the envelopes, none on the actual letters. He or she wears gloves. Paper you can buy anywhere.'

'They'd have to lick the stamps. There's something in spit.'

'DNA. Have you any idea how much a DNA test of the whole village would cost? And we can't force people to give samples. It's not a custodial crime. A nuisance, not a felony.'

'Nuisance! There's folk left their homes. I've a couple to see tomorrow moved out to a flat in Preston with two children and a springer spaniel. There's marriages broken. There's a woman on tablets for her nerves.'

'Can you prove she wouldn't be on tablets anyway? The Sergeant at Ackersley is doing his best, but as you say it's a low priority –' She had said nothing of the sort: it was she who had told him not to say it was a low priority. '– and anyway it's not a case for expensive forensics. It's not logical, it's psychological. Twisted motives. Think laterally. Don't get me wrong, Mrs Wainthropp: I'm delighted you're taking it on, but I tell you frankly you're on a hiding to nothing.'

So Hetty went home, thoughtful, from the police station. Perhaps she had acted too quickly in rolling over Robert's objections and taking on the job. Perhaps she had bitten off more than she could chew. Robert and Geoff would not say so, they would never tell her that she had acted without thinking and involved the Agency in failure, but she would be able to read their thoughts in their faces.

Ungrateful pair! They had forgotten that without her there would *be* no Agency. If you don't bite off more than you can

9

chew occasionally, you might never get anything worthwhile to chew at all.

She certainly had no intention of apologising if it all came to grief.

Meanwhile Geoff, who was also thoughtful for reasons of his own, had gone to find Robert on the allotment.

The afternoon was damp and cold; there had been rain and would be again. Robert was moodily communing with the Brussels sprouts, nipping out those which had gone bushy and would come to nothing. 'Six jobs on hold, all paying better money,' he said. 'I shouldn't be on the ground in this weather. Impacting the soil!'

Geoff was diffident. 'I've been thinking you and me might take on one of the other cases ourselves.'

There was a silence. Robert's right hand in a woolly mitten was curved over a sprout. 'We'd have to tell her.'

'Not immediately.'

'Which one?'

'Deckle-edge?'

'I've never kept anything from her, y'know. At least not very often.' Robert was dithering, but within the dither, Geoff could see, a decision was beginning to form. 'Nothing really important.'

'We'll need transport.'

'Not a car, Geoffrey. Once and for all—'

'It's an investment. We can use the reward money.'

'Which is invested already in the Leeds & Holbeck where it will remain. What's wrong with your friend's scooter?'

'We can't rely on it. She sometimes uses it.'

'Then find out if she'll sell. We might be able to afford that if you can get it cheap enough.'

Supper that night was a silent meal. All parties had something to conceal.

* * *

Morning at Shepton Fell. Mr Cullimore, once the respected village policeman, now a mere senior citizen without responsibilities, stood on the hill outside the village looking down on it. He was fond of this view; you could see the whole village spread out and count the houses, which were mainly in stone terraces with slate roofs – very little new building. It was a tourist village in summer, but this was not summer; the comings and goings were few once the rush hour of commuting yuppies was over. He could see the church, the village school, the general store, the sub post office. The fish van would be along shortly. Once a week, the fish. Mobile library tomorrow.

There was a car coming up behind him. Not the fish van. It was, he saw, that Mrs Harrow's car, and she had a passenger with her. The Harrow house was up for sale; perhaps the passenger was being brought to view – a respectable-looking body, he noticed, as the car passed him: it would likely be a change for the better.

The car stopped in a lay-by a little below the brow of the hill. Mrs Harrow would be giving her passenger a chance to admire the view. 'Shep! On our way! Home!' Mr Cullimore said to his dog, a collie, and stepped out briskly. He would be able to sneak another look at Mrs Harrow's passenger as he went by.

Mrs Harrow looked sulky, which wasn't new: Violet Dabney, who used to clean for the Harrows, always said that any inconvenience brought Mrs Harrow out in sulks. Her passenger wore a light blue beret and had a strong chin, a chin with some character to it, probably a chin you could trust. Mr Cullimore waved to Mrs Harrow and to the chin as he strode by.

Geraldine Harrow said to her passenger, 'If you're a detective, who's paying you?'

'I'm afraid I'm not at liberty to reveal the name of my client.' Hetty had caught Geraldine just about to leave for Shepton Fell where she had an appointment with prospective buyers to view the house, and had jumped at the chance of a lift which would provide a cover while she took an initial look around. But it had been an uneasy drive. It was clear that the woman would only co-operate with the investigation on her own terms, which included malice.

Geraldine said, 'You don't need to go to Shepton Fell to find out who's writing the letters. It's Miss Alloway.'

'How do you know?'

'Who else would it be? She watches everyone.'

'Selling your house and moving back to town, it's a big step.'

Geraldine put the car into gear. 'We haven't sold it yet.'

They came down the hill into the village and parked outside the house with its 'FOR SALE' sign. Geraldine glanced up at the first floor of the house opposite as she left the car, and Hetty thought she could see a woman step back from the window.

The rooms were bare. Their steps echoed. Hetty said, 'What did the letters accuse you of doing?'

'Personal matters. Private. All lies.' Geraldine looked at her watch. 'They're late. People don't think. I've a child to collect from school.'

'If they were lies, Miss Alloway wouldn't have seen anything because there'd have been nothing to see.'

'What she saw . . . she made something of it. But there was nothing, okay? We'd only been here two years. We wanted fresh air and scenery for the children. Then the letters. Just insults at first – calling names, yuppies and such. Then worse. Sick. And at the end – copies sent all over.' She was weeping, her face red with tears and anger. 'You can see everything from that bloody

12

window. And the village people looking at me from the corners of their eyes! Talking!' Silence. Hetty watched. Geraldine recovered herself and looked at her watch again. 'Quarter to twelve! What kind of time is that? If people are serious about buying a house, you'd think they'd be punctual.'

A car drew up outside. Hetty said, 'I'll go down the street for a while and ask about.'

She decided to start at the village shop, which seemed to be a combination of small supermarket and gift shop. As well as the cold cabinet of breaded cod and frozen peas and the packets of sugared cereals, jars of instant coffee and boxes of tea bags, there were racks of picture postcards of the village and its surroundings, souvenirs of wood and pottery which may or may not have been local though Hetty had her doubts, a display of jams with handwritten labels, cakes wrapped in cellophane and a pick 'n mix tray of candies – pink and white coconut ice, chocolate fudge, peanut brittle and a pile of bright orange lozenges which might have been anything.

'It's all local produce,' said the old lady behind the counter. 'Coconut ice – that's old village, and so is the fudge.'

Hetty pointed to the orange lozenges, 'And those?'

'Mango Surprise. New village: it doesn't sell. If you were thinking of jam, I've a good selection. Cakes – Victoria Sponge, which is what they mainly make at the WI. They take a stall at Ackersley market and the left-overs come to me.'

'I remember the village shop when I was a girl. They had Mint Humbugs in a jar.'

Mr Cullimore had left Shep outside the door and popped in for a packet of Lean Cuisine to heat up in his microwave. 'Gobstoppers,' he said. 'Licorice Bootlaces. Sherbet Cushions.'

'Those days are gone,' the old lady said. 'We mustn't hanker.'

And to Hetty, 'Have you made a decision?'

'Fudge. They mix in, do they, the old and the new?'

'They mix. "Mix in" might be overstating the situation. A pound of fudge, you said?'

'Half a pound.'

'Gift-wrapped? It is extra, but worth the expense.'

'Gift-wrapped. I was wondering who was mainly getting those poison pen letters, old or new villagers.'

Suddenly there was an atmosphere in the shop. The old lady went into slow motion with the weighing of the fudge: Hetty could see the stiffness come into her shoulders and hear a sharp, disapproving intake of breath from Mr Cullimore. Good! All reactions were interesting to an impartial investigator. They were looking at each other across her. Soon one would speak, probably the old man. Mr Cullimore said, 'You're from some bloody newspaper, aren't you? Pardon my French.'

'Do I look like a reporter?'

'They come in all sizes.'

'They've been here? Asking questions.'

The old lady gave Hetty the box of fudge, gift-wrapped, with the air of a prime minister shuffling his Cabinet. 'We prefer not to talk to the media. It's a private matter between ourselves. That'll be three pounds fifty.' Hetty was appalled. Did they take her for a southerner? 'Including the gift box with moorland view.'

She decided not to make a fuss. 'I'll require a receipt,' she said; the fudge would have to go down on expenses. 'I'm not one of your reporters, I've only come to see the village. Mrs Harrow gave me a lift from Preston. It was her told me about the letters.'

'Bad business!' Mr Cullimore said. 'Poor woman! Something like that. Everyone knowing.'

'Something like what?'

'Black lace came into it, as I've heard,' the old lady said. 'And latex underwear.'

'You believed it?'

'No . . . Oh, no.'

Mr Cullimore said, 'Nobody believed it.'

'But when it's been made public, it's bound to stick in your mind,' the old lady said.

'Makes for an unpleasant atmosphere.'

'Yes,' said Hetty, 'I can see that.'

Mr Cullimore walked her back to the Harrow house. Now that he was convinced that she was not a vulture from the media, he was free with his information.

'New villagers are yuppies – people with money . . . jobs in town . . . pay over the odds for their houses because it's an area of scenic beauty. When it snows, they work from home on lap-top computers.'

'And the old villagers?'

'Grub a living from traditional village occupations.'

'Mostly farming, I suppose?'

'Bed-and-breakfast, jobbing gardening, cleaning, living off the Welfare. There's not many agricultural jobs these days. Sheep aren't labour-intensive.'

They reached the house as the people who had come to view were driving away. Geraldine was standing in the open door. Almost automatically Hetty glanced up at the first floor window across the road, but Miss Alloway was not to be seen.

'Here she is, Mrs Harrow,' said Mr Cullimore, 'I've brought her back safe and sound. Good day to you.'

Miss Alloway's first floor was one long room from front to back. At the back, overlooking the garden, was her work-table with the computer. Miss Alloway was on the Internet. She put up

a menu of newsgroups, settled on 'Crime', went down the list to
'Crime, Community,' keyed in her code name, 'Country Girl',
and then the subject, 'Re: Poison Pen'.

The deckle-edged gentleman was a Mr Harold Skimmer. Robert
conducted the initial interview by telephone and closed the deal
at five hundred a week plus. Then he and Geoff waited for Hetty
to come home.

Geoff took a foil dish from the freezer. 'What's this? Hake à
la mode de Cannes? February 1989.'

'Better not.' Surprised, Geoff put the foil dish back again.
'She sees these things on TV but they never come out right. There's
some scrag end at the back of the fridge. We'll make hot pot.'

Geoff took potatoes and onions from the vegetable rack. 'How
are we going to tell her?'

'Straight out. Best way. Have we got any stock cubes? I'll
boil a kettle.' The front door was heard opening. 'She's back.'

'Don't you ever get tired of hot pot?'

'It's safe and easy. And entirely free from additives.'

Hetty came in from the hall. She looked tired and a little grim.
Robert abandoned the straight out approach. 'Had a good day,
love? You look tired. Shall I get you some Dubonnet?'

Geoff said, 'We've got something to tell you.'

'Won't it keep? That Mrs Harrow's been bending my ear all
afternoon. It needs time to straighten.' She saw the vegetables
on the chopping board. 'Hot pot, is it?'

Geoff waited for Robert, and Robert waited for inspiration.
Geoff decided to give the process a push. 'Straight out you said,
Mr Wainthropp.'

'Straight out what?'

'It's not important really.'

'Yes, it is,' said Geoff.

Robert said, 'You remember the deckle-edged notepaper, the man of substantial means? Well, Geoffrey and me are under-employed at the moment, and with so many cases pending there's an effect on cash flow, an imbalance, you might say, which requires correcting.'

'They need our services, Mrs Wainthropp, but they won't wait for ever and there's nowt for us to do here when you're out on your own. We've taken on a case.'

Hetty said, 'I'll have that Dubonnet now.'

John Winterton stood in the dark of the street in Shepton Fell, gazing up at Miss Alloway's first floor window. When he had gathered enough courage he rang the front-door bell and Miss Alloway came down to let him in.

She took him upstairs into the warm lighted room which functioned as both living room and study and drew the curtains. He was standing in front of the sofa, dripping rain onto the carpet. He said, 'You've heard?'

'Everybody's heard.'

'People say you write the letters.'

'How could I have known the details?'

'There are no details. It's not true. Nothing happened.'

'If you say so.'

Mr Winterton, head teacher, began to cry. He sank onto the sofa and sat there, arms tight across his chest, head bowed in hopeless tears. 'What am I to do?'

She came to him, and stood for a moment, looking down, her face expressionless. Then she sat beside him, put her arms round him and held him against her as he wept. 'Cry if you want to. It'll pass. Believe me, it will pass.'

* * *

'One case at a time. We'll come to the deckle-edged gentleman in a minute. DCI Adams said I was to think laterally. I'm not sure how to go about it.'

'Lie on your back on the floor with your eyes closed and say the first thing that comes into your head.'

'Is that really it?' Geoff nodded. 'He's got a funny idea of how we go on here. There's no room for that kind of behaviour.'

'If you don't mind me saying so, Mrs Wainthropp, why are you keeping this case to yourself?'

'I'm not. We're discussing it.'

'Discussing it's not the same as doing it.'

'Mrs Harrow wouldn't have talked freely in front of you, Geoffrey.'

'Do any of them? Talk? Freely?'

'None, come to think of it. They're afraid. Who's writing the letters? Whose turn next?'

'Does everyone get them?' Robert said.

'Can't tell. Seems they keep it to themselves until it's public and then say it's all lies. It may be something to do with old villagers and new villagers – the new villagers mainly get them. But I've too little to go on and I don't even know how to find out.'

'Lateral thinking.'

Robert said, 'You'd have to get one of the letters yourself.'

'You what?'

'If you was one of them – persecuted like by correspondence – on the receiving end – they might trust you.'

'You've not even laid down on the floor yet.' There was no doubt Robert did come up with some surprising ideas. 'I'd have to be living there. Temporary.'

Robert looked at Geoff and Geoff looked at Robert. If Hetty were to go and live in Shepton Fell for a while, they'd have a clear hand with Mr Skimmer. Five hundred a week plus. How long would she be away?

They were such children sometimes. Did they believe she didn't know what was in their minds? 'All right,' said Hetty, 'I'll give it a try. Now . . . the deckle-edged gentleman!'

Robert coughed. It was a case conference and he was in the chair. 'He's thinking of getting wed – a serious intention. He wants us to check up on the lady in question.'

'We don't do divorce.'

'They're not married yet.'

'It'll end in divorce. Bound to, if he's already checking up on her before the wedding.'

Geoff said, 'He saw a programme on telly. They do it in America. Hire a private eye to make sure your intended is the faithful type.'

'How?'

'The way it's usually done . . . well, you get someone to make themselves agreeable like, and if she responds . . .'

Robert was uncomfortable. 'You could call it—'

'Entrapment,' said Geoff.

'In the nicest possible way.'

Hetty looked from one to the other. 'And which of you two clowns will be making himself agreeable?' They could not answer. 'Well, you can't start immediately, I'll need Geoffrey to go to the reference library first.'

Geoff spent the morning in the reference library with a copy of *The Beginner's Background to Modern Art in Ten Easy Lessons*, making detailed notes which Hetty committed to memory on the journey to Shepton Fell. She arrived by the afternoon bus from Ackersley. Her costume, in which thornproof tweed, denim and waterproof plastic made an uneasy *ménage à trois*, was a compilation from every charity shop within range. She wore stout brogues and carried a heavy rucksack on her back; a camera in a waterproof case hung around her neck and a sketch pad and portable easel were fastened to the rucksack. She was that dauntless artist Tara Hall, a painter of rocks.

She returned to the village shop where, on the previous day, she had noticed cards in the window advertising Bed and Breakfast. She would need directions, information about what sort of accommodation was on offer and, if she was going to have to traipse around the village, somewhere safe to leave her rucksack.

Mrs Garbet, the old lady behind the counter, was doubtful. 'Bed and Breakfast? Well, I don't know. I really can't say.'

'Don't you remember me? I came yesterday for a quick look-see at the village. I was fascinated. It's got such possibilities.'

'I thought you were one of them reporters.'

'I'm a painter. Tara Hall. Perhaps you've heard of me?'

'No.' The only other customer in the shop, Mrs Fairbrother, a lady even older than Mrs Garbet, put down the packet of Atora Beef Suet which had held her interest so far and came to join the discussion. 'Have *you* heard of her?' said Mrs Garbet to Mrs Fairbrother.

'I've never heard of her.'

'Surprising that,' Hetty said. 'I've quite a reputation among Royal Academy circles. But maybe you don't get to the Royal Academy as often as you might like.'

'It's radio I mainly listen to,' Mrs Fairbrother said. 'I don't watch the television because of my eyes. I've been waiting two years for the cataracts but the call never comes.'

Mrs Garbet remained suspicious. 'Painters come in summer. We get no winter painters here.'

'I'm on a field trip. Just sketch pad and camera and a change of undies: I'm used to travelling rough. Rocks are my speciality. There's a card in your window – the Old Forge.'

'Old Forge never do B&B in the winter. They've got his mother with them.'

Mrs Fairbrother said, 'Glebe Cottage she might get in if she don't mind mice.'

'I do mind mice.'

Miss Alloway came into the shop. Hetty, who was facing the counter, did not see her enter, but the two women at once became stiff and ill at ease.

'Good morning!'

Mrs Fairbrother said sourly, 'Miss Alloway'll know. She knows everything.' And Mrs Garbet said, 'This lady's a painter of rocks looking for b&b.'

Hetty turned to face Helga Alloway and said, 'Tara Hall.'

Helga had not been warned of Hetty's arrival, far less that the Founder of the Wainthropp Detective Agency was a mistress of disguise, but she did not blink an eye. 'Rocks? I think I've heard of you. Rocks . . . yes: wasn't there something in one of the Sunday colour supplements?' and then to Mrs Garbet, 'Beryl Pacey might take her. They've converted the pigeon loft.'

'That's right: they have.'

'Summer visitors, but they might take one early.'

'I'd never have believed it,' Mrs Fairbrother said. 'Jim was in love with them birds.'

'Love fades when you've got osteoarthritis.'

'It *is* warm?' Hetty said.

'Don't worry. There's a paraffin heater. And en suite bathroom where they used to keep the corn.'

Mrs Garbet said, 'I'll phone Beryl.'

'Has it got a north light?'

While Mrs Garbet dialled the number, Hetty explained her technique to the other two women. 'First I capture the essence in charcoal, and work it up into a masterpiece in my studio later.'

'Where is your studio?'

'Accrington.'

Mrs Garbet said, 'Beryl there's a lady here wants to rent your pigeon loft. No, she's not a fancier; she paints rocks. Rocks – R,O, – that's right. And she'll need a north light.' She turned to Hetty. 'Will you be requiring packed lunches and an evening meal?'

It looked as if the pigeon loft was available and would suit. Helga Alloway went with Hetty to show her the way. Hetty said, 'All their defences went up the moment you walked into the shop.'

'I told you; they think I write the letters.'

The loft turned out to be a wooden structure on a concrete plinth. If you wanted to be complimentary you might say that it looked a little like a Swiss chalet. But there was hot and cold water and electricity and a comfortable bed into which two people might fit snugly and one easily. The windows were double-glazed, there was a haircord carpet on the floor, the walls were papered with a motif of doves holding up trailing ribbons of pink and blue, and the furniture, what there was of it, was solid and clean. High up in one wall was a tiny window with a wooden shelf of the same width beneath it. This was where the pigeons used to enter after an outing.

Helga helped Hetty off with her rucksack while Beryl Pacey showed off the room.

22

'Through there to the bathroom and toilet. I hope you like a shower.' Since no option was on offer, Hetty said she did. 'Wardrobe, writing table, chest-of-drawers, armchair, it's a bit of a squeeze but I'm sure you'll manage. There's no TV. You're welcome to watch with Jim and me if there's owt you don't want to miss.' There was a tapping at the little window. 'Shut up, Bertie.'

Hetty and Helga looked up. A racing pigeon was outside the window tapping at the glass. Beryl waved at it to go away. 'That's Bertie. We couldn't bear to have him put down. He keeps trying to get back in. He doesn't understand, y'see, about the change of use, but we expect he'll learn. There'll be tea and fruit loaf in the parlour in ten minutes. Let me know if you need anything.'

And she had gone. Helga said, 'I'm sure you'll be comfortable. They're good people.'

'How long will it take before everyone in the village knows I'm here?'

'Old village by this evening. New villagers don't always notice.'

'I need them to trust me.'

'Unlikely.'

'I thought . . . if I was to get one of the letters . . .'

Helga looked at her, appraising Robert's idea. 'Ah! Good! Very good!'

'I'll write it myself. I brought some of that cheap paper and a black pen.'

'Wouldn't be convincing. You'd never be able to bring yourself to write the words. I'll do it myself now and get it into the post by half past four.'

Meanwhile outside the village an elderly saloon car had been parked in the lay-by used by Hetty and Mrs Harrow the day before. John Winterton was slumped in the driving seat. He appeared to be asleep. One of the rear windows was not quite closed and a rubber hose had been jammed through it, projecting into the car. The other end had been attached to the exhaust pipe. The engine of the car was running.

A cyclist wheeled his cycle over the brow of the hill, mounted thankfully, and began the downwards ride to the village. He glanced at the car in the lay-by as he passed and before he had gathered speed, but continued on his way.

Then the penny dropped. The cyclist jammed on his brakes, turned his cycle, went down four gears and began the painful grind back up the hill.

Geoff, dressed to kill in the suit bought from the Sue Ryder shop which he wore for client interviews, came downstairs to join Robert, who was also wearing his best suit with a white handkerchief in the breast pocket and a dazzling white shirt. He had shaved (for the second time that day) and there was a small piece of bloodstained cotton wool on the side of his chin. Geoff said, 'Just as well I can iron shirts. Will you be taking off that bit of cotton wool before we get there?'

Meanwhile Hetty had settled in, consumed fruit loaf and tea with Beryl and Jim Pacey, who seemed to have very little in the way of general conversation, and made a tour of the village, watched from behind curtains by the old villagers, unnoticed by the new. She stood outside the Norman church, looking at the bulk of it against the night sky. There was light inside – not the whole body of the church, just the area of the choir and altar. She decided to go in.

As she pushed open the heavy door she heard the sound of a

vacuum cleaner and advanced towards the lighted area where a woman unknown to her was vacuuming the choir stalls and Mr Cullimore was polishing brass.

'Is it all right to come in and sit?'

The woman switched off the vacuum cleaner. 'It's a church. All welcome.'

Mr Cullimore said, 'You're that reporter.'

'Painter.'

'Of rocks. We know that now.'

The woman said, 'I didn't.'

'Then you must be a newcomer.'

'I wouldn't say that. Five years.'

Mr Cullimore grunted. 'Twenty more, and you may begin to qualify.'

'Twenty more years, George, and you'll be dead. *We'll* be the old villagers then.' And to Hetty, 'I'm Janet Bransby.'

'Tara Hall.'

'I'll put you on the grapevine for one piece of news anyway, Janet, 'cos I know it'll interest you,' said Mr Cullimore. 'John Winterton. Les Padmore found him this afternoon in his car up the hill.'

Mrs Bransby's tone was bleak. 'I've heard.'

Hetty said, 'Who's John Winterton?'

'Head teacher at the school where Janet's little boy used to go. Tried to end his life. Coward's way out. The Good Lord decides when it's your time to go.'

Mrs Bransby switched on the vacuum cleaner. Hetty sat for a quarter of an hour with her eyes closed hoping that the little grey cells might receive inspiration, but they did not: the noise of the vacuum cleaner was too intrusive.

* * *

Geoff sat in the front passenger seat of Mr Harold Skimmer's
Rolls Royce which was parked a little way down the street from
Club Jericho. He had never sat in a Rolls before, and would have
liked more people to see him, preferably people with whom he
had been at school – Lizzie Ollerenshaw might have been top
favourite – but Harold, who occupied the driver's seat, was shy
of observation. They could see the neon sign of the club and hear
the distant music and what Harold was sure was the sound of
lascivious revelry.

Harold was in his mid-forties, five foot seven and a half in
platform shoes, with sparse hair brushed forwards over a shiny
pate. He wore spectacles with thick lenses in a heavy frame,
sported a Hitler moustache and hoped that he would command
respect, but his hope was vain. He had inherited a family bakery
founded by his grandfather and built up by his father. By the time
his father died, when Harold was twenty-five, there were branches
all over the north.

Since then the business had run itself, and Harold had lived
with his mother in domestic contentment: she wore the trousers.
Now his mother was dead also. It was most unsettling. He had
not known how to replace her. But there was a young lady at the
chemist's where he used to take his mother's prescriptions, who
had always been cheerful and friendly in a respectful way, and
was probably quite the thing if you liked that sort of thing, and
they had got into conversation and one thing had led to another
and the upshot was that Harold had proposed marriage. And then
the doubts had begun.

'We're famous for Eccles cakes and parkin – the true taste of
the north.'

'Yes,' Geoff said. 'You told us.'

'I'm a good catch, y'see. Those were mother's very last words

26

– "You're a good catch, Harold, for any young lady. You must be wary."'

'You said.'

'Every Friday they go out, the four of them. Girls' Night.'

'An innocent outing. Old school friends. You said.'

'Right. But *they're* all married and she's divorced. Can Mr Wainthropp see her through the window, do you think?'

'Discos don't have windows, Mr Skimmer.'

'Is she enjoying herself a little too much? Dancing close with strangers and such?'

They could see Robert now coming towards them on his way back from the club. 'I never thought when I first saw her on the cosmetics counter that it would come to this,' Mr Skimmer said.

Robert had reached the Rolls. 'They won't let me in. Members only, they said, but I think they took against the suit.'

The table was laid for Hetty's breakfast – orange juice, a boiled egg, toast, butter, honey and tea. There was a letter propped against the tea-cosy, a cheap envelope addressed in black capital letters to 'Miss (!) Tara Hall, Old Hatch Cottage, Shepton Fell, Ackersley, Lancs.'

Beryl Pacey said, 'There's a letter for you.' She stood over the breakfast – her first breakfast for her first paying guest – as if to present it. Her husband Jim, badly arthritic with a stick, was by the door.

'Can't be. Nobody knows I'm here.'

'Didn't you leave a forwarding address?'

'I'm a free spirit, Mrs Pacey. Us artists are. Anyway I didn't know where I'd be staying.' Hetty picked up the letter. 'Local postmark.'

'I don't see how it could be local.'

'Only local people know.'

Hetty opened the letter and took out a single sheet of the same lined paper with the capital letters walking across it. The Paceys were watching her. They knew what the letter was all right, had known from the look of the envelope. She started to read.

It was like being hit in the stomach. She felt sick. Obscene suggestions, explicit about what the writer would like to do to Tara Hall, the words – Miss Alloway had been right: she would never have been able to bring herself to write such words in such a letter. When the chips were down, Hetty was chapel through and through.

'It's vile, is this.' She put the letter down. 'There's been a mistake made.'

Mrs Pacey was defensive. 'It's addressed to you.' Her husband moved forward to take it. 'I'll tear it up.'

'I'll keep it.' Hetty put the letter away in Tara Hall's thornproof pocket. 'Seems to me . . . You're not surprised.'

'We are surprised.'

'At me getting the letter, yes. But you knew what it was before I opened it.'

She looked from Jim to Beryl Pacey. Neither could meet her gaze. Jim said, 'What you're asking . . . have we ever had one like it?'

'That's part of what I'm asking, yes.'

'No, but we know folks as have.'

'I walked round the village last night. I went into the church. They told me what happened to the head teacher at the school.'

Jim was harsh. 'Nothing happened to him. He did it himself. And even then he made a muck of it.'

He left the room angrily, his stick thumping on the floor. Hetty sat down and finished her breakfast before taking her sketch pad and camera out to the seventeenth-century stone bridge over the river Hodder a mile down the road, where she had arranged to meet Helga Alloway for a bit of a conflab.

She sat on a stone slab under the bridge, protected by one layer of plastic, two of good woollen cloth and one of terylene, and sketched with a stick of charcoal as they talked. Helga's car was parked on the road above them.

Hetty said, 'There doesn't seem to be much sympathy for him in the village.'

'I suppose they believe what was in the letter.'

'And was it true?'

'There is a history. It was long ago just after he left training college, somewhere in the Midlands, I think, and never more than affectionate behaviour. Here he's kept out of trouble and done a good job. Until the letters started. Kept on. Got worse.'

'If they were anything like the one you wrote me . . .'

'Sorry to shock you but I wanted you to know what you're dealing with. John Winterton's were horrible – terrified him and yet inflamed his imagination. He cracked under the stress and did something stupid. Then the last letter arrived. Copies to the boy's mother, the local paper and the police.'

'You seem to know a lot about him.'

'Knowing about people is my hobby.'

Hetty put down the sketch pad. 'I wish I could draw. I know art's supposed to look odd these days but not as odd as this.'

'I brought you something.' Helga took a folded piece of paper from her pocket. 'From my own computer. A map of the village showing who lives in every house, who's old village, who's new, and who, as far as I know, has heard from Poison Pen.'

'These letters with copies made – just five so far?' Helga nodded. 'Are they always the truth?'

There was a silence. Was Miss Alloway holding something back? Then she said, 'Can't say for all cases.'

'True about John Winterton. And that Mrs Harrow . . . I had a feeling.'

'Gentlemen callers in the afternoons.'

Hetty stood up. Artistic creation was over for the morning. 'Can you drive me to Preston and I'll get a taxi back on expenses?'

It was possible that entrapment might be one of those activities which are easier to discuss than to do.

Geoff and Robert pressed their noses against the glass of the chemist's window and surveyed their potential quarry, Cheryl, behind the cosmetics counter.

Geoff said, 'I don't know how to begin.'

'The way Mr Skimmer did it, they just fell into casual conversation.'

'It can't be rushed, Mr Wainthropp. Observation is the basis of investigation.'

They continued to observe. Cheryl was in her late twenties, superficially confident and self-possessed; her manner with the customers was friendly without being forward. She looked like the girl next door grown up, but the world had bruised her; she had been married, Harold had told them, but it had not worked out and the divorce had been bitter. Now she was looking for security.

'We can't stay here for ever. We'll be noticed. There's a man in a lovat overcoat been looking at us most peculiar.'

'We'll walk down Parsons Street and on round, and when we come back I'll go in.'

It was lunch time. Hetty had reached Preston and been directed to a wine bar by the porter of the office block where Ben Harrow worked.

She had a description and accosted him on his way back to a table with a plate of quiche and salad in each hand. She was still wearing the clothes of Tara Hall, but thought it better to present herself as Hetty Wainthropp, detective. This bemused him, and a bemused subject is more likely to give himself away. Was there any chance that the accusation in the poison pen letters might be true?

'Why should I answer?'

'Because whoever sent the letters forced you out of the village, and I'm trying to find out who that was.'

'There's every chance it could be true. Now please get out of my way.'

He admitted it! And so coolly! 'You knew what was going on?'

'I don't think you understand our kind of marriage, Mrs Wainthropp. Let's just say there may be faults on both sides. But we have two children whom we both love.' He manoeuvred himself and the two plates round her without spilling so much as a lettuce leaf. One could tell that wine bars were this man's element. 'And now if you'll excuse me, this is a working lunch.'

The woman who was waiting for him at the table with a bottle of white wine and two glasses looked to be in her thirties, blonde, elegant, a woman of the world. He joined her, said something to her which Hetty could not hear, and they both looked in her direction and laughed.

Hetty found that she was blushing and her anger at doing so only made her blush the more. She turned back to the bar. 'I'll have a glass of Dubonnet, please, and a Scotch egg.'

* * *

31

Geoff stood at the cosmetics counter. His mouth was open, but no words came out.

'Cat got your tongue?'

'Me throat's gone dry.'

'What are you trying to say?'

'I had it all worked out when I came in. Give me time.'

Cheryl looked at the lad standing in front of her red-faced and tongue-tied. 'Oh, is that it?' she said.

'I expect so. What?'

'There's no need to be embarrassed, young fellermelad, not in this day and age.' She pointed to a display unit next to the pharmacy. 'They're over there – gossamer light, peppermint flavour, all different colours and sizes. Just pick up a packet and pay. Nobody'll think anything of it.'

Defeated, Geoff left the shop and rejoined Robert who was waiting across the street. 'We'd better come back later, find out where she goes after work, and you have a try.'

Hetty left the taxi a mile from the village and walked the rest of the way so as not to arouse suspicion. Jim Pacey let her in. He looked at her rather grubby sketch pad. 'You don't get much light for your drawing in winter.'

'Enough. Gives me time to brood.'

'About rocks?'

'I've been brooding about that anonymous letter I got this morning. My first full day in the village. It doesn't add up. I thought I might talk to some of the other folk who've had them.'

'Talk if you like. You'll find *they* won't.'

She went on into the converted pigeon loft, took off Tara Hall's outer gear, dried her hair and examined the computer print-out given to her by Helga Alloway. The five people whose final letters had been copied and widely distributed had been separately identified with a note of what had happened to them. The Harrow family had left the village and so had a couple named Davenport who dealt in antiques and had been accused of not being fussy where they found them, John Winterton had attempted suicide and was still in hospital, Harry Parmby, a local farmer, had died of an accident with farm machinery. Only one, Mandy Salthouse, an unmarried mother was still in the village. Hetty decided that she would put her feet up for a bit, have a cup of tea if there was one going, and then have a talk with Mandy.

She folded the print-out and put it away. Painters! They led funny lives. With no place in the outlandish gear they wore for a second-best handbag, where did they keep anything? She kicked off her shoes and lay back on the bed, her hands behind her head, staring at the ceiling. She wondered how Robert and Geoff were getting on at the business of entrapping Mr Skimmer's intended. At the very idea of it she began to smile and then to laugh.

Truth to tell, they were not getting on well. They had followed Cheryl to the saloon bar of the Weaver's Arms where she was meeting a female friend, and Robert had attempted to buy her a drink and get into conversation. Geoff watched the encounter from just inside the door. He saw Cheryl shake her head, smile and give Robert a friendly tap on the shoulder as she left him at the bar. It was heart-breaking to see him sitting there on his own, cast down by rejection.

Geoff went to sit next to him. Robert said, 'She doesn't seem to regard either of us in a romantic light.'

'She called me "young fellermelad".'

'She called me "granpa". We've got to face it, Geoffrey, when it comes to entrapment you're too young and I'm too old. We'll have to find someone more suitable.'

As for Hetty, she found Mandy Salthouse in a poorly furnished council house on the edge of the village and was taken into the front room, where there was a threadbare carpet over bare boards, a cheap battered sofa and armchair, a bare overhead light with no shade, an old TV set, an electric fire and a coin meter. A six-month-old baby went with them in its carrycot.

Mandy was happy to talk. She relished the company.

Hetty fed the meter with enough coins to last the evening and beyond while Mandy talked non-stop. 'I shouldn't ever have been left to manage like this, me being from an old village family. The old villagers look after their own usually. Get someone in the club and you're bound to wed. But with me mum dead and me dad gone and me not being certain, y'see – could've been one of three – I had nobody to exert that kind of pressure. I feel the unfairness but what can I do?'

'Why did you stay in Shepton Fell?'

'Nowhere else to go. Anyway what's to hide?' She indicated the baby. 'I still get the letters, y'know.'

Hetty was surprised. 'Poison Pen?'

'It's a comfort in a way. Nobody else writes to me.'

'What do they say?'

'Just general abuse. But he puts a ten-pound note in the envelope.'

'He?'

'A woman wouldn't send money.'

So ended the first day of Tara Hall's visit to Shepton Fell.

On the morning of the second day Hetty was woken by the sound of tapping on the little window and looked up to see Bertie, the displaced pigeon, looking down. 'Why don't you find yourself a bird sanctuary somewhere down south?' she said, washed, dressed and went over for breakfast, passing Jim Pacey in the yard rattling corn in a dish.

There was another letter on the breakfast table, just like the first one, the same capital letters, the same cheap paper. 'Two days in a row. I do find that interesting,' Hetty said, and, bracing herself against what message she might find inside, opened it.

There was a single sheet of paper inside, and a single sentence, one word to a line:

WHAT
ARE
YOU
UP
TO?

She passed the letter to Beryl Pacey, watching for a reaction, but it was clear that the message meant nothing to Beryl.

Someone was rattled. Good! Hetty sat down to her breakfast egg as Jim Pacey came in from the yard carrying the empty dish. 'I won't take a packed lunch today,' she said. 'I want to ask around. Your Poison Pen seems to have taken a fancy to me, and I want to know more about him.'

'Her,' said Beryl.

'Why "her"?'

Jim said, 'Always is, isn't it?'

Afterwards the Paceys watched her set out down the street, a confident swing to her walk, *sans* rucksack, *sans* sketchbook, *sans* portable easel.

Jim Pacey said to his wife, 'What *is* she up to?'

* * *

Robert and Geoff were back across the road, opposite the chemist's shop. It was a clear day. Through the window they could see Cheryl behind the cosmetics counter.

They had enlisted paid help. He had not been paid yet but he would be. No sanction had been obtained from Mr Skimmer: he would have to go down on expenses.

His name was Kevin; he was twenty years old; he had been at Geoff's school, but two classes ahead. He worked in a slipper factory but had taken the day off; they would have to arrange for a sick note. Kevin was short-sighted and wore spectacles with thick lenses and heavy square frames, but in his day, Geoff told Robert, he had been known as the best-looking boy at school and broken many hearts. Robert had not been sure it would work; Cheryl was no teeny-bopper but a well-balanced young lady who knew what side her bread was buttered. Still they might as well give it a go; they had no one else.

'What do I say?'

Geoff gave Kevin a ten-pound note. 'Buy something expensive and tell her she's beautiful.'

'You could have done that.'

Robert said, 'When it came to the test, he found he couldn't.'

Kevin crossed the road. They watched him enter the chemist's shop.

He went straight to the cosmetics counter, gave Cheryl a respectful smile and selected a chunky hexagonal jar in thick glass with a black and gold label. It was Colorado Springs, a Facial Moisturising Cream for Men, guaranteed not to have been tested on animals. 'Has it got organic collagens for after-shave dermal nourishment?'

'Full of them,' Cheryl said. 'And a delicate yet totally masculine fragrance to enhance personal freshness.'

'While we're on the subject, I think you're beautiful, so would you like to come out with me?'

'Sorry. I'm spoken for.'

'Oh!' Kevin was disconcerted. He dipped into this pocket for the ten-pound note. 'Well, I'd better just have the—'

'Wait!'

He waited, his hand still in his pocket.

'Take your glasses off.'

He took off his glasses.

'How about this evening?'

Hetty had walked five miles to reach Harry Parmby's farm, where she found his widow, Joyce, and her teenage son, both in oil-stained dungarees, working on a piece of worn-out farm machinery in the barn.

'I heard your husband had an accident with a tractor.'

'He had a lot worrying him. Farms are dangerous places when your mind is distracted. Wrench, please.'

Hetty passed the wrench. 'I hope you won't take it amiss but, from what I've heard, there was talk of fraud.'

'Talk's cheap. There was nothing proved.'

Everything was run-down; she had noticed that coming across the yard. Hetty said, 'I can see it's not easy for you.'

'Oh, I'm not so badly off now. We got the insurance and I've sold the milk quota. It was my husband trying to hang on to the farm.'

The teenage son was looking at his mother. He had loved his father, loved the farm, had hoped to inherit. So much was clear to Hetty. 'But you're still here,' she said.

'We won't be when I've sold it.'

* * *

37

That evening an unmarked car arrived in Shepton Fell and parked outside the Paceys' cottage. The driver, DCI Adams, walked briskly to the front door, rang the bell and was admitted by Jim.

Hetty and Beryl were having tea in the kitchen. Jim showed in the visitor. 'Your nephew's come to see you.'

'Hello, Auntie Tara,' the DCI said, 'I was just passing so I thought I'd drop in.'

Hetty said, 'Don't call me "auntie". You know I don't like it.'

After tea she took him over to the converted loft. 'The sergeant at Killerby had a letter from our anonymous friend this morning,' he said. '"Keep your grass off my patch."'

'Do they think he's a landscape gardener?'

'Technical terminology. "Grass" is an informer, "patch" the territory for which a policeman is responsible. Interesting use of language, except that there are so many police series on telly these days, the punters pick up the language.'

'I had a letter myself – "What are you up to?"'

'And what are you up to?'

'Not a lot. I've asked a lot of questions but I'm not sure the answers add up.'

She brought him up to date on her enquiry. He said, 'Right! You've established a pattern. First it's like a scatter-gun. Letters sent out all over – general stuff – sexual abuse – death threats. Then Poison Pen picks a few people to concentrate on, usually one at a time, softens them up, then gets specific.'

'And sends out copies. And it's always true.'

'But the sergeant at Ackersley knew most of this already. It doesn't get us any further towards finding out who writes the letters.'

'Why have you come?'

'Worried about you.'

38

'There's been no violence.'

'One fatal accident and one attempted suicide. You have to accept the fact, dear Auntie Tara, that I've really grown quite fond of you.'

Hetty was embarrassed. The man was a Detective Chief Inspector. She didn't know what to make of it. 'Cheeky monkey!' she said.

He shook his head sadly. 'What a way to talk to a senior police officer. Why Tara Hall, by the way?'

'It was a poem we learned at school – the harp that once in Tara's halls.'

'All I can remember of my school poems is "The Wreck of the Hesperus". It ended badly. Make sure you don't.'

She looked after the car as he drove away. Should she have told him that she had grown quite fond of him also? It was the truth, but better not.

Just where he had parked there was a sign on the street lamp, 'Neighbourhood Watch'.

They had promised Mr Skimmer that Cheryl and Kevin would be under their surveillance the whole evening. They had supplied Kevin with a hundred and fifty pounds in cash from the Agency float (he had beaten them up from a proposed hundred). Now they watched anxiously from the bar of the Mulberry Tree Dine & Dance Restaurant as Kevin and Cheryl took the floor.

Cheryl said, 'I've been hurt once already in my life, Kev. I've had a bad marriage and the break-up was painful. You can't blame me for wanting someone rich but steady.'

'I don't.'

'If you tell people you're twenty-nine everyone thinks you must be thirty. But I am only twenty-nine, Kev.'

'I'd better put my glasses on. We're bumping into people.'

'Bump. It adds to the excitement. I can't spend my whole life behind the cosmetics counter. All my friends have settled for boring marriages; if you're a woman you make your own amusement in this town.' They cannoned off a couple who seemed to have taken root and ended up near the bar. Cheryl noticed Geoff and Robert, both of whom immediately looked away. 'I'm sure I've seen those two before. What can they be doing in a place like this?'

'Selling drugs probably,' Kevin said. 'They look the criminal type.'

And when, at the end of a very enjoyable evening, Kevin paid the bill, there was little left out of the Agency's hundred and fifty pounds, and what there was paid for a taxi back to Cheryl's place. She looked at him, sitting up in bed, naked but for his specs, under an embroidered sampler 'GOD BLESS OUR HOME' and thought, This is what has been missing out of my life for far too long. And Kevin said, 'The trouble is, my mother doesn't understand me.'

Cheryl closed the curtains and shut out the rain which was lashing against the window. 'This job you do . . . Stock control, you said, in a slipper factory?'

'Aye?'

She came back to the bed, sat facing him, and slowly removed his spectacles. 'How could you possibly afford to spend so much money taking me out?'

There was a flash of lightning, clearly visible through the curtains, and a rumble of thunder and the sound of the rain outside the window pane beating even more strongly. Outside, across the road, Robert and Geoff were seated on the scooter, keeping watch on the house. Their crash helmets were no protection against the weather and their overcoats were no more than shower-proof. They were both soaked to the skin, their best suits ruined. Geoff said, 'If we had proper transport, we'd be dry.'

So ended the second day.

There was the same tapping at the little window. Hetty was lying flat on the floor fully dressed, her head on a pillow, her eyes closed, doing lateral thinking.

She opened her eyes and saw Bertie looking down at her. 'Go away, you loathsome bird,' she said, 'and stop distracting me.'

She began to get herself off the floor, and found the process painful. 'I'm too old for this game,' she said. 'It's logic I need, and I've been missing something.'

She crossed the yard to the kitchen. Again Jim Pacey was rattling corn in a dish. Nothing changed in Shepton Fell. He said, 'Had a bit of a lie-in?'

'I've been thinking laterally. It's murder on the back.'

On her second piece of toast it came to her what she had been missing and she went back to the council house where Mandy Salthouse lived with her baby.

'You were five months pregnant and you had nobody to exert pressure and make the father marry you?'

'I told you – could have been one of three. And I didn't really like any of 'em anyway.'

'So what were you going to do?'

Mandy shrugged. 'There's my Auntie Jessie in Readsby. She's a witch. She knows ways.'

Hetty knew there were witches in Readsby, since a case had taken her there, though most of them seemed to use their unnatural arts in aid of muscular dystrophy. 'To get rid of the baby?'

'Wi' herbs and such.'

'But when the letter arrived? With all the copies?'

'Everybody knew so I thought I might as well have it.'

'Thank you, Mandy.'

She turned and left. The missing piece had clicked into place. It was so simple. She must marshal her thoughts and put things clearly, irrefutably, the chain of logic stretching neatly with every link connecting the deed to the doer. She went to see Helga Alloway and was received in Miss Alloway's first-floor room with the window which overlooked so much of the village.

'At first I thought it was to do with old and new villagers,' she said. 'But that hare won't run.'

'No, it won't. Both get letters.'

'This morning I realised it's not to do with Poison Pen either, not in the usual sense.'

'Explain, please.'

'The letters most people get are just a smokescreen. Mostly lies. But the final letters are true, and they get results.'

Miss Alloway considered the proposition, both hands in her lap, the fingers of one tapping against the back of the other. Hetty watched. 'Harry Parmby's death was an accident.'

'Easy to arrange with a tractor. Better than going to prison.'

'What's the result for Mandy Salthouse?'

'She didn't get rid of the child. She gave birth to it and she's rearing it.'

Miss Alloway's hands were still now. Both women were looking at each other, Hetty challenging, Helga appraising. Helga said, 'You've come a long way in a short time.'

'I've come further since. It's all about controlling people. Someone who made herself responsible for the whole village.'

'You think it's a woman?'

'I do. Dishing out punishment, preventing abortion. Disguising

42

it all behind the poison pen letters.' No reaction. Hetty said, 'You never expected me to solve this case, because even if I did, I wouldn't be able to prove it. And meanwhile you'd been the one to call in a detective. Proof of innocence, Miss Alloway.'

Now it had been made. The direct challenge. According to the books, at this point the criminal should crumble. Instead Miss Alloway calmly considered the points put to her. 'You've decided I'm the Poison Pen?'

'I have.'

'Good. Very good. Classic.'

Hetty was thrown. The initiative seemed to have passed. 'And what's that to do with the price of potatoes?'

'The person who brings in the detective is really the criminal all along. Classic plot for a detective story.'

'Doesn't mean it's not so.'

'You want to know the real reason I came to you? I knew weeks ago who the Poison Pen is, but I can't prove my case either, and since I'm already the prime suspect nobody would believe me. But if the Supergran Sleuth points her finger at Poison Pen, that's another matter.'

Slowly Hetty took it in. 'You've been using me?'

'If you like.'

She felt her anger growing. 'I don't like. You've been making a fool of me, Miss Alloway. I don't like it at all.'

'Please! Don't undervalue yourself. You got further in three days on your own than I did in three months with a lot of help. And you're right: it *is* all about control, though I'm not the controller.'

A lot of help? 'What help?' Who in Shepton Fell could have helped her?

'I gather facts. Put them out over the Internet in my computer.

43

I have friends there – my only friends. A retired police chief in Tucson, Arizona. A student of neurology at the University of Lausanne. And others. We consult. Compare similar cases. Reach a conclusion. Now I need you to do what I can't do myself. Confront the real Poison Pen, using my evidence.'

Hetty said, 'Who?'

The bell-ropes were down in the belfry of the church. Mr Cullimore looked after the bells as he looked after so much else in the village. Hetty said, '"Keep your grass off my patch". That's police language, Mr Cullimore. And you were the village policeman.'

'I don't expect you to understand.'

'Try me.'

'A village policeman knows everything if he can read the signals, but I only used my knowledge when I needed to. I kept my village in order. Then they retired me. They took it all away and left me to rot.'

'There was still work to do. You could help people.'

'I do help people. Help: that's my middle name. Help the school kids with their reading. Keep the churchyard tidy.' He indicated the bells. 'Bell-ringing – keep the team in practice and maintain the equipment. Help folk in their gardens when they grow past it. You name it; I help with it.'

'And the letters? Was that helping?'

'It was. People need keeping in order. They're happier. We haven't got a village policeman now. There's still a job to do.'

'The letters were vile. The language – I felt sick.'

'I knew what to write.'

She looked at him. He hadn't even the grace to look away. 'You feel no shame, do you?'

'I was doing my duty. I always will. You can't make an omelette without breaking eggs.'

'Well, I don't think you'll be making any more omelettes in Shepton Fell, Mr Cullimore.'

'No. Go away now, please.'

She had done what she came to do. She left him in the bell-tower. As she descended the stairs she heard a single bell begin to toll.

She left the church with the bell still tolling. It was like the bell which tolls for the dead. She looked up the village street and saw a scooter approaching. Geoff drew up level with her, stopped and gave her the crash helmet attached to the pillion. 'All right?'

'We'll have to collect my gear. I'll leave the sketch pad and easel, but there's a rucksack and it's heavy.' That rucksack and the camera would have to go back to Miss Apthwaite.

'Have to be careful, then, on the bends.'

When they arrived home, Robert had a plate of ham sandwiches ready and a pan of soup on the stove. That was one of the many virtues of hot pot: the left-overs could be used in so many ways. 'Did you get the final payment?'

'She gave me the cheque before I left.'

Geoff said, 'Not bad for a week's work.'

Hetty said, 'And the deckle-edged gentleman?'

'There's been a bit of a problem. We've not been paid.'

'Not even expenses?'

Robert thought of the hundred and fifty pounds on top of Kevin's fee. It was a bitter thought. 'We were too successful. She gave Mr Skimmer the push and Kevin's moved in with her. Mr Skimmer says he may sue us.'

Hetty sat and took a sandwich. 'Dare say it's left you feeling a bit dirty.'

'Mebbe a bit.'

'As if you'd been used.'

'You could say that.'

'Same with me,' Hetty said. 'We'll have to pick our cases more carefully from now on.'

Mr Cullimore walked up the hill outside Shepton Fell, his shotgun under his arm and his dog Shep trailing some way behind. He reached the top, and turned to call the dog.

'Shep!' The dog came running up to him, and together they went over the hill and out of sight, man and dog in company.

For a moment nothing moved on the hill. Then two shots were heard, one a little after the other.

Runaways

Bridsea in early February at three in the morning. High waves battered the promenade wall, shooting foam and spray skywards to land on the duck boards of the deserted pier. In the distance further along the promenade there was the bobbing light of a pedal cycle. No police, none of the townspeople, certainly no trippers were about at that hour. The cyclist was alone.

His name was Bernard. He was twenty-nine years old, but – since he had learning difficulties – unused to undertaking adventures on his own, and consequently nervous of every shadow, afraid that some person in authority would appear to stop him. The bike itself was extremely old, rusty and without accessories. Strapped to the rear was a battered leather suitcase. He was on his way to meet his girlfriend, Susan. Their intention was to spend the weekend together away from Bridsea. They had never done such a thing before and consequently had thought it better not to tell anyone what they intended to do until they had done it. Susan also had learning difficulties.

Susan was a resident at the Hotel Clare, a run-down bed-and-breakfast hotel, once used by summer visitors in the days before such visitors spent their summer holidays on package tours to Majorca, Ibiza, the Canary Islands and the Costa Brava, now used by the Social Services to house people in need of community care. Now she stood listening at the door of her room in semi-darkness. Beside her were an expensive travelling case and a holdall. She listened to the silence, opened the door of her room and went cautiously downstairs with her luggage.

Bernard reached the front of the hotel where a street lamp illuminated the entrance. He dismounted, leaned the cycle against the wall, and crouched to look through the letter box. He could see nothing but darkness, but could hear bolts being withdrawn cautiously. The door opened. At Bernard's level what he saw first were the two pieces of luggage.

They had agreed on one case each. He looked up and Susan was looking down at him, smiling at her own cleverness at having negotiated escape without discovery. He said, 'Can't carry all that, girl,' meaning that he could carry it but there was no room on the cycle for themselves and the luggage. She ignored him, slid the suitcase and holdall out towards him, then came cautiously through the door herself, closing it behind her even more cautiously. Bernard pulled the cycle away from the wall, piled the suitcases on the crossbar, the holdall on the handlebars, and set off away from the hotel at a run. Susan ran after him, still smiling. After they had travelled some way further down the promenade, Bernard stopped for her to catch up, and they leaned towards each other across the cycle and the luggage as though over a garden wall, and kissed. Then they resumed their journey, one on each side of the cycle, at a walking pace.

By dawn they had reached the outskirts of the town and found a roadside mobile refreshment stall in a lay-by off the main road. They sat on their luggage, eating thick sandwiches with cans of coke; the cycle lay on the ground beside them. Bernard took his wallet from his pocket: although he had learning difficulties he was a wage earner. The wallet had been given to him by his mother. He removed a small newspaper clipping from the wallet and read from it to Susan. He read slowly and with difficulty, and was mostly remembering what he had been told the words meant. Susan listened, nodded and smiled, encouraging him to get the words right.

'Ro-mantic hol-i-day of life-time? Or simp-lee week-end a-way from it all in bew-tee-full surr . . . surr . . . ound-ings? Try Chigs-wick Manor Ho-tel . . . homey-lee-est Lanc-a-shire wel-come.'

'That's good, Bernard.' Susan had finished her sandwich. She got up, lifted the cycle and gave it a push which sent it rolling into the ditch. Bernard watched, a little alarmed, but did not try to prevent her.

Susan walked to the edge of the lay-by and stuck her thumb out towards the passing traffic. Bernard remained where he was, looking after the luggage.

Two lines of action were about to cross. The first had begun earlier, at tea-time of the day before.

Gerald was in the kitchen of Thurston Farm with his mother. It was not a working farm because there was nobody to work it. The land had been sold off, all but the farmhouse in which Gerald and his mother lived and the farmyard and barns which nobody wanted. Gerald himself drove a lorry, his own lorry, an old 5-cwt pick-up truck, one of the few remaining vehicles in Britain on which it was still necessary to double-declutch, and found work where he could in the area, mostly transporting feed for farmers.

The kitchen table was crowded with unwashed dishes, a tool box, some electric cable, empty jam jars, out of date newspapers. The fire had been allowed to die and Molly, his mother was raking the ashes from the grate, watched by Maggie, a German Shepherd bitch. Gerald had a mug of tea and some sliced bread with margarine. He took from his pocket four ten-pound notes folded into a thin wad and put it on the table. Molly wiped her hands on the piece of sacking she wore as an apron and came to look.

'Is this it?'

'It's all there is this week.'

She stared at him. He looked away. She moved slowly round the table to meet his gaze and hold it. He looked down at the table. Finally she spoke. 'What's her name this time?'

'Whose name?'

'The slut with expensive tastes. The cow who's got the rest of my housekeeping money.'

It was a game she played with him, an unpleasant game, which Gerald loathed and his mother seemed to enjoy. It happened whenever he'd had a bad week. No comfort and consolation from Molly. Instead there was contempt and anger and always the same game of question and answer. 'Housekeeping?' Gerald said, 'When has this house ever been kept by you?'

A cackle of laughter. 'If it's escape you're planning, go while I can just about walk. Don't wait till I've seized up altogether. You'll hate yourself when they find my bones rotting on this floor.'

So much else was rotting on the floor, would anyone notice? Gerald said, 'Stop it! It's pathetic.'

Smash! She slammed a plate down on the table, leaning over so that her face was close to his. Maggie's ears went forward; she knew when trouble was coming. '*You* stop it,' Molly shouted. 'Stop thinking I can feed us on this. Stop piddling around and get yourself a man's job. Best of all, stop taking whores off Preston Docks behind the Flag and Whistle, sapping your strength with my food money.'

He could feel himself flushing, the tears coming into his eyes. He would not, must not give her the satisfaction. 'When was it your money? When was there enough to buy sex even if I . . .' He could not finish. The words trailed away.

'Even? Even what? Even if you were capable? Even if you hadn't been at the back of the queue when they handed out equipment?'

She had gone too far as she so often did – taunted him beyond bearing to make him break. He took her shoulders and shook her while the dog growled. Molly's false teeth shot out of her mouth and landed amid the filth of the floor. She mumbled and moaned as he shook her but she had pushed him too far for him to notice that her distress was real.

'You . . . always . . . say . . . that. It's not . . . not . . . not . . . True. What chances do I get? I'm always here looking after you.' She was trying to point to her false teeth. Maggie, the dog, was barking. He was too far gone to take notice of either as he shook his mother harder and harder like a doll. *'Who was it? What's her name? Has she got VD? Disinfect your privates, Gerald. Where'd you learn how to do it anyway? Where'd you find that was dark enough? Didn't she laugh at you? Asked when you were starting and you told her you'd finished? Eh? Eh?'* He was crying now, his voice almost strangled with sobs as the dog grew more agitated. 'I've never ever been with a woman. I'm forty-six and I've never been with anyone. Do you understand what I'm saying?'

He dropped her. Molly fell, one arm sending crockery crashing to the floor. As she fell, her head hit the corner of the table. Then she was lying on the floor, oddly, her eyes open, her head askew.

And the dog was whining.

Gerald stood, looking down at his mother with disbelief. Then he spoke to her, very gently now. 'You're the only other person who has ever touched this body. I never had the courage to ask for a second opinion about it.' She did not reply, had not moved. She must understand; the game was over now. 'Don't tease me. I really don't have any more money to give you. Honest.'

Still no reply. Had she been knocked out by the fall? He had not intended that. He filled a pan with water and spilled it over her face. Still no reaction. He started to collect up the broken crockery, all the time waiting for her to come round, and she did not come round. He picked up her false teeth and slipped them into the pocket of her apron. There was a little blood from the cut on her forehead, not much, and it seemed to be drying.

The dog licked at the blood on the cut as if to wipe it away. She would never allow that. And blood, he remembered, ceased to flow when you were dead. Her blood was not flowing. He realised that if she were found like this nobody would understand.

'Got to move her,' he said to the dog. 'Get things tidied up. Looks wrong. She fell, hurt herself; you saw what happened, didn't you?'

And he began to tidy up so that it would all look proper for whoever found her. He could not leave her on the floor. He carried a chair into the dairy – which was no longer used as a dairy or for anything at all – and sat her on that to wait.

Later he dialled 999 at a public telephone box, asked for 'Ambulance' and tried to report the accident. But when the Ambulance Service answered, he could not find the words. Someone else would have to report it. If he, Gerald, reported it, they would think he had killed her.

Only Maggie the dog knew the truth, and she could not speak. She had left the house with him. They sat together in the cab of his truck sharing a bag of chips in the lay-by where they would spend the night. 'Best if I say you and me weren't home when it happened. Get someone else to find her. Stuck there in the dairy, bound to keep her cool, but she's not going to last forever.'

It had been decided at a specially convened meeting of the directors of the Wainthropp Detective Agency that, as a once-for-all item of capital expenditure, Geoff should approach Miss Apthwaite with a view to buying her scooter outright. Robert gave him a blank cheque and strict instructions about the need for economy. Geoff discussed the purchase with Miss Apthwaite in a frank and open way, filled out the amount of the cheque and handed it over, and brought the scooter back to the Wainthropp residence. The Agency now had transport of its own.

'I know that hang-dog expression,' Robert said. 'He paid too much for it.'

Hetty said, 'You were supposed to beat her down.'

'She beat me up.'

The telephone rang in the hall and Robert went to answer.

'She said, with all the publicity her scooter had become our emblem and that it gave us a corporate identity.'

'Wainthropp Detective Agency.'

'What is a corporate identity anyway?'

'Something between a cap badge and a regimental goat.'

Robert returned. 'The Mayor of Titterslow would like to see you in his parlour pronto. If he offers you the freedom of the city, tell him you're holding out for a season ticket to Blackburn Rovers.'

In fact, as Robert knew perfectly well, Titterslow was not a city but a small town of no great distinction, the administrative centre of a cobbled together conurbation with Bridsea to the west and Utterbourne to the north. And the Mayor's parlour was his own front room, in which there was a bar with its own lights and mirrors, a carpet with a pile deep enough to smother a hamster and furniture of white imitation leather. Everything in the room informed visitors that the people who lived there had money.

'Nobody must know the real reason you've come here,' Mayor Makepeace said.

'Nobody does.'

'If it was to get out the Mayor of Titterslow was consulting a private detective, I shudder to think. So many free newspapers without a scrap of news to print! The moment we leave this house, with or without the Bentley and the mayorial robes and chain, there's a fleet of cub reporters in Fiat Unos trailing us along the ring road.'

'So what do you want us to do?'

Mrs Makepeace as a girl had never got beyond the final ten in the Miss New Brighton Competition, but the years had given her thrust. She cut into the polite preliminaries. 'Susan, our daughter, has gone missing.'

There was a photograph of a pudgy little girl in a Laura Ashley print on one of the little tables, some holding lamps on Regency fluted columns, which dotted the room. Hetty picked it up. 'Is this your daughter?'

'Aged twelve. She's twenty-seven now. I'll give you a more recent photo.'

'The trouble is,' the Mayor said, 'she has learning difficulties.'

Hetty did not know that 'learning difficulties' meant what used to be 'mentally handicapped' and even 'backward': she thought it was to do with bad teaching, inadequate outdoor lavatories and holes in the classroom roof. But Geoff knew and therefore also knew that anyone with learning difficulties who disappeared was a major cause for concern. These people should be talking to the police not to a private detective agency 'When did you notice she'd gone?'

'We didn't.' Mrs Makepeace was bitter. 'Susan lives apart from us in a run-down seaside hotel.'

'Sheltered accommodation,' the Mayor said. 'Social Services use it for their Care in the Community. And there's a Day Centre close by she attends sometimes. Brenda and me thought Susan should get used to being independent while we're still alive to catch her if she comes unstuck.'

'She doesn't think of herself as handicapped. She thinks she's just like any other woman. Following fashion and current music trends are very important to her. She'd hate to think she was behind in any way,' said Mrs Makepeace.

'What do the people in the hotel think has happened?'

'The woman there can't get staff to stay; she's run off her feet. She saw nothing, heard nothing. Nobody noticed Susan had gone until one of the other residents went to her room to borrow money. The others live on social security and Susan likes to play Little Princess to the paupers.'

'How much money would she have on her?'

'That's difficult to say.'

'Does she have credit cards?'

'No, thank goodness,' the Mayor said. 'I wouldn't allow it. She has a building society account, and she's very good at making withdrawals from that.'

'You give her an allowance? A generous one?'

'More generous than it need be. And she gets money from grandparents and aunts. It's difficult to keep track of what she's got.'

Mrs Makepeace said, 'These abductions you read about . . . young women who are . . . well, like she is. She's not exactly slow or all that innocent, but she is too trusting. And much too vulnerable.'

Good, Hetty thought. *The mother has feelings*. 'Why come to us and not the police?'

'Susan went walkabout once before.'

The Mayor grunted. 'Some mischief-maker took her to an all-night rave near Grange over Sands. Later she was pictured topless in a Sunday tabloid under the heading "Sexy Susan's Daddy Is Mr Mayor".'

'So you understand the need for secrecy.'

Time to consider carefully, but not much time with an impatient client already fumbling at his cheque book. The girl lived on her own in a seaside hotel. She followed fashion and current trends in music and had been to at least one all-night rave. She had her own building society account and liked to play Little Princess to the other residents in the hotel. Her learning difficulties were clearly not enormous. But she was trusting; she was vulnerable. Hetty knew enough about police priorities to know that any ordinary Missing Person would not be high on the list; she remembered the heavy patience with which the police had treated the parents of Malcolm Stone, profoundly deaf and without speech, who had been the Agency's second case. Someone with learning difficulties was not ordinary, but these Makepeaces were clearly not going to go to the police; if she refused the case, they would find another private detective.

'You'd better give me the address of the hotel and the Day Centre,' she said. 'And phone to tell them to co-operate with our enquiries. We'll be there this afternoon.'

'But you don't understand. They mustn't know. It mustn't be talked of.'

'They know already, by your own account. The guests at the

hotel know and any of them who use the Day Centre will have told their friends. We'll take this case on our terms, Mr Mayor. That's how we do business.' The Wainthropp chin was well in evidence. Even the Mayor of Titterslow could not withstand it.

Gerald had spent the night with Maggie in the cab of the truck: they had kept each other warm. Not long after dawn she whined and woke him. She was a good dog, a clean dog, house-trained as a puppy; she would be wanting to do her business. He had opened the door of the cab, and she had jumped out, crouched at the side of the lay-by and then, instead of returning to her master, high-tailed through a hole in the hedge and run away. He had shouted after her, but it had done no good. He could not understand it. There had been rows with his mother before, and he had walked out and spent a couple of nights in the truck, and sometimes Maggie had come with him, but she had never run off before.

Bernard and Susan had made slow progress. Traffic was not eager to stop for them. Perhaps it was the suitcases. At the junction of the A682 and the A65, as Susan stood with her thumb out and Bernard sat discreetly a little distance away on the luggage, a very large lorry with automatic doors signalled and pulled up.

The door on the passenger side opened with a whoosh. Susan shouted, 'Chigswick Manor Hotel?'

'Where's that?'

'Chigswick.'

The driver shook his head. 'Pass.' And the door had whooshed shut again, and the lorry pulled away. Susan flushed and bit her lip. Pigs! Didn't they realise she was the Mayor's daughter? Men were all the same except for Bernard, who could always be relied upon to do what he was told.

A double-glazing van took them a good way down the A65,

and let them out at the junction of a minor road which, the driver said, would take them to Chigswick. They were wet by this time, but took heart because this seemed to be the last stage of their journey. Then they discovered that there was a notice to say that the road was closed for repairs but by this time the double-glazing van had gone on.

What were they to do? Would there be more vans, perhaps even cars (not one car had stopped) if they went on down towards the repair? Was it far? Could they walk? The luggage was heavy. While they stood at the junction discussing their predicament a battered old truck stopped beside them and the driver said, 'Closed down there.'

The driver was Gerald. The two lines of action had come together. They scrambled with some difficulty into the cab of his truck, since it only had two seats, and put the luggage in the back.

There was so little time that Hetty and Geoff decided to split the work in Bridsea. She would start enquiries at the Hotel Clare, he at the Day Centre.

The proprietor, Mrs Mottram, had been instructed to offer co-operation, but it was clear that she resented the instructions. She took Hetty to Susan's room and watched from the doorway as Hetty, who had no idea what she was looking for, cast about for places to look.

'She's a spoilt little madam and a bit of a loose cannon in some ways, but as long as I'm firm about no men in her room the parents are very supportive.'

Hetty had decided to start with the wardrobe. 'You've no idea what she took with her?'

'Clothes? Toiletries? I don't keep tabs on her wardrobe and

she certainly doesn't take me into her confidence. There's a fair-sized suitcase and a holdall gone. She could be anywhere.'

It was not a kidnap. The girl had not wandered out and been tempted away by some stranger. Two pieces of luggage. Her disappearance had been planned. It began to look like an elopement. Hetty moved to the dressing-table on which there was a photograph in a silver frame of Mayor Makepeace and his wife. She had left daddy and mummy behind without a qualm. Hetty opened the top drawer of the dressing-table and began to rummage.

It was odd that there seemed to be no other residents of the hotel about. She would have to talk to some of them. Who had wanted to borrow money from the Little Princess and why? 'Nobody stays in during the day?'

'Goodness no!'

'Not even in bad weather?'

'A place like this, we have to have a few rules for everyone's sake. It's easier in the summer of course. Some of them go to cafés, the cinema, bus station. That's the advantage of the seaside; there's almost always somewhere warmish to kill a few hours.'

One of the disadvantages of a private detective's work was that one kept meeting people one would like to bury in cold bread pudding and was not allowed to do so. Hetty kept her lip buttoned and rummaged in the second drawer. 'What's this?'

Clare Mottram came to look. 'It's newspaper. Used to line the drawer.'

'There's a piece missing.'

'I don't think that affects its usefulness as drawer lining.'

A piece had been cut out neatly and cleanly leaving nothing to indicate what it might have been. 'Can Susan read?'

'If it's not too complicated. Bits out of magazines and

newspapers. I don't think she goes in for books. She's pretty independent, all things considered. Most of the others have a social worker to keep tabs on them, but Susan doesn't need one.'

Hetty took the page of newspaper out of the drawer, folded it and tucked it away in her handbag. 'I'll keep this. If it was important enough for her to cut out, it's important enough for me to find out what it was. Meanwhile I'll just mooch around a bit if you've no objection. My colleague will be meeting me here, so I might as well fill the time. No need to come with me.'

In the Day Centre simple tasks were performed by service-users with different degrees of difficulty in learning. Nuts and bolts were sorted, raffia seats and backs woven onto wooden chairs already constructed, dolls' vanity sets packed into boxes of leatherette and imitation velvet. Geoff sat next to Mary. He had been told by the Day Centre leader that Susan usually sat next to Mary, a young woman with Down's Syndrome, whenever she could be bothered to put in an appearance.

'Susan didn't tell you where she was going, I suppose?'

Mary shook her head. Mary was shy. So far Geoff had not succeeded in getting a word out of her.

'On the days she did turn up what sort of things did she talk about?'

Mary shrugged.

'Gets boring, this work. You must have gossiped a bit.'

Mary shrugged.

'It's all right, Mary. We're just trying to find out a bit more about what sort of person Susan is.'

Mary nodded.

'So what did she talk about?'

The dam broke. Mary spoke forcefully and rather too loud,

much to the amused approval of the other people at the table.

'Men! Never stopped! Men, men and more men. All the time. Mel Gibson, Alan Shearer, Brad Pitt, Tom Cruise. Just about anyone in trousers.'

'Does she have a boyfriend?'

'Thousands. Man-mad, that one.'

'Anyone steady? Any favourites?'

'Said she'd save herself for Ryan Giggs.'

'And you've no idea where she might have gone?'

Mary thought for a while, then shook her head. 'Never go on her own without a man. She's frightened of dogs and the dark.'

It was not a lot but it was something, and probably all he'd get. 'You've been a great help. Thank you very much.'

She could not look at him, but managed to ask, 'Where do you live, Geoffrey.'

It would not do to rebuff this girl. Quick as a flash Geoff replied, 'With Mrs Wainthropp. She's my boss.' Mary nodded sympathetically, but was clearly disappointed.

Hetty mooched in the kitchen of the Hotel Clare, where there seemed to be little in the way of food beyond tins of own-brand baked beans, a sack of potatoes and some wilting carrots. She mooched in the dining room (where the residents did not dine but were given breakfast) but that did not take long since the dining table almost filled the room. She mooched in the common room, where cheap armchairs were crowded together to face the TV set and a depressed parrot brooded in a cage by the window. Finally she mooched in the yard.

The weather was cold and promised a return to rain. There was not much in the yard, certainly no plants, just paving, a shed and a wooden fence round three sides with a gate giving onto the

alley behind the hotel. Hetty opened the gate and looked out at
the alley which had a gutter running down the middle and rows
of dustbins. She closed the gate, turned back into the yard, and
discovered that a small portable camp-stool with a canvas seat
had been set up between the side of the shed and the back fence
out of sight of the back windows of the hotel, and sitting on it
was a middle-aged woman, knitting.

The woman looked up at Hetty, smiled and nodded affably.
'What's your name?'

'Hetty. What's yours?'

'Maureen Ethel Dabbs, that's all of my names. Marilyn Monroe
Suite. Hotel Clare. Bridsea.'

'You what?'

'They've got names for all the rooms. Social worker had that
done. It's easier to remember and it makes us feel special.'

'What are you knitting?'

'Haven't decided yet. Could be a sweater, could be a scarf.
Depends how I feel.'

'Depends if you get bored.'

Maureen grinned. 'Right. No flies on you, eh? You're not
eleven pence to the shilling, are you? You know what side your
bread's buttered.'

'So do you by the look of it.' Obviously Maureen had found
herself a place of her own, which was at least more private than
a shelter on the promenade and cheaper than a sea-front café.

'We don't get butter. She's a miser when it comes to food.'

'Have you been here long at the hotel?'

'Five Christmases. We get a party with crackers and pudding.'

'And before that?'

'St Leonard's Hospital, Chorlton.'

'How long?'

Maureen put the knitting away into a shopping bag and did sums on her fingers. 'Twenty-three. And another hospital before that.'

'All your life in hospitals?' The nod and grin again. 'Why?'

'Told you. I'm not eleven pence to the shilling. None of us was. Some more than others. They let me be cow-girl on St Leonard's float at the Preston Guilds. That was special. Chosen. Best of our ward. Mary Beattie Ward. I've got a photo upstairs.'

'Must be nice now, having your own room, with your own things around you.'

'We've to be out by ten.'

Mrs Mottram was staring out of the kitchen window, wondering why the private investigator was spending such a long time mooching in the yard and whether she ought to do a bit of investigating herself. Hetty moved in closer behind the shed. 'Did Susan Makepeace have to be out by ten?'

'Susan's not on the Social. Her daddy's the mayor.'

'Would you like to tell me a bit about her?'

'All I know?'

'All you know.'

Meanwhile Geoff at the Day Centre was looking at his watch. He had found out as much as he could and ought to be getting back to meet Mrs Wainthropp at the hotel. 'Goodbye, then. And thank you.' He had taken three steps towards the door when Mary called after him. 'Course she might have been swept off her feet.'

All the other women at the table were giggling. Geoff turned back. 'Sorry?' He looked round the table at Mary and the giggling women. Their intention was clear: they were telling him something. 'Swept off her feet? That's a clue, isn't it?' Everyone at the table was nodding. 'Brush? Broom? Carpet salesman?'

It was like one of those games where you have to act syllables.

'Chimney sweep?' Mary had placed her hands in front of her, half-closed, pushing and grasping an imaginary broom. 'Got it! Roadsweeper.'

And Hetty, who had also got it, but with less difficulty from Maureen, confirmed the information. Maureen had seen the two of them from the top of a Number 92 bus. 'A street-cleaner. He works for the very council Susan's father lords it over.'

Gerald said, 'Aren't men and women kept separate any longer in the sort of place you come from?'

He was uncomfortable. If he had realised the two hitch-hikers were retard bastards he would probably not have picked them up, but now he was landed with them. Okay, Gerald had nothing against retards if they kept their place and were properly grateful for any kindnesses shown to them, but these two were shameless. They were crowded together, the young woman in the passenger seat and the man crushed uncomfortably between with his bum on cold iron and his feet her side of the gear level. He had one arm round his shameless retard bint and she had her head against his chest. Now she was unbuttoning his shirt, feeling his nipple beneath his vest. He should have made them travel in the back of the truck, rain or no rain, and if they went on like this, he would.

The man was kissing the woman, first a peck on the top of the nose, then, as she responded, the kissing became passionate. Shameless, shameless. Had they no idea what this sort of behaviour could lead to? He said, 'I asked a question. Don't they keep you separate?'

'Sorry?'

'They teach you all about unwanted babies and that, do they?'

'Who?'

'The mental nurses. Orderlies. Warders. Whatever they call themselves these days.'

'We don't come from a hospital.'

Susan said, 'Bernard's got his own job. He lives with his mum. And my father is Mayor of Titterslow. So I do know babies get born, thank you very much.'

He drove on in silence for a while. At least they had stopped canoodling; he had achieved that at any rate. 'Don't like to think of innocent kiddies suffering, that's all.' He felt an idea beginning to stir. 'What's this place you're heading for, again?'

Bernard took out his wallet and showed the clipping. 'Chigswick Manor Hotel. Chigswick.'

Susan said, 'Thought you told us you know where it is.'

'I do. We go right by.'

Hetty and Geoff were looking for roadsweepers on the route of the 92 bus. They started by following a bus for a while, but had to stop – usually suddenly – whenever it stopped, and also the bulk of it blocked their view. So they had decided to let the bus go, and thereafter work from bus stop to bus stop keeping a keen eye on the gutters.

'There's one,' Hetty said. He was their third. The first two had not responded helpfully to the question, 'Excuse me. Does one of your colleagues have a girlfriend with learning difficulties?', being clearly of the opinion that mental handicap need not stop with the girlfriends of workers in the field of Public Cleansing but might just as possibly affect senior citizens on scooters as well. This one was young with long hippyish hair and a trolley of cleaning gear and, as Hetty saw as they passed him, wore a string of beads which may have been made of wood but could as easily be human bone.

Geoff stopped the scooter to allow Hetty to dismount and stand in the way of the young beadsman.

'Halt!'

He looked at her, worried, made a decision to treat her as an immovable object, wheeled his trolley carefully round her (but without actually cleaning any part of her) and continued on his way. Hetty followed.

'If keeping on the move is part of your contract of employment, I shall neither tarry nor dally with you. Brush an answer this way and I'm history.' He quickened his step. She called after him. 'Look, I'm a human being just like you, and I'm in need of your assistance.'

He stopped and turned. And told her what she wanted to know.

Bernard and his mother lived in a small terraced house in a back street. She must have been watching the street from a front window because she had the door open before Hetty had time to ring the bell.

'Don't tell me.' She held up her hand to silence her visitors and spoke as if on their behalf. 'It was a mugging. Come in quickly before I faint. Some youths at a bus stop thought he was laughing at them. He has a smiling, open nature, fatal with teenagers of a certain sort. Tea! That's it. Strong sweet tea for the shock.'

She was a woman hardly higher than a hedge-sparrow. Her name was Doris Lavery. They followed her into the house. She led them to the kitchen and put the kettle on, talking non-stop the whole time.

'Or was it a hit-and-run driver over the limit? Didn't notice Bernard's dayglo anorak and smashed him into that lamp-post at the Jubilee Intersection?'

'I'm afraid you don't understand.'

'Just tell me where to go, the hospital or the mortuary. There's no easy way of doing your job. It was good of them to send a woman. Men never understand the wherewithal of bereavement. They just stand about looking nervous and fiddling with their shirt fronts. Is that your son or a lad on Work Experience?'

'This is my associate, Mr Shawcross. We're private detectives.'

'It was murder, then, was it? Done to a dreadful death for the fifty pence mad-money in his sock and the pound note sewn into his vest.'

Geoff said, 'So you do know your son is missing, Mrs Lavery? You've been expecting someone to arrive with news about him?'

'They phoned from the Council. Wanted to know why Corporation Street was unhygienic to the public. I couldn't speak, couldn't answer. I thought he must have come on sick over something he'd put his broom to, poor little mite. They do uncover the most unusual and disgusting things left in those plastic supermarket bags.'

'You'd no idea he'd gone until then?'

'He goes to work so early I've had no time to prepare meself against the ravages of the day. He must have smuggled that suitcase out when my back was turned.'

Hetty said, 'Then why are you afraid dreadful things have happened to him when you know he took a suitcase with him?'

'There's no way my Bernard would stay out all night of his own accord. He may have difficulties learning but he's not unaware of my weak heart. Stress to my heart is like a red rag to a bull. Once it starts galloping it never knows when to stop.'

Hetty said, 'We've no reason to believe anything unpleasant has happened to him. On the contrary, we think he's with his girlfriend, Susan Makepeace.'

It was as if she had turned off the tap. Doris could not speak.

She stared at both of them in turn, then turned her face to the wall. She had anticipated every form of mayhem, including murder, but not this.

The kettle began to whistle and, since Doris made no move to do so, Geoff took it off the gas.

Then he said – gently, to reassure her, 'The Mayor's daughter.' No response.

There were questions to be asked. The investigating team needed to know how the runaways had departed and whither. Hetty said, 'Are we to take it that Bernard doesn't drive?' No reply. She took it that Bernard didn't drive and persisted. 'Was there anything he took with him that might indicate where they were heading?'

No response.

'If you can't help us we'd better be going, but we may have to come back. We've been engaged by Mayor Makepeace to find his daughter and we've already used up most of today.' Hetty took one of the Agency's cards from her bag and put it on the table since Doris made no move to take it. 'I'll leave our card in case Bernard should phone. I'd have liked to ask how severe his learning difficulties are. It might have helped us.'

Doris spoke without looking at them. 'When you find him, don't let him know he's just taken twenty years off my life, will you?'

'I think you can rely on us never to disclose that kind of detail.'

'Why should a girl with money want a man with learning difficulties, except for his body?'

'Perhaps because she has similar difficulties.'

Now Doris turned to face them. All the silly self-dramatising had gone, leaving a concentrated and genuine hostility. 'You mean this woman he's gone off with is like him?'

'In that respect, yes.'

'You stupid, stupid woman! You don't realise, do you? You don't think.' Geoff saw the look on Hetty's face, and put a hand on her arm. People did not talk to Mrs Wainthropp like this, and if they did, they shouldn't. Doris said, 'My son mustn't ever sleep with anyone who's mentally handicapped. What sort of child might they produce?'

Geoff could feel Hetty's arm stiff and tense under his touch. He said, 'I think we should go now. Mrs Wainthropp.'

'In a moment. I've a word to say first.' She removed his hand from her arm and spoke gently to Doris. She would not meet anger with anger. What was said must convince. She remembered Maureen, sitting patiently on her camp-stool, knitting as she waited to be allowed back into the Hotel Clare.

'I'm sorry,' she said, 'but you really have got it wrong. You see, I had a great aunt who spent most of her life in the Royal Albert Hospital, Lancaster. She'd been put there at a time when to miss the last tram and spend a night away from home was thought to be immoral. When I was thirteen I was allowed to go with my mother to take Aunt Ruth new hair ribbons and scented soap. She'd have been about sixty then. What being in that place all those years did to her was far more immoral.'

Doris had not softened. Hetty continued to speak gently but now found herself, for some reason she did not understand, on the verge of tears. 'You're not disabled, nor was Bernard's father, yet you produced Bernard who is disabled. Contrariwise, people with learning difficulties like Bernard and Susan's are no more likely to produce a child with the same difficulties as anyone else.'

She moved back towards the door, Geoff watching her closely and following. They were done here. Perhaps the woman had learned something. 'My own son's in Australia,' she said. 'I haven't seen him for more years than I care to count. You don't know how lucky you are.'

Doris did not move. They saw themselves out of the house. Back on the scooter, Hetty said, 'Reference library and then home. That bit cut out of the *Record* is the best chance we've had today for a positive lead.'

And so it proved. Susan had cut out an advertisement for a small country house hotel, Chigswick Manor. 'They'll be dolling themselves up now for the Cocktail Hour, I shouldn't wonder. We'll get there by breakfast time tomorrow, bright and early.'

Gerald stopped the truck. 'This is it.' Bernard and Susan climbed out of the cab and took their luggage from the back, two suitcases and a holdall. They looked about them. There was a gate and a track leading to a stone building about a mile away in the valley. 'Down there,' Gerald said. 'I expect they'll have warmed the double room you booked.'

He put the truck in gear and moved off, leaving them standing on the road. They looked again at the distant house in the valley. There was no smoke coming from the chimney. Susan gave Bernard a worried glance. She hoped her great idea was not going to turn out bad. But the lorry driver had said he knew the place and this was it. Together they began to move down the track, Bernard carrying the two suitcases and Susan the holdall. They did not even notice the sign on the broken-down gate reading, 'THURSTON'S FARM'.

Half a mile down the road, Gerald glanced sideways and noticed that the wallet from which the retard had taken the bit of newspaper had been left behind where the young man had been sitting. He braked, then sat where he was, wondering what to do.

He always needed money but was not a thief; he wouldn't keep it. He had intended to punish them, not to rob them.

Yet he could hardly go after them. He opened the door of the cab and looked back, but they had left the roadside and would be well on their way by now.

He had intended to punish them and more, much more importantly intended them to find his mother's body and report it, as he himself could not. He could not report the death because he had not been there when it happened. There had been no quarrel. She had not fallen and hit her head. It was nothing to do with him. The two retards would discover her sitting quietly in the dairy and then they would find someone to tell. It was their business now.

He would think what to do about the wallet, would get it back to them somehow. Meanwhile let them get on with what *they* had to do.

Tired and already beginning to be disheartened, Susan and Bernard looked at Thurston's Farm. The buildings were broken down, badly in need of repair and appeared to have been abandoned. Bernard looked doubtfully at Susan and recited what he remembered of the advertisement like a spell against disappointment. 'Homely Lancashire welcome awaits? Wood fires and piping hot water in every bedroom?'

'We'll go in. Shout!'

Bernard knocked at the door and shouted. 'Hullo? Is anybody there?'

There was nobody there to hear. Certainly the person sitting on a hard straightbacked chair in the whitewashed dairy off the kitchen did not hear the shout or the knock since she was dead.

Bernard said, 'Be dark soon,' and knocked again. He tried the handle of the door and it opened. He looked again at Susan for instructions.

Susan said, 'If they come back to catch us, it was you what broke in,' and flounced ahead of him into the farm. He picked up the two suitcases and the holdall and followed.

There was nobody inside to greet them. They opened doors and looked in cupboards but did not try the door of the dairy. Dust – there was dust everywhere. The kitchen was a pit: Gerald had tidied up all signs of the struggle, but this kitchen had been a pit for many years and, being used to that, he had not noticed it.

Suddenly there was the sound of the fridge turning itself on. It made them jump, but told them there was electricity. Bernard turned the overhead light on at the switch by the door, but as he did so, the bulb popped, so they would be in the dark after all. Susan looked in the fridge for food, but found very little: the milk was off. There were tins of beans, pineapple chunks, and peaches in an alcove behind a greasy curtain. Was there water? Bernard turned on a tap at the sink and it gurgled, spluttered and then gushed so that water sprayed onto his chest.

'Bloody hell!'

'I beg your pardon.'

'Gracious me!'

'That's better,' Susan said. She would not permit profanity. 'If you're expecting me to stay here in this rubbish dump for the night, we need a fire.'

Bernard did not answer. He had begun to open the door of the dairy, as they had opened the other downstairs doors, to see what was inside, but his attention had been distracted before he could go in. A hen had entered the kitchen from the farmyard and was looking up at him with its head on one side.

'Bernard!'

He came out of his study of the hen to answer, closing the door to the dairy without going in. 'Fire. Yes, fire. Get us warmed up, that would.'

There were matches among the clutter on the kitchen table, sheets of newspaper on the floor and bits of broken wood outside in the yard. It was wet but would soon dry if they used plenty of paper. They found a packet of firelighters under the sink. Bernard knew what they were – his mother used them – though Susan did not. They would help the paper dry the bits of wood.

Soon they had a good fire going in the grate of an upstairs bedroom, and they had found a box of candles with the firelighters so there was plenty of light. The room was dominated by an old-fashioned iron double bed and a large mirror-fronted wardrobe. Bernard squatted in front of the fire, holding up damp blankets from which steam was rising, while Susan stood looking at her own reflection and that of the room behind her in the wardrobe mirror.

'I'm creepy, Bernard. That's somebody's bed. Where they gone to?'

'If they come back and catch us, you ate tinned peaches.'

Tentatively Susan moved her hand to the handle of the wardrobe door and opened it. Inside skirts, dresses and an overcoat were hanging, all clothes for a woman, nothing for a man. Susan moved in closer, reached out to touch them, then looked up at the shelf above. A fox-fur stole reeking of mothballs dropped from the shelf onto her upturned face. She screamed, lashing out with her hands.

'It's alive. Stop it! Help me! It's alive.'

Bernard dropped the blanket and jumped to help her, pulling off the fur and holding it dangling at arm's length so that she could see what it was. He put his other arm round her. 'Nosey parkers find more than they're expecting.'

He led her to the fire, and they sat together on the floor in front of it. Susan said, 'Wouldn't tell on me about the peaches, would you?'

'Oh, yes. Here she is, this is the one you want.'

She had her arms around him, kissing his face. 'They can't have me when I'm all yours.'

'Told you a fire would warm us up good and proper,' Bernard said. Cuddling and snuggling they moved over to the bed, pulled each other up the side of it and onto the mattress, where they rolled around, giggling.

Outside Gerald waited in the dark looking up at the lighted bedroom window.

Hetty and Geoff reached Chigswick Manor Hotel at breakfast time, expecting to find the runaways tucking into scrambled eggs and black pudding, but they had not arrived. Jessie Mann, the proprietor, remembered the booking. 'It was clear from the hesitant way he asked the questions – how much? – was there a double room free? – that someone was prompting him. At first I thought it might be school children playing a practical joke until he said, "Thank you for being so kind". I mean, after the pushy money-talks types we sometimes get, he sounded so considerate. But, as you see, they never turned up.'

Hetty chewed her lip and said nothing. It was a puzzle. Geoff rubbed the tip of his nose. Jessie turned the Wainthropp Detective Agency's card in her hand. 'You think something may have happened to them?'

'Her father's rich, but they have learning difficulties. We're pretty sure they started out.'

'Hitch-hiking?'

'Seems likely. Public transport wouldn't bring them from the coast right to your door. And if they'd hired a taxi, they'd have arrived.'

'Let's look at the map.' Walkers used the hotel in summer: there was a large-scale map in a frame on the wall. 'They'd have used main roads, at least to begin with.'

'We'll have to make our way back to where they started in Bridsea, asking at every road junction along the way.'

'When you can find someone to ask. This isn't the most populated part of the North West. And once you get back to the A65 it'll be just as bad in a different way with too much going on for people to have noticed a couple of hitch-hikers—'

'—with suitcases,' Geoff said. 'They'd be bound to stand out.'

'Even with suitcases.'

Hetty said, 'Where should we start, do you think? We came via Clitheroe because it's our shortest way but it wouldn't be theirs from Bridsea.'

Jessie indicated a road on the map. 'Normally I'd say here – the Hodder Bank road – but it's closed for road works so they'd have to find another way round. Or *was* it still closed yesterday? You'll need to know if you want to retrace the route they would have taken. Come with me a moment. Gerald will know.'

She took them into the bar, where a man in his mid-forties, unkempt and ill dressed, sat at a table mopping the last vestiges of a fry-up from his plate with toast and supping a mug of tea. 'Just in time. This is the man you talk to about roads around here. Gerald, was the Hodder Bank road closed yesterday?'

'Yeah.'

'I was right. Thanks.'

'Why?'

'This lady and gentleman are private detectives searching for a young couple who've gone missing.'

'Oh, aye? Good luck, then.' He was already on his way out.

Geoff said, 'They're hitch-hiking with suitcases. They'd look odd. You didn't spot them yourself, I suppose?'

'No. Sorry.'

Jessie said, 'Don't go without some scraps for Maggie.'

Gerald shouted over his shoulder, 'She's not with me today,' and was gone.

'Maggie?'

'His dog. I thought she'd be with him in the truck. That poor dog is piggy in the middle whenever Gerald and his mum have a row which they do every few months. Either Molly throws him out or he leaves. Then he hangs around here, living in his cab in the car park and using the facilities until he can't take the inconvenience any more and goes back to make it up.'

'We'd better start on the Clitheroe road then, the way we came, and work back up the A59 to the A65.'

'Speaking from bitter experience,' Geoff said, 'the trouble with hitch-hiking is that, however much you try to take the shortest way, you always end up going round about.'

They were two children playing house. They knew perfectly well that this was not the Chigswick Manor Hotel, but in one important respect it was better; it was theirs. Nobody else was about. They could be a married couple, they could do what they liked.

They dressed up in clothes they had found. Bernard wore a boiler suit and Susan a dirty old mackintosh and a man's flat cap. They followed the hen and found eggs which they boiled in a pan on the fire and ate with baked beans from a can. There were tea bags but the milk was off and the sliced bread was mouldy. It was not a substantial breakfast. Bernard said, 'I'm still hungry.'

Susan was the busybody, walking about importantly, looking for pencil and paper. 'List. We make a list. Write things down. Help us remember. Count our money. How much for us to spend? Can't make chips without potatoes, Bernard, and that's that.'

So Bernard went upstairs to get his wallet from his jacket while Susan began to make the list which they would take to a shop wherever there was a shop. If they just walked along the road they would be bound to find one.

There was a howl from upstairs. Bernard's wallet was not in his jacket. 'Wallet! . . . Wallet!' He pulled out all the pockets, and there was no wallet, searched the floor before the fire and under the bed, shook the blankets, lifted the mattress, pummelled the pillows and there was no wallet. He looked on every mantelpiece and in every chair in every room, rummaged among the newspapers on the kitchen floor, moved the pots and pans and the cans of tinned fruit, beans and luncheon meat behind the greasy curtain, lifted and sifted the pile of broken bits of wood for the fire. There was no wallet.

There were tears on Bernard's face and on Susan's. He stood at one end of the kitchen by the open back door, pressing his face against the jamb, unable to look at her. After a while she moved slowly towards him, put one hand gently to his cheek, turning his face towards her, then pressed her own face against his.

She began to rock slowly and gently. His body rocked with hers.

Gerald still had the wallet, but they did not know that, had no idea they had left it in the cab of the truck. If they had looked out of the front door and up the track they might have seen his truck on the road at the top. He was collecting the mail from the postbox, nothing of interest, just circulars from firms which believed that Thurston Farm still functioned as a farm. He had not yet decided how to return the wallet to them. It depended on when they found his mother in the dairy.

Hetty and Geoff started on the road to Clitheroe, stopping at every turn off and, where there was not a house at the turn itself, proceeding a little way up every side road to find someone to ask. Jessie was right. It was not an overpopulated area.

They had the photograph of Susan with them. Nobody could remember having seen her with a man. Nobody could remember two hitch-hikers with suitcases. Downhill the scooter showed a tendency to gather speed. They came too fast round a bend on a moorland road and skidded between sheep. They worked back from the A59 to the A682 to the A65, the A687 and the A68̈, showing the photo at every junction, every tea bar and lay-by, every Welcome Break and Happy Eater. They worked their way back to the edge of Bridsea and saw a rusty old bike abandoned in a lay-by off the main road. People had no consideration, said Hetty; they would junk anything anywhere.

From Bridsea they worked forward again, and had a piece of luck with the driver of an articulated lorry who remembered a girl hitching in the rain, trying to get to some bloody Manor House, and a boy sitting on suitcases close by. But that was it. Darkness found them sitting in a transport café, ready to give up.

'Nothing!'

Geoff said, 'We know they made a booking. We know they started out. Know they got as far as the junction of the A682 and the A65 because that lorry driver saw them. It's not nothing.'

'If they reached the road works on the Hodder Bank road, they'll have taken side-roads with no traffic and got lost. They have learning difficulties and they've never hitched before. They may be anywhere and nowhere and wherever they are they're freezing.' Hetty stood up. She had made a decision. 'We've no choice. We report what we've discovered so far and tell his Worship the Mayor to call in the police.'

She made her way to the pay telephone in the corner of the café while Geoff bought himself another ring doughnut. She inserted money, dialled the Makepeaces' number, and was connected immediately with the voice of Mrs Makepeace at her most genteel. 'This is the Mayor of Titterslow's residence. I am afraid there is nobody available to take your call at this moment.' Answering machines! Nobody these days had time to talk. Hetty left a message, definite and succinct. If the Makepeaces needed any more information, they could phone her at home, but meanwhile the police might as well start tuning up their helicopter to scour the moors.

'I think we've got visitors,' Robert said.

Two heavily padded chickens, bright yellow and orange, were getting out of a taxi in front of the house.

The doorbell rang and Geoff answered it. 'Is Mrs Wainthropp at home?' the first chicken said, and the second chicken added, 'Please, it's urgent.'

'Whom shall I say is calling?'

The first chicken lifted its beak and told him.

Geoff announced the visitors. 'The Right Honourable Mayor and Mayoress of Titterslow, Councillor and Mrs Makepeace.'

Hetty said, 'I thought you didn't want to be seen coming to the house.'

The chickens cut in on each other, tumbling over themselves to explain.

'Since we were coming close by—'

'—we thought if we changed taxis—'

'—we could risk dropping in on our way.'

'It's a Charity Ball.'

'Fancy Dress.'

'We'd never have known,' Robert said.

'In aid of endangered species,' the first chicken said. 'I don't mind putting on a silly costume for a good cause.'

The second chicken backed him up. 'In our position we have to support these functions. One can't grudge the expense. You said on the answering machine that our Susan is with a boyfriend.'

'They booked into a Country House Hotel.'

'I told you that girl had too much money,' the first chicken said to his spouse, and then to Hetty, 'Where is this place?'

'They didn't turn up and might be lost. They could be anywhere in the Ribble Valley. Unless we use the media to ask the public for help we could search for weeks without finding them.'

'Let's not lose our heads. Is this boyfriend person sane and responsible?'

'From what we know, the young man appears to be quiet, hard working and good to his mother. And he has learning difficulties just like your daughter.'

There was silence as the two chickens took in this information. Then the second chicken said, 'Oh my God!'

The first chicken said, 'He has a job, then?'

'He's a hygiene operative.'

'No, please,' said the second chicken. 'Not a lavatory attendant.'

'Bernard is a roadsweeper with your own Borough Council's Public Cleansing Department.'

The first chicken exploded. 'No media! No newspapers! No

television appeal! Understand? I engaged your services by paying a deposit, and I demand secrecy. Not one word about Susan and this road cleaner. Not *one* word. My God! If this was to get out . . .'

He crossed to the window and looked out, almost as if he were expecting the press to have arrived already. 'Wait, Charlie, wait!' the second chicken said. 'What if they've had an accident? They could be dying slowly in a ditch somewhere.' Hetty decided that the woman was not all bad. There were finer feelings somewhere. A mother's heart still beat beneath that orange and yellow fancy dress.

'I don't believe it!' Now the first chicken sounded like Victor Meldrew, but with some reason. Outside in the road two pigs had found the taxi. One was brandishing a handful of notes at the driver. The other was climbing in. 'There's a couple of porkers hijacking our taxi.'

Robert said, 'That'll be the Jessups from Number 46.'

'Stop! Stop!' The first chicken flapped his wings but it did no good; the taxi drew away. 'Well, he won't get *his* licence renewed.' He looked at his watch. 'Oh God! We'll miss the official opening by HRH and we're due to be presented.

'We're finished here. Mrs Wainthropp, you've got your instructions.' He moved back to his wife and began to move her towards the door, but she resisted, saying, 'We'll have to phone for another taxi. I'm not waiting at bus stops for public transport dressed like this.'

Robert said, 'Ernie Outhwaite at Number 7 does a minicab service.'

'We'll take it. Let's go.'

'Why can't he come here?'

'Brenda, sweetheart, don't start, not now.'

'You're bending my plumage, Charlie.'

Hetty said, 'I'm going to have to put a time limit on your secrecy, Mr Mayor. One more day; that's all you get. After that it's a police matter. Geoffrey, would you please show our feathered friends to the door.'

Outside the kitchen of Thurston's Farm the wind was howling. The fire was almost out, just smoke and damp wood, and there was none in the bedroom. Susan, wrapped in blankets, moved from the dying fire to the alcove in which the tins of food were kept. Two left, neither large, one cheap salmon, the other fruit cocktail.

They had found a torch with a weak beam, the batteries not quite dead, and Bernard had taken it to light his way to the barn where he might find more wood. Shutters and half-doors banged in the wind. There were bits of rope and a rusty harness hanging from nails on the wall and zinc feeding troughs on the floor.

He had found a couple of logs and a fence-post. They were enough for one load; he could come back for more. He had left the door open, but suddenly it banged closed behind him. He jumped and turned quickly, his knee hit something sharp and he gave a cry of pain, fell sideways, grazing the sharp thing and dropped the torch. The beam went out. He was lying helpless and in total darkness on the floor of the barn among straw, dust, muck and goodness knew what else. He shouted for help, but who could hear him? Not Susan, in the kitchen with the door locked, not with a gale blowing.

Not even Gerald, who was nearer. He had left his truck on the road and come to prowl. He had to know what was going on, whether they had found his mother in the dairy, and what they had done about her. Could he have made a mistake? Was his mother still alive, just knocked out and had made a recovery? Were they all three laughing at him? He moved cautiously in the shadow of the out-buildings, drawing closer to the house.

Susan was at the back door, willing herself to open it. Within the sound of the wind she could hear – or believed she could hear – the howl of a distant dog. She was afraid of dogs and the dark. It was not fair. Nobody could expect her to open the door until Bernard knocked and asked for entry. But Bernard had not knocked, and had been gone too long; he should be back. Was there another sound in the wind, someone calling? Was it Bernard?

She closed her eyes and turned the key. She did not see a face pressed against the kitchen window – Gerald's face. She opened the back door slowly. She would prop it open with a chair so that she could see her way across the yard to the barn by the light from the kitchen. She did so and went out. Gerald watched her go.

'Bernard? . . . Bernard? . . .' He was not in the farmyard. She would have to look for him in the barn. She could see the door but it was shut. There was a cry now from inside; she could hear it. 'Help! . . . Susan! . . . Help!' She tried to open the barn door, but the wind was so strong that it resisted. Unseen, behind her, Gerald went into the kitchen.

She struggled and pulled at the door, and it opened suddenly, almost knocking her backwards. She could not see well enough to find something to prop it open, but she could hear Bernard moaning.

'Bernard?'

'Over here. Be careful. Come slow.'

She came slowly towards him as instructed. There were obstructions and a dank smell. She reached and touched him.

'Can't move.'

She had not endured so much in order to find him only to be told that she had wasted her time.

'You have to move, Bernard. It's cold here.' She got her hands under his arms and began to drag him out of the barn.

Gerald had found his way into the dairy. There was a small window but it did not face the farmyard; he could switch on the overhead light. He did so. His mother was still there as he had left her, sitting bolt upright in the chair. He touched her face. It was cold. 'Leave the door open,' he said. 'Bound to find you then. Report you. Can't do it myself. Folk won't understand it was just a game. Sorry, mum.' She stared back at him. It was not like his mum just to sit there with nothing to say for herself.

He turned off the light and came out of the dairy, being careful to leave the door open as he had said he would. One more job to do. Return the wallet. He propped it up on the mantelpiece in clear sight. He could hear the two retards talking to each other in the farmyard. Out the front, then: he could work his way round to the back again when they were safely inside and watch them find his mother and the wallet; he did not care in which order.

Susan dragged Bernard backwards across the farmyard towards the light from the kitchen door she had propped open. 'Got to get you inside. Brass monkey weather.'

That was rude, he knew. In spite of the pain from his leg he began to giggle. 'Quick as you can, then, girl.'

She dragged him back into the kitchen; he helped as much as he could, using his hands and his good leg. She left him on the floor and began moving furniture out of his way, so that he could crawl to the fire. If he had found any firewood he had not said and anyway would not have been able to carry it; they could burn a chair. 'Get you warmed up again.' In moving furniture Susan closed the door to the dairy, not even noticing that it was now open when it had been closed before. Gerald, who was still making his way from the front to the back of the house, did not see her do so.

Bernard crawled to the fire. 'Did very well. Didn't know you had such big muscles on you.'

Susan banged the leg of a chair against the side of the table, and being old and worm-eaten and the glue mostly gone, the chair fell to pieces. She fed the fire, then put the kettle on and noticed the wallet propped up on the mantel.

Gerald had reached the back window by this time. With two of them in the kitchen to see him, he dared not look in, but he could listen. He heard Susan cry, 'Bernard! Look!' and his reply, 'Don't point. It's rude. What you staring at?' It was enough. They had found her. He moved away swiftly from shadow to shadow across the yard.

Susan took the wallet from the mantelpiece and opened it. 'Must have been there all the time.' Perhaps it was easier for her and Bernard to accept this than it might have been for many people. Both of them knew that objects mislaid did have a way of turning up even after having been searched for.

They ate the tinned salmon and fruit cocktail and built up the fire. Only the first chair counts: after that burning furniture becomes easy. They used what fuel they could find, including lino from the bedroom. They found a mail order catalogue of leisure wear, beach wear, garden furniture, an electric wok, humidifier and all sorts of useful objects offering Mrs Molly Putnam of Thurston's Farm both substantial discounts and the opportunity to win a Ford Cortina if she placed an order within fourteen days, and Susan used it to give Bernard a reading lesson. He endured it for as long as he could and then said, 'Leg hurts bad.' And it did. It had swollen up and hurt whenever he tried to move it.

'Talk about something else.'

'Promise you'll go find someone tomorrow morning.'

She shook her head. It was unreasonable of him to expect her to go out into unknown country on her own and explain their troubles. People were there to look after Susan. Susan did not look after people. She had done more than enough already, going out into the dark of the barn.

Bernard said, 'You got to help me, Suzy.'

'Lino from the bedrooms burns different colours, look.'

Gerald sat in the bar of the Chigswick Manor Hotel, eating a huge breakfast. He did not pay for such meals. Any hotel needs an odd-job man and Gerald was paid in food for any bits of carpentry, gardening, plumbing or electrical work he did.

Jessie came in with a large mug of coffee which she placed on the table. 'Got any work on today with the truck?' He shook his head. 'I've fixed up a nice little job for you. Hire of you and your transport for the full day, chauffeuring those two private detectives.'

It was Robert who had told Hetty that searching for the runaways by scooter was a dead loss because they could not see over hedges and needed to be higher, and Hetty had remembered the man with the truck who knew all the roads around the village of Chigswick. While Gerald, much alarmed, was still trying to think of a reason to refuse, Hetty and Geoff had already followed Jessie into the bar and it was too late; Jessie, already assuming that he had accepted, was asking them if they would like a bite to eat before setting out.

Geoff said, 'I wouldn't say no to a bacon sarney.'

Hetty said, 'You've had your breakfast, Geoffrey.' He looked at her with a real concern. When would she realise that any meal eaten before six-thirty in the morning was not breakfast but an extension of supper the night before? 'Oh, all right,' she said. 'I'll have one as well. It's going to be a long day.'

Soon they were on their way. Every side road was to be explored and every track wide enough to take a truck and two passengers. Geoff sat where Bernard had sat earlier, between the two front seats, but since he was smaller than Bernard, found it a little less uncomfortable, though he still bounced about on the rougher roads.

'How does this casual haulage work come your way?' he asked. They would have to get to know Gerald if they were to be in his company all day, and he showed no disposition to make conversation without being prompted.

'Word of mouth.'

'Do you live somewhere close by?' Hetty remembered that Jessie had told them Gerald lived with his mother, but had walked out because of a quarrel. 'When you're at home, I mean.'

'Over Blackleg Fell way.' A lie but a necessary lie. Gerald hoped that he would not have to lie too often. It was so easy to trip oneself up.

It had not been possible for Bernard to climb the stairs to the double bed, and anyway they had burned so much of the bedroom lino it made the room look squalid. So they had spent the night by the kitchen fire lying among a tangle of blankets and cushions.

Bernard had been woken by pain whenever he moved his leg, and even in sleep he whimpered. Susan had been kept awake by the noise and by her own thoughts. It was so unfair, so obviously unfair, that she should be expected to get help, when it wasn't her fault Bernard had hurt himself. She had looked at his face, all screwed up, by the light of the fire, felt his restlessness, heard him whimpering.

She had no notion of anyone's being dependent on her. She said what she wanted and people did what she asked, and if they didn't she made a fuss. That was the nature of things; that was how life went on. Only this time there wasn't anyone else around. If she didn't put herself out to help Bernard, there was nobody else to do it.

And Bernard was hers, belonged to her, not to anybody else. He was not just somebody to cuddle and kiss and make love. It came to Susan with some difficulty that love was not just something you did; it was something you felt. And if you felt it, you had to try to look after the person you felt it for. Bernard was not just for carrying the luggage and playing house with. He was hurting and could not look after himself. She would have to go.

At first light Bernard fell into a deeper sleep, but his leg was still swollen as Susan could see. She snuggled him close to her, feeling his body helpless against hers, and, having made up her mind, slept also.

When Bernard woke it was to find the chicken back in the kitchen investigating his toes. He supposed that, since they had run out of food, they would have to kill and eat it, but he did not know how. Cut off its head, pull out its insides, put it in the oven. He did not think he could do it, but might have to try. His leg was still hurting, worse than before. Where was Susan?

He shouted and she replied from upstairs where she was pulling up floorboards to get more wood for the fire. When she came down to him with an armful of boards he saw that she was wearing an overcoat, headscarf and a pair of wellies, all the property of the woman who had received the catalogue. 'Don't burn all this while I'm gone,' she said.

He took in her appearance and understood her intention. Tears filled his eyes. He was so proud of her. 'You going . . . get help?'

'Been thinking. It's best. Don't be upset just 'cos it's a long way. Be all right.' He turned his head away. He was weeping, racked by sobs. He should be glad. Maybe he was hungry. 'I'll bring sandwiches,' Susan said, and set off up the track towards the road.

They were on a single-track moorland road, approaching a crossroads with a postbox and an elderly post lady emptying it, except that it was empty already. The post lady, who must have been in her sixties, wore a skid-lid and her transport, a motorbike with sidecar containing sacks of mail, was parked by the box.

Hetty's feelings were mixed. On the one hand approval, on the other jealousy. *She* was the one who wore a skid-lid; other senior citizens need not apply. 'Stop here, please,' she said. 'I'll talk to her.'

She climbed out of the cab. Gerald said, 'Her name's Bessie. Stay on her right ear. She's deaf in the left.'

Geoff said, 'Is that how they collect the post around here?'

'Used to be a push-bike: she was a devil on the hills. But it all changed when she got arthritis.'

Hetty stayed on Bessie's right ear, and Bessie removed her skid-lid. Yes, she had seen a couple of hitch-hikers. She pointed to the left. Back a bit up Tor Fell.

'Young man and woman?'

'Soaked to the skin. What folk do for pleasure!'

They drove on up to Tor Fell in heavy rain, with the road getting rockier and narrower the further they went, a steep drop on one side, increasingly damp and depressed sheep on the other. On top of Tor Fell, sheltering under the lee of an upended slab of granite erected to the memory of a seventh-century ravisher and sheep stealer who had turned Christian on his death-bed and been made a saint by administrative error, they found two very damp hitch-hikers, one male, one female, of about the right ages but without suitcases.

'Don't look much like our runaways to me,' Hetty said. 'But we've come so far, I'd better have a word.'

She climbed out of the cab and made her way to the upended granite. Geoff, left behind with Gerald, decided to try to establish a rapport. 'You've trouble at home, I've heard.'

Gerald looked at him sideways. What had the lad heard? Personal questions had to be discouraged. Better not to answer.

'It can be very distressing not seeing eye to eye with a parent. I had trouble in that direction with my own mother. That's why I left home. If you think it might help to talk about it, you only have to say.'

Gerald looked away. 'I'm all right, thanks.'

Hetty had reached the hitch-hikers, who regarded her without enthusiasm. It did not seem to them that she represented the likelihood of a lift. 'Excuse me. Are you Susan, by any chance?'

The young woman looked at her in amazement. 'I am. How do you know that?'

She was? That made a difference. Hetty delved through two layers of winter wear and produced the photo given to her by the Makepeaces. She looked from the photo to Susan. 'It's not a very good likeness.'

The young woman took the photo, looked at it, then handed it to the young man, who said, 'It's not a l . . . l . . . likeness at all.'

He had difficulty in speaking. What did that indicate? Hetty

said, 'If you don't mind me asking, have you got learning
difficulties?'

'Hasn't e . . . ev . . . everyone?'

The girl called Susan said, 'I don't know what you're on about.
I'm Susie Brierley, he's Stephen Slater. Learning difficulties. He's
the most brilliant biochemist of his year at Cambridge. He's been
on *University Challenge*.'

Susan had reached the road. Which way should she go? There
were no signposts. She tried to remember how far back there had
been houses when the man in the truck had brought them, and
could not; too much had happened since. Maybe if she went on
in the direction he had been going she would find somewhere.
She did not need a shop, not at once, just people she could tell
about Bernard's leg. The people would do something. People
always had; she was the Mayor's daughter. She would get
sandwiches afterwards unless maybe the people had some she
could take.

She walked. It was not easy in wellies which were too big for
her. They scratched the back of her legs.

Susan kept a good look-out for houses on either side. She did
not wear a watch, although she could tell the time. It was all up
and down hills and the mist and rain made it difficult to see.
Mostly the land to the right of her sloped up with not much room
for houses before the land became a ridge which could not be
seen over. To the left was the valley in which the farmhouse lay,
and that way you could see further and up the hill beyond the
other side. Meanwhile she was on a road and there would be cars
or lorries to give her a lift to wherever she was going.

She did not know how long she had been walking when, on
the other side of the valley across fields, she saw a stone building

which must be a house. She left the road and headed in that direction. They were large fields divided by low stone walls. If she tried to go from gate to gate through the fields towards the house, she would be going in a zig-zag and it would take too long. She tried to climb over one of the walls, but it was of a kind she had never seen before; it had just been put together with the stones piled one on another and nothing to hold them, so part of it came to pieces and the falling stones hurt her leg. She decided to go from gate to gate.

When she reached the stone building which must be a house, it was not a house, but an empty barn. The ground outside was muddy. Perhaps there would be a farmer in the barn. She went in, but there was nobody. A sudden rustling noise startled her. She turned quickly and saw a rat with a long tail. She ran whimpering from the barn, slipped on the muddy ground outside, and fell, grazing her knee on a stone. It hurt and she was frightened. She began to weep.

Susan, on her hands and knees, weeping and muddy, looked across the valley towards the distant road and saw first a van passing in one direction and then, after some time, a motorbike with a sidecar in the other. She had been wrong to leave the road. Her knee hurt where she had grazed it and the backs of her legs felt raw from the friction of the wellies rubbing against them. She did not move quickly as she limped back, zig-zag from gate to gate, and some of those gates were not easy to open.

Time passed. A lot of time, as her empty stomach told her. Back on the road she walked in the direction she had first started to walk, no longer bothering to keep a look-out on either side of the road since she did not intend to investigate any more barns; she would get a lift. But there was no more traffic. All the drivers would be having their lunch. Uphill then down again. A car came up behind her. It made very little noise, so she only realised that it was coming when it was already close, and had passed before she could get her thumb out properly. Nevertheless she did stick out the thumb of one hand and waved desperately with the other, and the car stopped about a hundred yards in front of her.

She ran towards it. In his wing mirror the driver saw a wet dirty muddy hoyden running with a curious lop-sided gait towards his car. He went back into gear and accelerated away. Susan sat down at the side of the road and sobbed.

Bernard sat in the kitchen, wrapped in blankets, and kept the fire going. His leg was all swollen, he could not walk, but he could get about by moving his bum along the floor. Susan was a long time but she would come back with people to help them. And bring sandwiches as she had promised. Meanwhile there was nothing to eat.

Hetty and Geoff were driven by Gerald along bleak moorland roads and saw nothing moving but sheep. Where there were isolated houses, they showed Susan's photo, but got no good of it. They stopped and ate the packed lunch Jessie had provided and drank from a thermos of coffee, and went on, and had no luck whatever. Gerald said very little throughout the journey.

Susan gathered herself together and continued her journey, not knowing where she was going or whether she would ever get there. After more time than she could calculate she saw another vehicle, but this one was not on the road. It was a Land-Rover, something like that, moving along a track or path two fields away, but heading towards her. Again she left the road and ran as best she could towards it. She reached a gate and pulled herself over. The Land-Rover was still coming her way. Then it swerved off, but she could see that there was a rutted track, and if she followed, even though she might not – clearly could not – catch up, it would take her where the Land-Rover was going.

So she followed and after some time the Land-Rover was out of sight, and after even more time the track grew less easy to follow and then disappeared altogether.

Bernard slept, his back against a door leading from the kitchen. He was awakened by a crash, and looked about him, still stupid with sleep, trying to work out what was happening.

Nobody in the kitchen. The crash must have come from behind the door against which his back was resting, and which opened onto . . . what? They had not opened it, had not explored in there. It would be a cupboard or another room, not the toilet because they had found that, somewhere they had overlooked when seeking for food or fuel. A crash. And now other noises. He pressed his ear against the door and heard a soft whining sound and a steady thump of something being hit against wood.

Was it human? Someone broken in? Was it Susan come back, found him asleep and now playing a joke?

'Susan?' He waited. No response. 'What you doing?'

It was not Susan. It was some person or thing had broken in. Could be anyone. Or anything. Keep the door closed. He pressed his back harder against it.

But he couldn't do nothing. Whatever it was, he must deal with it before Susan returned because it might harm her. He would have to look. There had been a crash. And whimpering, which still persisted along with the thumping sound. The person or thing had hurt itself, just like Bernard hurting his leg in the dark barn. They should have looked before.

Problem was, he couldn't stand up to open the door. The latch was out of his reach.

There was a broom leaning against the opposite wall. He went across the floor on his bum, and brought the broom back with him. He faced the door, put the handle of the broom under the latch and pushed. Up came the latch. Now all he had to do was to keep it lifted while he edged the door open. Fingers in the crack between the door and the doorframe, easing gently then pulling wide open.

Inside the room Bernard saw a German Shepherd dog, pushing its head against the side of a wooden chair, its tail thumping rhythmically. One of the chair legs was splayed out, coming loose from the spindle and ready to collapse. There was a woman sitting in the chair and staring directly at him. It would be the woman who lived here. Bernard said, 'Sorry we ate tinned peaches. We'll buy more when Susan gets back.'

Then the chair leg finally came apart from the spindle and the body of the woman toppled to the floor, her dead eyes still glaring at Bernard. And as Bernard screamed, the dog began to bark.

The two detectives were on their way back to Chigswick, just as dispirited as they had been the day before. Gerald, for some reason, had made objections to coming back by the most direct route, but Hetty had overruled him; there was no point in covering the same ground twice.

There were farm buildings in the valley down to their left and a gate with a track leading down to them. A notice on the gate, not easy to read since the gate was open. Thur something. Hetty said, 'Stop a moment. Let's ask at that farm. They might have seen something.'

Gerald did not even slow the truck but drove on regardless. 'Nobody lives there,' he said. 'It's deserted. There was an old woman owned it, but she died.'

The farm had been below and was now behind them. Geoff said, 'Thought I saw smoke.'

Susan, a long way from the road, drenched by rain and mist, every part of her hurting, had lost heart, but went on anyway. Road or track, field or bare moorland, it seemed to make little difference; there was nobody to help her and she was no longer sure of her way back. She limped, weeping and bedraggled along a ridge, and again saw the distant road and a truck moving along it.

Geoff said, 'Be dark soon.'

'Have you back at the hotel in fifteen minutes. Sorry you've had no luck.'

Hetty saw, far away on the ridge opposite, a solitary female figure walking. 'There's someone over there.'

Gerald looked across. He knew at once that the woman was Susan. She had changed course and was moving off the ridge back towards the road. 'It'll be Sharon from Barton Cross,' he said. 'She's out in all weathers,' and drove on.

Back at the Chigswick Manor Hotel Jessie gave them tea and thick chunks of fruit cake, which were consumed while Gerald laboriously wrote out a receipt and Hetty a cheque which – since Gerald did not have a bank account – Jessie would turn into cash. Once she had done so, Gerald quickly disposed of the rest of his tea and cake and drove off.

Geoff was looking at the receipt. 'He's written his address on here.'

'I told him to. Has to be official if we're to get the money back from the Lord High Chicken.'

'It says he lives at Thurston's Farm, Meatly Bottom. But he told us he and his mum were over at Blackleg Fell.'

'Thurston's Farm. Do you remember the deserted farmhouse

where it wasn't worth stopping to ask? Thur something on the gate.'

'And smoke from the chimney.'

Hetty said to Jessie, 'Do Gerald and his mother live off the Clitheroe road?'

'Just off. It's down in the valley.'

Hetty said to Geoff, 'An old woman owned it, but she's dead.'

'And when we said yesterday morning that we were looking for a missing couple he wasn't interested in who they were.'

'Well, at least it's on our way back,' Hetty said. 'We can look in,' and Jessie, rather uneasy, said, 'I suppose that's all right. Gerald's not dangerous as far as I know.'

But they were spared from danger by the arrival of a police car and DCI Adams wearing his most long-suffering expression. 'Your Robert is something of a tiger when he's roused,' the DCI said. 'He spent the morning brooding on the kind of publicity the Agency would get for agreeing not to involve the police when a disabled couple were missing, and the afternoon shouting at Mayor Makepeace. So I'm here to give you my official co-operation.'

It was already dusk. Susan had found her way back to the road and staggered as she tried to keep walking. Everything was difficult; she was so cold, if she shivered any more she would fall over. She could see the headlights of a truck coming towards her. It was going the wrong way, but any way was right now if it would take her to people. She broke into a sort of run, waving her arms. The truck stopped and seemed to be waiting for her.

As she grew closer it came to her that there was something familiar about the truck, but she could not be sure; the headlights still dazzled her. She slowed her pace, then stopped. The headlights were switched off, and she saw a man getting out of the cab. She knew who it was.

She dared not leave the road again, but knew she must. There was a gate into a field. She managed to get over and stumbled forwards into the dark where she might be able to hide. But her breath made such a noise as she ran. There was a wall ahead. She would not be able to get over but perhaps she had come far enough. If the man had followed her, surely she would have heard him. She would wait where she was until the truck drove away. She turned to face the road.

She had not heard the man, because he had not bothered to run after her. He was walking towards her, moving slowly, talking gently as to a frightened animal.

'Don't be afraid. I won't hurt you. I fetched an old coat to warm you up a bit.' She tried to run again, sideways this time along the dry-stone wall but found herself trapped in a corner as he continued to approach, still at the same unhurried pace. 'Please don't run away from me. I'm not bad, and I'm not mad either. I've no real experience with women, that's all. Never been close, not alone like this.' He had reached her now, and she could feel the warmth of his breath. 'Would it help warm you if we sort of cuddled a bit?'

He had hold of her shoulders and was very slowly moving his body closer to hers. 'It's Susan, isn't it? I remember your name. It's best you let me press myself against you like this, best for us both in the long run. I don't think you will find that too frightening, I really don't, not being pressed against gently but firmly.'

Susan said, 'Please . . . Just please don't do anything rude to me, will you? I am very cold, but I don't want to. Please don't hurt me.' There was wet on the man's face, not just the rain, but tears from his eyes. 'I love my boyfriend, so don't take my clothes off, will you?'

And a woman's voice said, 'If he so much as loosens a button, I'll have his guts for garters.' Hetty Wainthropp had brought another case to a successful conclusion.

Bernard and Susan sat side by side in the kitchen of Thurston's Farm, each with an arm round the other's shoulders, wrapped in blankets before a blazing fire. They had been given sandwiches and coffee brought from Chigswick and would be taken back to Titterslow in a police car.

'I think it's possible he's telling the truth – she fell during a quarrel and hit her head on the table,' DCI Adams said to Hetty. 'If that happened, Forensics will confirm it.'

'There's more to it than that.'

'Heavy psychological stuff. Getting someone else to find his mother, report her death, and so ease him of some of the guilt.'

'Why these two?'

'They fell in his way.'

'When I was a girl my uncle kept chickens – real ones, not these conveyor belt creatures you get nowadays. Any that was weaker than the others, they'd peck it to death.'

'Only the strong survive? Well, that's the Law of the Yukon, I seem to remember from my schooldays, but we'll try not to make it so in Lancashire. Eh, Bernard?'

Bernard had no idea what they were talking about, being far too much concerned with loving feelings for Susan, who had done exactly what she had promised, bringing both sandwiches and people to help, but he grinned and nodded anyway. Hetty said, 'I hope you two know how lucky you are. Any couple whose love survives the romantic holiday you've just had would certainly be daft to look around for anyone else.'

And so Bernard and Susan were married, a quiet wedding at a country church with no press coverage, and whether they will live happily ever after is too early to tell.

Hetty, Geoff and Robert were at the ceremony, as was Jessie, who had given a home at the hotel to the bereaved German Shepherd dog. Not long afterwards Hetty took a trip of her own to Bridsea and she and Maureen had tea together at a café in the High Street.

They sat among ladies in hats and shared a pot of tea for two and toasted teacakes with iced fancies. 'I don't usually come here,' Maureen said. 'Too expensive.'

Hetty told her about the wedding and the whole story of Bernard and Susan's adventures at Thurston's Farm. Maureen was particularly impressed with the conduct of the dog, travelling so many miles in bad weather to find its dead mistress. 'There's some folk frightened of dogs,' she said, 'but not me. Man's best friend.'

'Are you happy at the Hotel Clare, Maureen?'

'Better than the hospital.' She looked around the café, where the waitresses wore aprons and the cups were thin china. 'This is nice.'

Hetty said, 'We'll come again.'

The Astral Plane

In a ground floor room running from front to back of a semi-detached house in Aquinas Avenue, Burnley, eight people sat in a line facing a ninth. The eight had come to communicate with the Spirit World; the ninth, Maurika Rome, was their channel of communication. She lay, dressed all in black and silver – black dress, black shawl decorated with sequins, black stockings, black court shoes with silver buckles – on a chaise longue upholstered in red velvet. The communicants sat, three on a sofa, two in armchairs, one on a pouffe, two on red velvet cushions on the carpet. Each grasped the hand of the person on either side, except for the two at the each end of the line, whose hands were connected by a red velvet rope. Linked in this way they formed a circle of power, concentrating their spiritual forces.

The eight were local, or at least within a bus ride's distance. Two were men, both widowers, and of the women three were widows, one had lost a father and one a dearly loved elder sister. The only woman under fifty had long hair, thick spectacles, a broad beam and wore a dress she had made herself from material she had woven herself. She had not come to make contact with any particular departed, but hoped for spiritual enlightenment in a more general sense.

Mrs Rome was not local or a senior citizen; she was clearly in the prime of life and as for spiritual enlightenment she already had it in spades. She and her daughter had rented the house in Aquinas Avenue for the winter. Nobody knew where they came from. The daughter, Sara, stage-managed the proceedings, assisting those who had come for enlightenment to achieve the right frame of mind to receive it.

There were red bulbs in the ceiling lamp and in the candle-shaped fittings on the walls, so the light in the room was dim and red. The curtains of the french windows behind Mrs Rome were of the same red velvet as covered the chaise longue. The chaise longue, curtains, cushions and rope did not belong to the house but had been brought by Mrs Rome and even the armchairs, sofa and pouffe had been draped with red velvet throws that totally hid their own floral chintz which would have been out of keeping.

There were stereo speakers of dark wood with a red fabric front. Sara pressed a button. 'Eyes . . . closed. Floating. Relax. Lose the self.' The eight would-be communicants closed their eyes and went self-consciously limp. From the speakers came the voice of the young Ernest Lough in the well-known recording of Mendelssohn's anthem, *Hear My Prayer*, a re-mastering which had skilfully removed the crackle of the old 70 rpm record. 'Breathe . . . deep.' They breathed deeply.

Mrs Rome on the chaise longue with the red velvet curtains behind her had also closed her eyes and was also breathing deeply; truth to tell, it was more like a snore. She was in a trance, they knew, reaching out to the spirits. Suddenly she gave a little cry. 'I'm getting something.' Sara faded out the music.

'It's not clear. I think . . . Is it . . .? Yes, it's A. Does the letter A mean something to anyone here?'

Silence. The letter A was of no significance to anyone. Then one of the widows said, 'When I was a girl in Castleton, I had an auntie used to make alphabet soup.'

'No, I don't see soup. It's a man, I think, trying to communicate. Capital letter A – not very well formed.'

Another of the widows, Grace Todd, cleared her throat. She was shy and did not like to put herself forward. This was her first time at a séance, and she was not sure whether she ought to speak. However, since nobody else seemed to have anything to say . . . 'Could it be an H? Capital A does sometimes look like an H.'

'You're right. It's H. I've got it clear now – H. A definite H.'

'Harry.'

'Someone dear to you?'

'My husband. He passed over in January. His handwriting was never easy to read.'

'Harry? . . . Are you there, Harry? Is there something you want to say to this lady?'

Silence. Grace wanted to release her grasp of the hands of the people on either side. She wanted to sit up, open her eyes, hold her hands in front of her ready to reach out to him: Harry was hers, no business of anyone else's. But she remained as she was until suddenly there was a whoosh. Grace opened her eyes; so did everyone else but Mrs Rome. The french windows had been closed, as they had to be in this winter weather, yet now their red velvet curtains were billowing into the room.

And there was a scent. Unmistakable. She knew it. 'It's him. I know it is,' Grace said. 'I can smell his pipe tobacco.'

'They're called House Parties. The woman summons up the dead for small groups in her own front room. It's unhealthy.'

Hetty and Geoff stood in a biting east wind among polyanthus and a few uneasily flowering daffodils at a garden centre near Padiham where Amy Bartlett, only daughter of Grace and Harry

Todd, was the manager. 'What do you want us to do?' Hetty said.

'Expose her,' said Amy.

'It's not illegal.'

'Then it ought to be. Taking advantage of the bereaved at a vulnerable time.' She clicked her tongue. She had seen something untoward which required correction. 'You'll have to excuse me. That lady's corgi is lifting its leg on the chairanthus. I shan't be a moment.'

Amy bustled away to reprove a customer who, hampered by a trolley loaded with perennials, was trying to pull her corgi away from the display of flowers. 'I can't sell those. You've soiled the goods; you'll have to take them.'

Hetty looked at Geoff. 'What do you think?'

He shrugged his shoulders. 'It's all work, I suppose.'

'There's work and work. We've not had much to do with the supernatural up to now.'

The lady with the corgi put the tray of already wilting chairanthus on top of her trolley, pulled the dog up short on its leash, and made her way to the check-out. Amy returned to the two representatives of the Wainthropp Detective Agency. 'Mother goes twice a week. Twenty pounds and bus fares. The expense is horrendous. But there's worse. The House Parties are only a come-on. Folk go for the interest and get hooked. Mother's having private consultations as well at twenty-five pounds an hour.'

Geoff said, 'She must be getting satisfaction or she wouldn't go back.'

'We're not meant to get satisfaction in this world. We're meant to get through it as best we can, and hope for better in the next. I've asked mother to live with Jim and me but she refuses. She says dad talks to her through a Spirit Guide and tells her to stay where she is.'

'Why don't you go to the seance with her?'

'She says the spirits won't utter if they sense a hostile presence.'

'And if your dad really does talk to her?'

'We had him cremated. He no longer possesses the equipment to communicate through a Spirit Guide or anyone else. Will you take the job or not?'

Hetty was hesitant. This woman did not own the garden centre; she only managed it, and it did not seem to be doing well. 'You'll excuse me mentioning it; I speak as I find. Our fees aren't high – my husband's always telling me we should put them up. But even so . . .'

'I can afford a week.'

'It'll take longer than that.'

'Five days, as worked. You can slot it in with something else. We'll be in touch. Now, if there's nothing more, I've given you all the particulars you need – name, address, and so forth – and I've work to do.' And she was off again, shouting at a young man in a green boiler suit, 'Henry, I want you in the perennials PDQ, so stir your stumps.'

Hetty was still doubtful. Geoff said, 'Exposing fraud, Mrs Wainthropp. It's a public service if ever there was one.'

'She wants to get her hands on her mother's nest-egg before it's all squandered. Still, if this medium woman really is a fake, it's true she's taking advantage.'

Three evenings later Hetty was among the audience at a seance in Aquinas Avenue. She was calling herself Mrs Lola Hattersley and, on the principle that it is better to invent as little as possible if one wishes to avoid being caught in a lie, had given the late Mr

Hattersley the same first name as the living Mr Wainthropp. Dressed in deep mourning, with a hat and half-veil, she sat holding the hand of Grace Todd on one side of her and a woman in her late twenties on the other. Music she did not recognise (it was the *Pavane* from *Las Meninas* by Gabriel Fauré) lulled the group of nine.

'Eyes . . . closed. Breathe. In . . . Out. Deep breaths. In . . . Out. Feel yourself floating.' The stomach of the young woman next to her gave a gurgle. It was a form of floating, Hetty supposed. 'Eyes . . . closed. Minds . . . open. Ready . . . ready to receive.'

The music faded. *Here it comes!* Maurika Rome spoke, but in the voice of a little child. 'No! No! Nasty! Nasty, nasty!' Eyes opened. This was not, for at least some of the audience, what had been expected. Maurika spoke in her own voice, 'Not now, Tiny! Never at the beginning. You're in the way. Let the Red Indian gentleman through.'

Hetty whispered to Grace, 'Who's Tiny? A Spirit Guide?'

'Just a little girl. Rather naughty, I'm afraid. She interrupts the others.'

Several of the group shushed them crossly, and Sara said, 'No distractions, please. It can be dangerous.'

The child was back. 'Nasty! Jinga-jangle. Wivvery.' Maurika spoke in her own voice, 'Is it an astral presence, Tiny? Something from a lower plane frightening you?' The child began to whimper as if in fear. Then Maurika said, 'Oh, I see. Don't cry, my dear. It won't hurt you.'

The whimpering died away. Maurika came out of her trance. 'What happened?'

Sara said, 'It was Tiny. She was frightened.'

'Yes . . . I remember. There's hostility in the room, interfering with reception. I've felt it from the beginning, but it's stronger now. There's someone in this room who wants to destroy our work.'

How could they know? Hetty was a mistress of disguise. Had Amy Bartlett talked, maybe told her mother that she was sending a detective? Well, she would face out any accusations, make her excuses and leave. Hetty cleared her throat.

Sara said, 'Do you know the source?'

'Oh yes, I know the source.'

All eyes were open by now and nobody was relaxed or even breathing deeply. Maurika swung her body round on the chaise longue and faced her audience. 'I know which one of you it is. I can feel the bad vibrations creating astral static.' She seemed to be looking straight at Hetty. 'I must ask you to go now, please. The spirits will not speak to those with closed ears. All you can do is spoil the sitting for others. Your money will be refunded.'

Hetty returned direct gaze for direct gaze. She had been rumbled and had better leave. She let go the hand of the young woman next to her who, much to Hetty's surprise, got up and walked quickly, head down, to the door, followed by Sara.

Maurika rearranged herself on the chaise longue. 'When my daughter returns, we'll try again.' The man who was now sitting next to Hetty took her hand.

Hetty and Grace Todd walked back together to the bus stop round the corner at the end of the road. Hetty said, 'It's funny how you can't help feeling guilty. Mrs Rome looked right at me and I was all ready to get up and go; I thought I must be giving out the hostile vibrations with my unconscious mind.'

'Oh no, dear,' Grace said, 'anyone can see you're the sympathetic type. And you're one of us; you've sustained a loss. It's surprising your husband didn't make himself known; they usually do at the first sitting. They've been waiting to make contact, y'see. My Harry came straight through the french windows in a cloud of herbal tobacco.'

'Robert never liked putting himself forward. He'll bide his time, see how the land lies, and then make his move, I expect. Who was that young woman anyway – the one with the aural static?'

'Can't say. She's never been before.' They were round the corner and there was a bus coming. Mrs Lola Hattersley, well used to command, halted it with an imperious hand. As they got on Grace said, 'You ought to try a private consultation. It's more expensive but well worth the money. There's no competition – just you and the departed and the Spirit Guide.'

When Hetty reached home she heard the putt-putt of the scooter coming up the road behind her, and Geoff caught up with her as she opened the gate. 'What did you find out?' she said.

'Not a lot. They're a mother and daughter. Not local: they've rented the house for the winter. Keep themselves to themselves and cause no trouble.'

'You'll have to keep watching and keep asking until you find something.'

'Trouble with asking, folk want to know why. Then it gets back to them someone's asking questions. Which is okay if you want to put the wind up them, but do we?'

'No,' Hetty said, 'I suppose we don't. Not yet, any road. Point taken, Geoffrey,' and they went on in to be told by Robert that DCI Adams had phoned, only that minute more or less, and wanted to see her.

'Tonight?' Hetty took off Mrs Lola Hattersley's black hat with the black half-veil and put it on the kitchen table.

'Tomorrow. Would you drop in at the police station, please,

at your own convenience? That's a lovely hat.'

'What about?'

'There's a Dundee cake his wife made he'd like you to try. You look like Marlene Dietrich when you wear that hat.'

Was he making fun? She gave him a quick look, but he seemed to be serious. She picked the hat up again, and lifted it so as to try it on in front of the hexagonal mirror in the burrwood frame which hung on the wall over the sideboard.

She watched herself in the mirror, holding up the black hat. Marlene Dietrich! 'What rubbish!' she said and put the hat back on the table.

Nevertheless she was wearing the hat when she went next day for coffee and Dundee cake in the DCI's office.

It was excellent cake, moist with a touch of brandy. 'I didn't know you were married.'

'If we're not we don't get promoted. Of course the marriages mostly break up for lack of attention. Luckily my wife has a job of her own; it's just the children who feel neglected.'

She had grown used by now to never knowing when he was serious; he had once told her he did not even always know himself. Meanwhile she sipped coffee, looked wise and waited for the change of subject, which came soon enough.

'Tell me please, Mrs Wainthropp, what's your interest in Maurika Rome and her daughter Sara?'

He had done it again. She was amazed. 'I only went there yesterday evening for the first time. Are you having me followed?'

'I wouldn't dare. No, I had someone of my own at that seance.'

'A young woman?'

'Detective Sergeant Angela Gatting.'

'She got thrown out?' He nodded. 'And what's *your* interest, then, in Mrs Rome and her Spirit Guides?'

'You first.'

'A client of mine thinks she's fake. I said that wasn't illegal.'

'Technically it is – Fraudulent Mediums Act, 1951. But as long as the medium hears voices nobody else can hear, sees what nobody else can see, and the spirits use her own vocal chords to communicate, you can't prove it.'

'I'm being paid to prove it.'

'By?'

'Someone who thinks her mother's being taken advantage of. Now are you going to tell me what your lady sergeant was doing there?'

'Have some more cake.'

'I can't be bribed.'

'Detective Sergeant Gatting was, as you say, rumbled. But you, Mrs Wainthropp, were not rumbled. How did you explain your presence?'

'Said I'd read their advert in the *Psychic Herald*. Said my husband had recently passed away and I hoped to get in contact.'

The DCI was concerned. 'Robert? Has he?'

'No, he'll outlive us all if he's not prevented. I went in disguise under a flag of convenience – Mrs Lola Hattersley, a wealthy widow without dependants.'

'Totally without?'

'I haven't gone into details. That comes in the private consultations, as I'm told.'

'Will you be having one?'

'I'll have to consult my client. I'm not sure she'll be prepared to pay.'

'I have a small fund under my control which might cover it.'

Had he indeed? This was serious stuff. 'What's the problem?' Hetty said.

'Let's go for a little drive.'

So the DCI took Hetty for a little drive to the village of Dowerby Sutton. The villages of Lancashire come in two sorts, picturesque and industrial. The Wainthropps lived in the industrial sort: this was picturesque. 'I'm a churchwarden of this parish,' the DCI said. It was an aspect of him with which Hetty was not familiar.

They went to the church. The vicar had been warned to expect them and was waiting, thin and twitchy, in the porch. He led them to the vestry and took from the safe an old-fashioned leather-bound diary. It had belonged to his father, also a north-country vicar, who had retired in the fullness of years and gone to live with his wife in a rented flat in Grange-over-Sands.

'My mother died there suddenly eighteen months ago, he only recently. My sister found the diary when she was going through his effects. She's not very worldly.' The vicar did not seem to Hetty to be very worldly himself, but she judged this to be the effect of a country parish. In the Manchester area, she supposed, vicars would be worldly to a fault. 'She didn't know what to do with the diary; she gave it to me. We must do something.' He was looking at the DCI as if for guidance, and the DCI nodded gravely to tell him to go on. 'He took my mother's death hard, you see,' the vicar said. 'They'd always been very close, and with no parish work any longer, had grown closer: even my sister and I felt . . . surplus to requirements.' He was finding it hard to go on. 'He began to go to . . .'

The DCI helped him. 'Group seances in a private house.'

'Maurika Rome?' Hetty said.

'She'd rented a place for the winter. Just like here. Group meetings, private consultations after.'

'Everyone noticed the change in him,' the vicar said. 'Much

more cheerful to begin with, then like a man . . . tortured.' He opened the diary to show them. 'It's all in here. What he wrote is what he believed *she* told him – my mother told him through some Spirit Guide.'

'Which was?'

'Terrible things.'

'Lies,' the DCI said.

'We have to believe they were lies. Before her marriage my mother was a psychiatric nurse. What she told my father . . . is *said* to have told him . . . terrible things done to patients . . . ill treatment. You could call it sadism.'

'By your mother?'

'He believed so.' He showed them the entry. 'He writes here . . . "Nobody must know. They must never know." And when he himself died last month his savings were all gone. For nearly a year he'd been taking large sums out of the bank in cash.'

Hetty said to the DCI, 'He has these private consultations. His dead wife talks to him, telling him all about the dreadful things she's done and he believes her. Then he pays to keep it quiet.' So far, so clear. Then a thought came. 'But wait a minute. The medium's in a trance. She's not supposed to know what happens.'

The DCI said, 'Mrs Rome tape records the private consultations so that her clients can have a record of what their loved ones tell them. It'd only need one tape.'

'You've got the tape?'

'He seems to have destroyed it.'

'Blackmail?'

'And no way of proving it.'

As they left the parish church Hetty said, 'Aren't you always telling me you won't investigate any case you can't hope to clear up?'

'I told you, I'm a churchwarden here; the vicar came to me privately. If blackmail's going on, it won't be just his dad. Anyway, *you're* going to clear this one up.' They walked together down a weedy path through untended graves. 'And may I say? . . . I do like your hat.'

Amy was outraged. 'A special consultation? Twenty-five pounds!'
    'And bus fares.'
    'Why?'
    'You want me to expose her.'
    'Why can't you expose her at one of her evening dos? You'd have witnesses.'
    'She's a clever woman. She doesn't give herself away in public.'
    Geoff said, 'Anyone hostile affects the vibrations, so you get thrown out.'
    Hetty said, 'Please try to understand, Mrs Bartlett. The point is, she doesn't do anything: the spirits do it all. She just passes on what the spirits say, and the folk at the seance have to tell her if it has any meaning for them. So if there's a mistake made – wrong age, wrong colour hair, wrong sex, any sort of error – that's not her. The spirits got muddled owing to bad reception.'
    'What do you expect to get out of a private consultation that you wouldn't get otherwise?'
    'In private she might just take one step too far.'
    They had not told her about the vicar's father. It seemed to Hetty that this blackmail business should be kept on a need-to-know basis. As far as Amy Bartlett was concerned, at least at this stage, the Wainthropp Detective Agency had been hired to unmask Maurika Rome as fraudulent and the blackmail was gravy – a favour to the DCI. Hetty intended to cast her gravy upon the

waters that it might return to her again fivefold.

Amy's hands twisted against each other like snakes in a sack. 'Twenty-five pounds!' She glanced about angrily at all the seasonal flowers in the garden centre, at least half of which would wilt before they sold. 'A place like this – the waste! You've no idea.'

But she agreed. As Hetty and Geoff returned to the scooter, which had been chained to the railings, Geoff said, '"One step too far"! How do we manage it, Mrs Wainthropp.'

'We'll put together a life story of Mrs Lola Hattersley as soon as we get home, and I'll learn it by heart.'

The private consultation was at two-thirty on the Thursday afternoon following. Sara showed Mrs Hattersley into the same room as was used for the seances. The curtains at the front window were still closed for privacy, but those over the french windows were now open for light, and the furniture had been rearranged, the chaise longue pushed back against one wall, the sofa against another, and a small round table draped with the black shawl had been set in the centre of the room, with an armchair on either side of it. On the table there was a crystal ball in a black wooden stand.

'Come in, come in, Mrs Hattersley. You're a friend of Mrs Todd, I believe.'

'Both having lost a loved one recently, it does bring you together.'

'A loved one? That would be . . .?' Mrs Rome's manner was that of an undertaker sweet-talking the bereaved into a casket of best beech with brass handles.

'My husband. Mr Hattersley.'

'Mr Hattersley? You don't use his first name?'

'Not at first acquaintance, no. *He* may do so if he decides to make himself known. That's up to him.'

'I see . . .' Point to Hetty; she had wrong-footed the adversary and placed herself in a one-up position. Mrs Rome dropped the phoney sympathy and got down to business. 'Now you'll excuse me but we have to get one thing straight right from the beginning. I'm only a channel of communication: I cannot guarantee success. If your husband doesn't wish to communicate, there's nothing I can do about it.'

Hetty baited her hook. It was time for Mrs Hattersley to become distressed. 'But he must want to communicate; he must. He's always looked after me. He's left me all this money . . . the house . . . the business. He went so sudden. I don't know what to do.'

She heard the front door close. The daughter had gone out. Mrs Rome motioned Hetty to one of the armchairs and the two women sat on either side of the little table with the crystal ball. The game was about to begin.

From further down the street, Mrs Wainthropp's associate watched the suspect's daughter leave the house, dressed for the outdoors in overcoat and tam o'shanter and carrying a shopping bag. He followed.

'Take the crystal in both hands.' Hetty picked the crystal out of its stand and held it as instructed. 'Feel the warmth. Look deep into it. Deep . . . Yes. Such secrets there! Put it back, please.'

Hetty put it back. It had felt oddly warm when one considered that it was just a piece of glass on a cold day and the only heat in the room one of those flickering electric fires pretending to be coal.

'First I'm going to study your aura. Close your eyes, please.' Hetty closed her eyes. 'What's an aura?'

'The astral part of you. Everybody has one. It's just light – a

115

mist of light, like you see round a street-lamp on a rainy night. Yours is purple. That's the colour of grief.'

Time for Mrs Hattersley to be impressed by all this mumbo-jumbo 'I'd never have known.'

'Open.'

Eyes open. Make the first cast. 'Grace said something about a tape recording.'

'I was about to ask.' Mrs Rome left her chair and went to the tape recorder, which, it now seemed, had other uses besides the playing of relaxing music at the evening seances. 'It's a little extra, but many clients like to have a record of any communication from the departed which may transpire.'

'Oh, I don't mind the extra; that's the least of my worries. I just want to be sure I've got everything straight in case Mr Hattersley gives me any complicated instructions.'

Mrs Rome inserted a blank tape. 'I shan't have to turn it over. It plays for an hour on each side.'

Round the corner was the bus stop. Did the suspect's daughter intend to catch a bus? If so, Mrs Wainthropp's associate would have to run back for the scooter and follow the bus from stop to stop until she got off. A shopping bag suggested shopping, not visiting friends or confederates. But with just the one shopping bag, it would not be a major shop, not a bus journey to a superstore at the edge of town. A little way down the main road, the houses gave way to a stretch of shops. She would be going there. Following her on a shopping expedition probably wouldn't lead to anything, unless what she bought had some significance, but it made a change from standing around watching the house. He would maintain a slow and easy pace, let her get round the corner well ahead of him, then look round carefully, keeping himself well hidden, to see whether she was waiting at the bus stop or had gone on to the local shops.

What Mrs Wainthropp's associate did not know was that the suspect's daughter had been followed by young men before, and could distinguish a steady and purposeful footfall from a casual stroller, a householder walking a dog, or a mother with a pushchair. Sara liked gadgets and preferred to be aware of what was happening around her. Her wristwatch had a cover with a small magnifying mirror set on the inside. She looked down at her watch, pressed a button, and up popped the mirror. A teenager in a check jacket, walking in what he probably thought was a casual manner. Well, he looked harmless enough. She smiled and walked on.

Maurika Rome had returned to her place on the other side of the little table. Her eyes were closed. 'I see . . . an old man rocking.'

'Mr Hattersley wasn't old. He was cut down in his prime.'

'Rocking in his chair. There's a chamberpot by the side of it.'

'Rocking! Chamberpot! I didn't come here to play silly games. You put me on to my husband, please, and be quick about it. Rocking!' A thought hit her – hit Hetty Wainthropp not Mrs Lola Hattersley. A memory, suddenly very clear, a picture in her mind. 'Oh my goodness. Goodness gracious! Well, cover me in a suet crust and bake me in a moderate oven.'

'You know the old man?'

'Grandad. He had sciatica very bad. He had to rock to get out of his chair.'

'And the chamberpot?'

'Used it as a spittoon.'

'He's your guardian in the Spirit World. He keeps an eye on you.'

Hetty was troubled. 'I don't know why. I never liked him. He was a little Napoleon to my gran.'

Mrs Wainthropp's associate, hot on the trail, extended his neck like a marmot and craned round the corner. The suspect's daughter was not waiting at the bus stop. Good!

He had allowed her to get some way ahead of him, and must now catch up a little. Quickening the casual pace, he rounded the corner and discovered that she was no longer in sight. The shops were a little closer than he remembered, but she could not have reached them so quickly without running, and she had no reason to run since she could not know that she was being followed. He forgot about the casual pace, and broke into a run himself.

The first of the line of shops was not a shop at all but an Indian restaurant and takeaway, The Khyber Pass. Outside it stood a wooden cut-out figure of a turbaned Rajput. Geoff slowed down to a walk, looking about him on both sides of the road. She had to be in one of the shops – a phone box – somewhere – but must not see him looking. The cut-out Rajput spoke to him as he passed. 'Why are you following me?'

Geoff's head turned sharply. But there was only a wooden figure. 'Eh?'

Sara stepped out from behind the Rajput. 'You heard.'

'I wasn't following you.'

'Don't lie. You're not good at it.'

'Well . . . if I was . . .'

'You were.'

'It was because . . . I . . .' Inspiration struck. 'Because I fancied you.' Second thoughts. Was this getting him in too deep. How could he escape from such an indiscretion? 'I suppose.' But that was as bad. Second thoughts in matters of the heart were insulting. He would never be able to worm himself into her confidence if he began by insulting her. 'No, that's it,' he said. 'I saw you. I

118

fancied you. I followed you. The story's as old as time.'

'Most stories are,' the suspect's daughter said.

At the private seance Mrs Rome was still in a light trance, a very useful state which allowed her to communicate both with her Spirit Guide and with the client. 'F,' she said.

Hetty was wary. She had felt put-down by the encounter with the old man in the rocking chair and did not know what to make of it. She could so easily have given herself away, although obviously Mrs Hattersley must have a grandfather too. Now it was being suggested that someone whose name began with F was trying to get in touch. 'F?'

'Florence? Florrie? Flora?'

There it was again: the F had to do with Hetty herself, not with Mrs Hattersley. There seemed to have been little point in committing a whole imaginary life history to memory if her own relatives were going to keep popping up. She allowed Mrs Hattersley to become impatient. 'Auntie Florrie lived in Bamber Bridge and her husband worked on the railway in a supervisory capacity. We never had much to say to each other in this life and I can't believe the Spirit World will make a difference. Now may I speak to my husband, please?'

'I told you, my dear, I can't command the spirits. The ones who come are the ones with something to communicate. F . . . I don't think it's your auntie, but nothing is clear; I can feel impatience hindering the flow. F . . . I have the feeling . . . a child. A little girl perhaps. Is there some buried unhappiness in your mind connected with a child?'

'Mr Hattersley and I never had children. We married late in life.'

Maurika lifted her head and looked directly at Hetty, except that her eyes were still closed. It was most unsettling. Hetty shifted uncomfortably in her chair, and looked away.

She had been given – felt strongly that she had been given – an opportunity. She must play the game carefully. 'He had a lady-friend for some years before our marriage, but we never spoke of her.'

'And what was the name of this lady-friend, my dear?'

The fish was hooked. Immense control was needed. She must not let triumph show. 'Fiona,' Mrs Lola Hattersley said, then clinched it with another F. 'Freeman. Fiona Freeman. We never discussed her between ourselves: Mr Hattersley had too much delicacy.'

There was a place that sold milkshakes just up the street past the Do It Yourself. Geoff and Sara sat at a table well away from the other customers, each with a milkshake and a slice of pie. Sara said, 'Why aren't you at work?'

'I'm unemployed at the moment. That's why I have to keep wandering about. Killing time like.'

'If you're unemployed how come you're buying the milkshakes?'

'I had a piece of good fortune with some careless person left his car unlocked.'

'You're beginning to grow on me. I've been wondering what you're like in bed.'

This had come out of left field. Geoff choked explosively on his pie. She watched him, well pleased with herself and amused by his reaction. When he had recovered his voice and his dignity he said, 'I've had no complaints.'

'Maybe you've had no opportunities either.'

This completed Geoff's discomfiture. She was laughing at him, had seen right through him. His pride was badly dented but he would not show it. 'I don't know how to reply to that.'

'Don't worry. I was just trying to knock you off balance.' She had succeeded. 'In my business you learn a lot about people from their reactions.' Opportunity. He could now ask her what her business was, and learn something. 'You're not a jack-the-lad looking for a quick pick-up. So why were you really following me?'

'I followed you because anyone can dream,' said Mrs Wainthropp's associate.

Meanwhile in Aquinas Avenue the bait had certainly been taken. Maurika Rome continued to be extremely interested in the person whose name began with F. 'Has your husband's lady-friend passed over, do you happen to know?'

'They lost touch. She went south to Dunstable for her health and he never heard from her again.'

'For her health?' Maurika's trance was now so light as to be almost transparent. The tone of her voice suggested that nobody, in her opinion, would go to Dunstable because the air there was like wine. 'To have an abortion, my dear, or to have the baby?'

Suddenly her body jerked and she gave a cry of pain. The trance was not so light after all; it was as if she were being dragged back in spite of herself into the Spirit World, there to be physically attacked by the lady whose name began with F. 'Ow! . . . ow! Whoever it is, she's extremely anxious to communicate.'

Enough was enough. Hetty needed time to think. Too much had occurred which would have to be discussed at a Case Conference. Anyway Mrs Hattersley's hour was almost over. 'Please inform Miss Freeman that I do not wish to receive any communication she may be trying to make, and if she and Mr Hattersley have taken up again on the astral plane, I shall have something to say about it when I pass over myself. It is my

husband and only he with whom I wish to communicate. There's
two hundred and fifty thousand pounds tied up at an extremely
low rate of interest, and I need better advice than I'm getting
from the bank.'

That should hold her. Let the fish swim a little: the hook was
well lodged.

'There you have it,' said Hetty. She was in high good humour.
'Twenty-five pounds of Amy Bartlett's money for an hour of
communication with the departed and my dear husband never
gave me so much as the time of day.'

'Of course I didn't. I'm not dead yet.'

'You've not had a lady-friend called Fiona either. As far as I
know.'

'You and I were married too young. I never realised my
potentialities. I might have fancied a Fiona if Fate had thrown
one my way.'

Geoff said, 'It was funny about your grandad though.'

'It was. Rocking in his chair! And the chamberpot to spit in
for his bronchitis! My grandad, not Mrs Lola Hattersley's. That
medium couldn't have known.'

Geoff had been distrait through supper. Poached egg on toast
with beans had not received his usual singleminded attention.
'She could be genuine,' he said.

'No way,' said Robert. 'There was a lot of old men had sciatica
in your grandad's day. And bronchitis.'

'Keeping an eye on me from the astral plane, she said. Well,
why not if he enjoys it? The important thing is, genuine or not,
she's taken the bait. The bleating of the goat—'

Geoff and Robert came in together on cue. '—excites the tiger.'
'Some goat!' said Robert.

'A wealthy goat with no children. And now there's her husband's ex-lady-friend trying to get through with a message about a little girl. I do find that interesting.'

'Did she give you the tape recording?'

'Next session. She has to make a copy for her own records.'

'That's how she blackmailed the vicar's dad. Kept a copy.'

Robert said, 'It's not blackmail this time.'

'Maybe not,' Hetty said. 'But I expect that little girl will turn out to be in need.'

Geoff went to bed early. He too needed time to think.

He sat by the window, looking out into the night sky. It was clear, with the moon only half way to full.

'I followed you because you're a suspect. It's my job to follow you.'

His face was close to the window pane. His breath misted the glass. In the mist Sara's face appeared, at first serious and sad. Then she smiled at him.

Geoff wiped the glass clear, got into bed and closed his eyes.

'Anyone can dream.'

Next morning, while Hetty was at the police station reporting on her progress to the DCI, Geoff went to see Robert at the allotment. He felt in need of a private conversation.

Robert was planting seed potatoes, first slicing them into pieces in the polythene greenhouse, then planting them with a dibber in a trench already prepared.

'She's not thought it through, Mr Wainthropp: that's the trouble.'

'Hetty never does think things through. "Little grey cells!" – Rubbish! It's instinct with her and always has been.'

123

'I've not thought it through: that's the trouble,' Hetty said to the DCI.

'Explain.'

'When I began all I was going to do was go to a couple of seances, get her to give me a message from my dead husband, and then expose her because Robert isn't dead and anyway I'm not Mrs Hattersley. She'd have wriggled out of it somehow, but it might have been enough for Grace Todd, and I'd have done my duty to the client.'

'And now?'

'There's the blackmail business. I've laid a bait and she's taken it.'

'The little girl. Not so little now, I suppose. Born to Mr Hattersley's ex-lady-friend and now in need. Who has not yet appeared.'

'And may not appear if Mrs Rome gets scared off. How does this not so little girl get in touch with the wealthy widow? Geoffrey and me made up a life story for Mrs Hattersley, but she's going to need more than a made-up story. Where does she live and what's her phone number?'

The DCI said, 'Don't worry. I'll find you an address and an answerphone. And Mrs Hattersley will need a cheque book. It can all be arranged.'

Geoff was not finding matters quite so easy to manage. He was handing Robert bits of cut-up seed potato which Robert was popping into holes made with the dibber. 'I wanted to have a talk with you. Man to man.'

Robert was worried. 'It's not the facts of life, is it? I had to do them with our Derek. I got rather muddled up, to tell you the truth.'

'It's not the facts of life – at least not exactly. It's more . . . I mean, the way we live . . . you and me and Mrs Wainthropp . . . there's not the opportunity to . . .'

Robert's worry had, if anything, been increased by this explanation. 'To what?'

'If I was meeting someone. A girl, say.'

'Oh!' Robert discovered that he had squeezed one of the pieces of potato into a squidgy mess between his fingers instead of planting it. But if it was only about meeting someone. He rejected the squidgy piece and popped in another. 'Well, y'right. It's quiet for you here with us.'

'I'm not complaining.'

'Well, when I say quiet I don't mean the Detective Agency aspect. Witches . . . arsonists . . . the Mafia sort of thing. They're not always welcome, but they do make a change. But what I mean . . . you're a teenager.'

'I am.'

'You've got urges.'

'I have.'

'It's a problem.'

'It is.'

'Hetty doesn't always understand men's feelings. She gets proprietorial, you could say.'

'It's a family, Mr Wainthropp. I like that. I haven't had a proper family for a long time: I'm grateful. And, as you say, the work – it's a challenge: it stretches me. Only . . .'

'You ought to get out on your own from time to time. Every lad should. I'll have a word with her.'

Of course Geoff could get out on his own if he was on Agency business, and since his task was to find out all he could about Maurika Rome and her daughter, he could take the scooter to

Burnley if he wished without any other explanation. Meeting Sara, getting to know her, going for a walk together, that was all part of his job, yet he did not mention it when he left the Wainthropp house.

They walked together along the bank of the canal, which is on an aqueduct above the centre of town. The view of the bus station, shopping precinct and multi-storey car park is impressive and the movement of the water soothing to a troubled heart. Geoff told Sara that he was unemployed and lived with his grandparents in Darwen. He had prepared a more elaborate background if it were necessary, but hoped not to have to use it. Sara told Geoff that she worked helping her mother, who was a medium.

All open and above board so far, and all part of the job for Geoff. 'What about your dad?'

'The women manage things in my family.'

'Is it a good trade being a medium?'

'It's not a trade, it's a calling; you have to have the gift. As for money, we don't charge much. A lot of the clients are old age pensioners. It's like being a hairdresser. We give them reduced rates.' They had reached a bench. 'Let's sit down for a bit.'

So they sat down for a bit, side by side, and watched the water. Geoff said, 'Have *you* got the gift?'

'Yes, I think so. It's in the family. My gran had it, and her gran; it goes way back. You can put your arm round me if you like.'

Geoff put his arm round her, looking around nervously to see who was watching. Sara said, 'Try to enjoy it.'

'Haven't you got a regular boyfriend?'

'If I like someone I might go with him for a bit, but nobody claims me. Anyway I don't know anyone in Burnley. We're only here for the winter.'

'What about the summer?'

'Seaside.'

'I thought we might go to a disco later. I could collect you and take you home after.'

'Have you found another careless person left his car unlocked?'

'I wouldn't ask if I couldn't afford to take you.' He would need a sub from expenses and would have to explain to Mrs Wainthropp where he was going and why. It would be complicated but Robert would understand.

'I work most evenings.'

So much for complicated explanations, 'Shall I kiss you?'

'I might enjoy it.'

Had he really heard what he had heard himself say? Had he really heard her reply? He had. He kissed her, at first respectfully, then as she responded the kiss became passionate. After some time they moved apart. Geoff was shaking.

Sara said, 'Not bad. You'll get better if we practise.'

'Let's practise.'

So they practised and Geoff got better.

When practice was over, at least for the moment, Sara said, 'Would you do something for me, Geoff? Since your time's your own.'

'Ask.'

'You said you live in Darwen. There's one of our clients lives there – a widow, Mrs Lola Hattersley; I'll give you the address.'

The Romes had an address for Mrs Hattersley because Hetty had been back for a further session. And already they were checking up. Geoff was wary. 'What about her?'

'She doesn't feel right to us. Usually when folk want to communicate with a loved one it's loneliness. With her it's all

127

money; love doesn't come into it. That's not how you approach the Spirit World.'

'What do you want me to do?'

'Find out all you can about her. Ask the neighbours. She could get hurt if she's going into it for the wrong motives.'

'How hurt?'

'Not all the spirits are good. You get some evil. We'll practise again for a bit, if you like, and then you'd better get back home.'

So he had to tell them after all.

Hetty's face was like thunder. Robert hovered behind her, extremely worried.

'You what?'

'In the course of making general enquiries in the area—'

'No flannel. I don't want flannel, Geoffrey.'

'I came to make the acquaintance of the subject's daughter.'

'And never told us?'

Geoff looked at Robert. This was the time for him to explain to Mrs Wainthropp about a teenager's quite natural urges. Robert accepted the mute appeal and coughed to clear his throat in preparation. Hetty swung round to face him.

'You spoke?'

'He told me he'd made the acquaintance of a young lady. He didn't say who. I was going to talk to you about it.'

'How dare you keep secrets from me! You've had one go at solving cases on your own, and it came to no good. Now you want to take over the Agency.'

Geoff had appealed to Mr Wainthropp for help, and Mr Wainthropp had tried to help, and now he was getting stick for it. It was unfair. Geoff lost his temper and shouted. 'It's got nothing to do with the Agency.'

Hetty the tiger turned from savaging one helpless piece of prey to a second. Geoff knew he must be calm. He could not engage in a shouting match with his employer. He took a grip of himself. The room quivered with the tension created by Geoff's calm. 'My feelings for the young lady are private, Mrs Wainthropp. They have nothing to do with the Agency.' He received a basilisk stare from Hetty, and weakened. 'Until now. Maybe they have now.' The unfairness of it hit him again. It was not he, but Mrs Wainthropp herself who had aroused their suspicions by talking about money. 'But you've got to look at things from their point of view.'

'*Got* to?'

'Give the boy a chance, Hetty. Let him explain.'

'Explain.'

'There's your grandad. And your Aunt Florrie. Mrs Rome got both those right. She didn't know who you were because you were pretending to be someone else, but she got those right.'

'And my dear husband who passed over and his lady-friend Fiona – also passed – who wants to tell me about a little girl?'

'She didn't say that?'

'Am I losing my mind? Are you telling me what this medium did or didn't say when you weren't even there?'

'I'm sorry, Mrs Wainthropp, but from what you've told me—'

'God give me patience!'

'I do so hope He will,' said Robert.

'All she actually said was that there was a message about a little girl — something to do with the letter F. She's never succeeded in communicating with Mr Hattersley and all that about Fiona was what you told her yourself.'

The silence was heavy. Robert cleared his throat again. 'I

suppose . . . strictly speaking . . . that might be true.'

'Then why does this daughter, this Sara person, want Geoffrey to investigate Mrs Hattersley?'

'She thinks there's something strange about you. She thinks you're obsessed by money and you may be at risk.'

Hetty was near to bursting. 'Me! At risk! I'll tell you who's at risk, young man. I'll tell you who's obsessed, and it's not with money; it's with sex.'

The telephone rang in the hall. Robert went to answer it. Hetty said, 'I'm not speaking to anyone.'

'It may be the DCI.'

He left the door from the kitchen to the hall ajar. Hetty and Geoff heard him pick up the phone. 'Wainthropp Detective Agency?' The pitch of his voice changed. 'Who? . . . Derek? . . .'

Hetty was up immediately and on her way. 'It's the baby. Something's happened.'

Geoff could hear Robert on the phone. 'My God! It must be four in the morning out there. Is everything all right? . . . She's coming now.' He handed the phone over to Hetty saying, 'They've had a little girl. A week early but she's perfect in every way.'

He went back into the kitchen, closing the door to give Hetty privacy in the phone call. 'Four in the morning,' he said. 'It makes you think.'

'Good news?'

'They've had a little girl. With the two boys, they wanted one, but . . .' He wiped his eyes. 'There was a miscarriage before and they thought they might lose . . . but it's all right, everything all right, no complications. They're going to call her Felicity. That means happiness, you know.'

Geoff said, 'Felicity. F. A little girl.'

In the hall Hetty, tears running down her cheeks, was saying to her son, 'Felicity . . . Oh yes, it's a great name. It's most appropriate.'

Robert stared at Geoff. 'Y'right. F. Felicity. A little girl. That woman couldn't have known.'

Hetty went back to see the DCI. 'I'm giving up the case.'

'Why?'

'She's not a fake. There's too much she's got right. First my grandad. Then my Auntie Florrie of Bamber Bridge.'

'But *you* identified your Auntie Florrie. All Mrs Rome gave you was an F.'

'You're right. I'm so confused.'

'Take your time.'

'It's that F. The little girl. She's just been born.'

'In Dunstable?'

'In Sydney, Australia. She's my new grand-daughter Felicity. And Mrs Rome couldn't have known. So maybe what the spirits told that vicar's dad was true. Maybe his wife really did all that.'

'Who cares?'

'I care. So should you.'

'Whether Maurika Rome is a fake or not, whether the vicar's mother ill-treated her geriatric patients or not, blackmail is still blackmail and it's a blackmailer you're after. So tell me, please, what is Geoffrey going to say to the girl?'

Geoffrey was to tell Sara that Mrs Hattersley lived alone in a detached house in the select area of Darwen with a moorland view from the back windows. All the neighbours agreed that she and her husband were a devoted couple. Rich. Well respected. Rather old-fashioned views – pro-hanging, anti-abortion. She was utterly dependent on him, he was her all in all, and consequently she had no close friends, and since she had no brothers or sisters either, nobody came to see her. Her telephone number was ex-directory but Geoffrey had managed to get it by sweet-talking the cleaning lady. And he would pass it on to Sara.

'And I tell you now,' Hetty said to the DCI, 'nothing will come of it.'

So Geoffrey sat by the canal on the aqueduct, hunched and broody. He looked at his watch. Past time. He looked down the canal bank and saw Sara at a distance, coming towards him. He got up and stood looking at her. She ran towards him. Somehow he found his arms opening, found that in spite of his errand, he was glad to see her. She ran into his arms. They kissed.

Later he gave her the piece of paper with Mrs Hattersley's ex-directory phone number written on it.

And something did come of it. Next day the telephone rang in a detached house (with moorland view from the back windows) in the select area of Darwen.

An answering machine clicked on and the caller heard a recorded message. 'Mrs Lola Hattersley is not available to take your call at the present time. Please leave a message after the tone.'

When the message had been left Detective Sergeant Angela Gatting rewound the tape. Wendy Freeman from Dunstable had called. She was sorry to trouble Mrs Hattersley but the matter was urgent and since she was in the area, staying with friends, she hoped that it would be convenient for her to call. She would phone again at four p.m.

'Then,' said the DCI, 'Mrs Lola Hattersley had better be there to answer the phone. Get me Mrs Wainthropp, please, at once.'

Hetty said she would pack a bag and move in pronto. She would have to take a taxi on expenses. They'd never get Mrs Hattersley and a suitcase on the back of the scooter.

Geoff said, 'Do you want me to come with you?'

'She has no children.'

Robert said, 'Shall I come?'

'Her husband's dead. I don't suppose there'll be any food in that house. I'd better take a carrier bag of bits and pieces.'

The taxi drew up at the gate of a house Hetty would really not have minded owning, and Detective Sergeant Gatting opened the door and carried in the suitcase. Then, since there was an hour to kill before the phone call, they had a cup of tea and admired the moorland view.

Quarter to four. There was a large carpet bag open on the carpet of the long ground floor room of the semi-detached house in Aquinas Avenue and into it Maurika Rome was packing the moveables of her trade – the shawl, the crystal, tape recorder, red velvet curtains: the chaise longue stood at one end of the room by the french windows ready to go.

Sara was looking out of the window at the front, looking out at the road. A beat-up old van, driven by a young man with long dark hair, drew up outside.

'Danny's arrived.'

Three minutes to four. Geoff and Robert were seated at the kitchen table, staring at the clock. Geoff said, 'Doesn't time pass slowly when you're not enjoying yourself?'

One minute to four. The DCI was at his desk. He looked at his watch.

Four o'clock in the drawing room of the detached house in the select area of Darwen. The carriage clock on the mantelpiece began to chime. The telephone rang. Hetty answered it.

Half past four. Robert and Geoff were in the front room watching on TV the highlights of a football match played days

133

earlier. The telephone rang and Robert answered. It was from Hetty. The young woman would arrive, accompanied by her cousin, at ten o'clock tomorrow.

'Cousin?'

'I suppose she thinks she needs protection.' Robert and Geoff were to get their own suppers from the freezer and join her at the Hattersley house at eight a.m. The police were already with her, getting the place ready.

'Replace that picture,' said the DCI to the Detective Sergeant. It was a Stanley Spencer print. 'Doesn't fit the character. Find another – Constable, I should think, or Watteau. And there probably ought to be little glass animals and a lot of Benares brass.'

Hetty said, 'I thought you'd be putting in hidden cameras and bugs and such.'

'We shall. No expense spared.' Then to Detective Sergeant Gatting, 'And wedding photos in silver frames.' To Hetty, 'Can you supply those?' He was clearly enjoying himself. It warmed the heart to see him.

'Not the frames.'

The DCI took three steps backwards and held up his hands to make a frame. He was looking at Hetty critically, not as a trusted comrade, but as an actor in a set. 'What would Mrs Hattersley wear to receive her guests? I've a fancy for a negligée of apricot silk with ostrich feathers at the throat.'

Detective Sergeant Gatting gave a warning cough. 'Animal rights, sir.'

'From nylon ostriches, of course. And artificial silk.'

Time passed slowly. Robert and Geoff found a foil dish labelled *Poulet Sauté à manière de Metz June '94* in the freezer, created from a recipe which Hetty had found in a dentist's waiting room and remembered incorrectly, and ate it in tribute to her. After supper they watched television for a while, flicking from channel to channel unable to settle, until Robert went to bed early with indigestion.

Hetty sat up trying to concentrate on a paperback copy of Stanislavski's *An Actor Prepares* left for her by the DCI, found that she couldn't make sense of it, strongly doubted whether anyone could, put it aside and listened to music on Radio Two.

The house in Aquinas Avenue was locked up, quiet and empty. If any members of the Spirit World were around they did not make themselves known.

At just after ten next morning, Mrs Lola Hattersley in a negligée of artificial silk with nylon ostrich feathers at the throat, received her guests. The Stanley Spencer print had been changed for one of a ballet dancer in the style of Dame Laura Knight and there were glass animals and Benares brass on most plane surfaces and flying ducks on the wall. Robert had brought wedding photographs, but the DCI had decided that Robert and Hetty looked too young on the day they were wed to pass for Mr and Mrs Hattersley, who had married late in life. Instead a studio portrait of the two of them standing by a potted plant, taken in Manchester on the occasion of their Silver Wedding, stood on top of the piano.

The two guests, Wendy Freeman and her cousin Daniel, sat side by side on the sofa. Both were dark-haired, dark-eyed and wore dark clothing. Daniel's hair was worn long and curly at the back; his black trousers were snug on the hips, his shirt a dazzling white and his black jacket did not match the trousers. Wendy's dark brown dress was loose, cut like a maternity dress, and indeed she said – it was almost the first thing she said – that she was pregnant.

'I know you wouldn't want me to have an abortion.'

'Would you like some coffee? I have the Georgian silver coffee service all ready in the kitchen with a plate of *petits fours* and a boy to serve them.'

The 'boy' was Geoff, dressed up in a white coat, standing ready in the kitchen to serve coffee to Mrs Hattersley's guests if required, while Robert had his ear to a pottery funnel pressed against the wall between kitchen and living room so that he could hear all that went on. The police, waiting upstairs in a first floor bedroom, could already hear all that went on, but, where Hetty's safety was concerned, Robert preferred to leave nothing to chance.

'It would be your husband's grandchild, you see.'

'The milk has of course been boiled.'

Daniel said, 'Are we getting through to you, Mrs Hattersley?'

'Oh, yes. This lady says she is my husband's illegitimate daughter by the late Fiona Freeman, and that she is now about to have an illegitimate child of her own, which she does not wish to abort.'

'My mother refused to have an abortion and so do I.'

'I don't think you need be too upset. There are plenty of single mothers these days and nobody thinks the worse of them.'

Upstairs the DCI grinned and said, 'She's wonderful.' He thought the Stanislavski paperback was responsible for what was in fact a natural talent.

'My mother never asked for a penny from your husband. She struggled on her own to bring me up. I only discovered who my father was after she died.'

'Am I right, my dear, in thinking that, unlike your mother, you are about to ask for money?'

Daniel said, 'She shouldn't have to ask. You should offer,' and Wendy said, 'I want to start a new life in Canada with the baby.'

'And how much would that cost?'

'With the air fare . . . and getting on my feet . . . three thousand. I've booked the ticket – put down a deposit: you wouldn't see me again.'

Mrs Hattersley rose from her armchair and walked about, indecisive, wringing her hands, the ostrich feathers waving. In the kitchen Robert was attempting to remove wax from his listening ear, using the blunt end of a pencil wrapped in cotton wool.

'Oh dear! This is really very disturbing. Three thousand! I mean, there's no proof. My husband never mentioned . . . he never spoke about Miss Freeman after our marriage.'

'There is proof, Mrs Hattersley. How else could I know so much about you?'

Hetty Wainthropp might have suggested how but Mrs Lola Hattersley continued to dither. 'I've no responsibility. Three thousand! I mean, if you're pregnant you must know who the father is. You don't have to go to Canada. There's something these days called the Child Support Agency. He can be made to pay.'

'He's a married man. Like your husband was.'

'Mr Hattersley and I were not yet married when your mother went south to Dunstable for her health.'

Daniel said, 'Makes it worse. I don't think you understand, Mrs Hattersley. My cousin wants to bear your late husband's grandchild and make a new life for them both. You should be happy to help her. If you won't she'll have to get what she can where she can.'

'Meaning?'

'This is it,' said Robert to Geoff in the kitchen. 'Crunch time.'

'Sell her story to the Sunday papers. History repeats itself kind of thing. Like husband, like wife.'

'That's blackmail.'

'No. Blackmailers keep coming back. This is a one-off. She'll be in Canada. You'll never hear from her again.'

'Three thousand . . . I haven't that much money in the house.'

'Write a cheque. Pay cash to bearer. Phone the bank and tell them to honour it. I'll get the money and come back for my sister. Then we'll go.'

They watched Mrs Lola Hattersley, deep in thought, come slowly to a decision. 'Very well. I'll need a receipt. Mr Hattersley always used to insist on a receipt.'

Robert said to Geoff, 'She's making out the cheque. Money has to pass, then the police take them in. I don't think you'll be serving coffee.'

The police would take them in. Then they would take Mrs Rome in. And Sara. Geoff could see it, hear it, imagine the whole scene as the two women, tearful and distressed, were bundled into a police car with its blue light flashing outside the house in Aquinas Avenue.

He took off his white coat. 'Then if you don't mind, Mr Wainthropp, there's something I have to do. You don't need me here,' and left the house quickly by the back door.

Robert was surprised. 'Eh?' But Geoff had already gone. 'Suit yourself.' He took a *petit four* from the tray and ate it thoughtfully before going back to his listening at the wall.

In the living room Hetty stood with the cheque in one hand, the other held out to receive the receipt. It was signed and exchanged for the cheque which Wendy handed to Daniel. 'Before your cousin goes to collect the money,' Hetty said, 'there's someone I'd like you both to meet.'

She went out into the hall, leaving the door open behind her. Wendy and Daniel looked at each other, puzzled and wary. They heard another door opening off the hall, and then Mrs Hattersley returned with an elderly man in tow, the artisan type.

'This is my husband, come back from the astral plane. Robert, this is your daughter by the late Fiona Freeman who actually never existed except in my imagination.'

And the police were already on their way downstairs. 'Congratulations seem to be in order,' said the DCI.

At Aquinas Avenue incomprehension was in order. Geoff parked the scooter outside the house, ran up the front path, and rang the bell. It was answered by a very large lady unknown to him.

'Yes?'

'Is Mrs Rome in?'

'Gone.'

'Where?'

'Who knows?'

Geoff was alarmed. 'Done a bunk?'

'You're worried about the rent. Don't be. They pay a month in advance. I've lost nothing.'

'They were here two days ago.'

'Right. They were going to stay till summer but they've terminated early. It's the way the wind blows.' He was staring at her, distraught. 'Look, I'm sorry, but I don't know where they've gone.'

'You know where they came from. They'd have given references.'

'Not one. Not needed. They paid the rent in cash and they've left nowt behind. Tidy. Even the dustbin's been cleared.'

He had to think. They'd had long talks, he and Sara. She was careful, of course she was, but she must have said something, some small unguarded confidence, which would be a clue to where they'd gone. He stared at the large lady, stared into her eyes, trying to divine some unnoticed fragment of truth in what had just been said. Little grey cells, where are you when you're needed? The situation required a Wainthroppian flash of intuition, and suddenly he had one.

'Cash up front?'

'Used notes.'

'The women manage things in my family.'

'You what?'

'Something her daughter said to me. The women manage things. And they paid cash up front. Sara Rome. Romany. They were going to stay till summer, then go back where they came from?'

'I said so.'

'Where does a Romany woman go in summer?'

'Seaside, fortune-telling. Everyone knows that.'

'Thank you. You've been very helpful.'

He ran back towards the scooter. The large lady watched him go. What a little love he was! She shouted, 'Wait!' and he turned back towards her. There was a touch of the gypsy in the lad himself, she shouldn't wonder, with those large black eyes. He'd be breaking hearts in a couple of years, but for the moment, she'd lay money, it was his own heart breaking.

'You going looking for her all the way up the coast on that thing?'

'If I have to.'

'You're in love.'

'Yes, I am.'

'Heaton Undercliff. The Pleasure Beach.'

He gave her a great grin and ran on. She watched him start the scooter and ride off, then went back indoors, well pleased to have kept the wheels of true love turning.

Mr and Mrs Wainthropp were not expected to go home by taxi. Instead they were given a lift by a police driver. There were people in the village who would be the subject of scandal if they were brought home by police car, but in Mrs Wainthropp it was only right and proper. Respected by the police, she brought lustre to the neighbourhood.

They got out of the car, Robert carrying the suitcase, and Hetty thanked the driver, who saluted respectfully before driving off, watched by five women from behind their front room curtains. 'Never said where he was going?' Hetty said to Robert. 'It's so unlike him. Maybe he's phoned. We should have one of them answering machines.'

'We have,' Robert said. 'It's me.' Faintly the phone could be heard ringing from inside the house. 'Phone's ringing now.'

He hurried to the door, dropping the suitcase, and fumbled for the key. The phone stopped ringing. 'How could you have let him go off like that?' said Hetty.

In the interview room at the police station, Wendy Freeman from Dunstable was defiant. 'Just tell me how I'm supposed to have conned money out of a woman who doesn't exist. If there never was a Mrs Lola Hattersley that cheque's a fraud for a start. It's her should be shut up in here, not Danny and me.'

It was true. They would not be able to make the blackmail stick, but the DCI had never expected they would. 'That's not the point. When do we ever make blackmail cases stick?' he said to Detective Sergeant Angela Gatting. 'The point is to warn them off and – by a little judicious harrying – get them off our patch.'

Hetty and Robert prepared food for lunch and discovered that neither could eat it.

Hetty pushed her plate away. 'I'd better go and talk to Grace. Wrap things up.'

'You can't go out. Anything might have happened to him.'

She snapped at him. 'He's eighteen. He'll phone or he won't. And if he has had a fatal accident, no doubt they'll phone and let us know.' She was pushing out her own worry at him as anger and they both knew it.

The phone rang.

Hetty said, 'You take it.' He went to answer. She closed her eyes. They would let her know. Please let this not be 'them' letting the Wainthropps know. She heard Robert say, 'Geoffrey . . .' Then he put his hand over the mouthpiece and called to Hetty, 'He's at the seaside.'

The Season proper at the Pleasure Beach of Heaton Undercliff begins after Easter. This was the pre-Easter run-up to the Season when there were still cheap rates at the resort's hotels and the possibility of a little sun to tempt the punters. Not many would be tempted, but those who were, with nothing else to do but walk up and down on the Esplanade shivering and grumbling in equal measure, would be there for the taking. So although many of the tiny shops and booths selling confectionery, hamburgers and hot-dogs, T-shirts with 'I went to Heaton Undercliff and All I got For You Was This Lousy T-shirt' written on the front, postcards, Kiss-Me-Quick hats of laminated cardboard and all the usual seaside trash were still boarded up, a few were open. Broadly speaking, as a guide to trading conditions, one might say that fudge and even rock were available for the punters to buy but not yet candyfloss.

Riding the Apthwaite scooter above 25 mph was impossible, below 5 mph inconvenient because it made complaining noises and emitted signals of black smoke from the exhaust. Geoff tried to maintain a steady 7 mph up the Esplanade but even so earned glares from chilly punters. Gypsy Serena was closed, so was Gypsy Petula. Was it too early, had he wasted his time and the money for petrol, would Sara and her mother still be tucked away for the next few weeks in a caravan on a lay-by near Chorley with piebald horses cropping grass at the roadside?

There was a wooden booth at an intersection where the buses came up from the town centre. Gypsy Maurika. It was open. Now that he had found them, what would he say?

He parked the scooter by the booth. There was a bead curtain over the entrance. He entered and found himself in an empty room with a round table covered by a black sequinned shawl and two armchairs. There was a crystal in a stand on the table and two chairs set on either side. The room was chilly. To his left there was another curtain, this one of red velvet, and from behind it came the sound of a Bugs Bunny cartoon.

He stood there, uncertain. If they were watching cartoons on TV in a side-room, how would they know when a client had come in? Was there a bell to ring? He could not see one. In the next room the TV was turned off, and Sara pulled back the curtain, entered and brought a blast of warm air with her from a two-bar electric fire.

Sara said, 'Have you come to have your fortune told?'

'I've come to warn you.'

'No need. They had to let her go.'

'Wendy Freeman?'

'My sister Katya. Did you really believe a Romany would be called Wendy? How did you find me?'

'Worked it out. Seaside, you said.'

'Fortune-telling in summer, spiritualism in winter. It's a good living, but there's a lot of us.'

'Is that why you have to make extra by blackmail?'

'Nobody blackmailed Mrs Hattersley. There was no such person. You lied.'

'And the old man at Grange-over-Sands?'

She looked at him steadily, biting her lower lip. No shame, not even surprise. 'Been doing your homework?' He could not reply. Even holding her gaze was difficult. Yet *she* was the criminal. 'There was no blackmail there either,' she said. 'He was a stupid old man who paid to keep it quiet what his wife had done when we'd have kept quiet anyway.'

'All his savings. Spread over a year.'

'Don't push your luck, Geoff. What you know, you know. The rest is silence.'

'Didn't it mean anything – you and me?'

'A kiss and a cuddle, what's that mean?'

'Something. A lot.'

'I told you, nobody has claims on me. When I want a man I'll pick one, and he won't be a Gorgio.' She became suddenly impatient. 'I liked you. I still do, if that's what you want to hear. But it means nothing. You'd better go. I'm sorry you've wasted your time.'

'Anyone can dream,' Geoff said, and left the booth. Outside as he mounted the scooter he saw a police car come up from the direction of the town centre. It stopped near him, and he watched a uniformed police constable get out and enter the booth.

Geoff rode away.

* * *

Hetty went, as she had said she would, to see Grace Todd, who lived on her own in a small terraced house in a back street of Burnley. Grace was neither surprised nor upset to know that her daughter had set a detective to break up her relationship with the Spirit World.

'The trouble with Amy, she knows nowt about feelings. Exposing Mrs Rome would have done no good. I've known for some time she's a fake.'

'You never said.'

'I thought you believed in her. I didn't want to put you off.'

'Put *me* off!'

'Put Mrs Hattersley off. No, I tumbled to Maurika Rome very quick, and I'll tell you for why. That Spirit Guide of hers, that shaman of the Attahachee tribe.'

'Big Chief Wet Blanket or some such.'

'My Harry would never discuss his personal problems with a Red Indian. And then he kept saying he was so happy in a better place where everything's perfect. That's not Harry. He'd find a bit of faulty workmanship in the gates of Paradise.'

'Then why did you keep going?'

'When someone you love dies, you think about them all the time . . . blame yourself for what you did or didn't do . . . forget they're gone, and pass the odd remark. It's wearisome for other people. They keep trying to take you out of yourself. Mrs Rome's big room with the tape recorder and the dusty curtains was the only place I could talk about Harry non-stop. It was worth twenty-five pounds an hour.'

'Amy wants you to go and live with them.'

'That's the other reason the money was worth it. I tell her Harry says I must be independent. You know . . . I put the bolster down the middle of the bed, and sleep beside it with one arm over, pretending it's him. Amy wouldn't allow that.'

Nine o'clock at night and a fine rain falling. The sound of a motor scooter, putta-putt up the village street.

Hetty and Robert were in the front room, supper over, about to watch the news. Robert lifted his head. He had heard the scooter. He turned down the sound. 'He's back.'

Hetty said, 'I'll go.'

She was in the kitchen, waiting, when Geoff came in by the back door. He could see Robert hovering in the hall.

He said, 'I went to warn her. She knew already as a matter of fact. You can have my resignation if you want. I'll go upstairs and pack.'

Hetty said nothing. He walked past her into the hall. Robert made a small move towards him, but Hetty put out a hand to tell him to stay where he was, and Geoff went on upstairs.

Hetty moved into the hall and remained at the bottom of the stairs. When Geoffrey had reached the landing she spoke. He stopped moving at the sound of her voice, and stood there rigid, his back towards her.

She said, 'Your supper will be ready in twenty minutes: we've had ours. You'd better have a bit of a wash. There'll be work to do in the morning, trying to get the rest of our fee out of Amy Bartlett.'

Geoff turned. His face broke into a great grin of relief, though there were also tears running uncheckably out of his eyes and down his cheeks.

'You're right, Mrs Wainthropp,' he said. 'You're right.'

Lost Chords

The case of the Lost Chords of Blainthorp has a special place in the annals of the Wainthropp Detective Agency because it was the only one in which Hetty was able to imitate the methods of her favourite fictional detective, Hercule Poirot. The chords, of course, were vocal chords and they were only lost for a couple of weeks, but that was enough.

Blainthorp was not the most notable town in Lancashire. It lacked architectural distinction, had no ruined abbey like Whalley, no castle like Clitheroe and Lancaster, none of the Victorian seediness of Bacup or the daunting grandeur of Bolton Town Hall. It had, of course, its fair share of abandoned mills, most of which had been turned into slipper factories. One might say that Blainthorp was to bedroom slippers what Kendal was to mint-cake, but it would not be saying much.

But it did have an annual music festival, which had been going fifty years. And it had the Oliver Hardiman factory where Hardiman's Herbal Healing Remedies were prepared. When these two came together the trouble began.

Hardiman's Herbal Healing was big in the North and Midlands; in Scotland and Northern Ireland its fame was not unknown. The pastilles and linctus, the tablets in three strengths – Strong, Superlatively Strong and Total Enfranchisement – were

John Bowen and David Cook

distributed as far north as Kirkwall, as far south as Kettering, to every town and city in the British Isles where catarrh blocked the sinuses and bronchitis inflamed the chests of those unhappy persons forced to live amid urban pollution. But all this was not enough for Oliver Hardiman, who had founded and built the company. He wished to extend the Hardiman empire, first to the South and West until all Britain was his, then into Europe by way of Britanny and the foggy Rhineland to Lithuania, Poland, Belarussia and right on into the Urals as far as Sverlovsk and Chelyabinsk.

In this jubilee year of the Blainthorp Music Festival, Hardiman's Herbal Healing had offered to sponsor an additional class, the Golden Voice Competition, with a gold cup, a cheque for five hundred pounds and a contract to promote Hardiman's Remedies countrywide in a campaign of advertisements (mostly radio) and special events. The preliminary classes had been held three months previously; the final would be the climax of the Festival, with the cup and cheque presented by a mystery judge.

There were posters all over town with photographs of the ten finalists under the caption 'WHO WILL BE THE GOLDEN VOICE OF BLAINTHORP?' Coverage by local press and radio had already been arranged: Mr Hardiman was a major shareholder of both companies. Only there was a problem. As the day of the Final drew closer, some of the finalists lost their voices. Eileen Hargreaves (mezzo) had turned bright pink and her face had swelled. Osbert Edrington (counter-tenor) and Ken Badgett (tenor) had both developed crippling hay fever from which neither had ever suffered before. Their photographs on those posters which were within easy reach of vandals had already been defaced with large Xs painted over in creosote.

Nerves, said the organising committee after Eileen Hargreaves

148

scratched; Eileen had often been bad with her nerves and the pink face seemed to indicate hysteria. But then Osbert. And Ken. And the crosses which were painted, nobody knew by whom, across the faces. And then Harry Hope (light baritone), geography teacher at the local comprehensive school, a man simply not given to nervous behaviour of any sort, lost his voice one afternoon while coaching the Blainthorp Combustibles, a teenage soccer team.

There were witnesses. His words were remembered. 'Pass it, boy! Pass!' Not exactly epigrammatic stuff but suited to the circumstances. 'Good! Dribble. Tackle him, Martin, you craven beast.' Then he had begun to cough. The coughing had begun on the craven beast, but Mr Hope had recovered from the first fit of coughing. 'Good boy, good! Jason, keep your position – you're a winger not a lead guitarist. Shoot, Gary! shoot!' And he had started to cough again. 'Shooo . . .' And then his voice had totally gone.

It was time, said Oliver Hardiman, to call in a detective. Obviously the police would not take it seriously. (He knew this because he had already spoken to the police.) They would have to pay somebody.

The senior partner of the Wainthropp Detective Agency and her associate sat in the living room of Annie Mosscrop, Chairman of the Organising Committee of the Blainthorp Music Festival (and therefore the *de facto* organiser since none of the others did any work), and listened to a message on her telephone answering machine.

'It's Marianne Hope, Mrs Mosscrop, phoning about Harry. It's his voice, I'm afraid. I've had him inhaling balsam since four o'clock but it does no good. His lower register's completely knackered, and as for his arpeggios, I wouldn't cross the street to hear them. He's certainly no Golden Voice of Blainthorp or anywhere else.'

Annie switched off the machine. 'And that's the fourth. With five days to go before the final. Leaving six.'

Geoff said, 'We saw the poster.'

'They're all over town but only a few are within the reach of vandals. If it *is* a vandal defacing them and not . . .'

'Not the nameless nobbler – serial silencer – marking up his successes at street corners for every passer-by to admire. Don't worry, Mrs Mosscrop. We'll have him. It's his own vanity defeats the criminal nine times out of ten.'

'Just take the notes please, Geoffrey,' Hetty said. 'I'll do the theories.' And then to Annie, 'Shall we start at the beginning? You're the Festival Organiser. It must be a great responsibility. Are you musical yourself?'

'Musicality isn't part of the job description. I was voted into the hot seat at my first committee meeting. Everyone else had done the job once and failed. It's all too easy to fall foul of your sopranos, and if you can't find someone frightening enough to keep the mothers out of the judge's eye line, you might as well raffle off the prizes.'

'What kind of prizes?'

'That's the point. Usually nothing much. But this year with the Golden Voice Competition—'

'Five hundred pounds and a gold cup. That wouldn't be solid gold?'

'No, no; it's like bathroom taps – gold leaf over brass. But there's also a glittering career beckons in radio and TV. Or so says our sponsor.'

Geoff consulted his notes. 'Hardiman's Herbal Healing.'

'You've certainly done your homework on that poster.'

'Is it just the cup? Don't the runners-up get anything?'

'Silver for the second, you mean, and bronze for the third? No, he hasn't thought of that. But all the finalists have already been presented with a gift set of Hardiman's Herbal Preparations for Nose and Throat in cut glass crystal with 18-carat gold stoppers – real gold this time, though rather small stoppers.'

Hetty said, 'You don't like Mr Hardiman much, do you?'

'Nobody likes him. Mr Hardiman isn't interested in being liked. He prefers respect.'

'You believe it's one of your competitors nobbling the others?'

'You're the detective, Mrs Wainthropp. It's not up to me what to believe.'

'You're the client. You're entitled to have an opinion.'

'Mr Hardiman's the client. I'm to look you over and take you to him if I'm satisfied. Which – there being very little time and nobody else suitable – I am, so we'd better make a start.'

Mr Hardiman lived in a Georgian manor house with Victorian additions, bought cheap in the early eighties during the collapse of the property market and after it had been refused by the National Trust. Annie parked her Citroën *deux-chevaux* in the drive and the three of them stood there looking up at the magnificent frontage.

Annie said, 'Mr Hardiman has a special feeling for the Blainthorp Festival. He was born the year it began and by the time he was fifteen he'd won twelve certificates with distinction and three cups.'

'Born in this house?'

'Oh no, backstreet Blainthorp, two up, two down. As he'll cheerfully tell you, he's of humble stock – not that you could ever use the word "humble" in connection with Mr Hardiman. He bought this place fifteen years ago when he married.'

'There's a Mrs Hardiman, then?'

'Was. She left. We'll use the kitchen entrance. He's left the door open. Nobody uses the front.'

Even the kitchen was of an imposing size and magnificently appointed. There was an 18th-century range, with antique cooking implements hanging above it, a microwave and a modern German electric oven with a rotisserie attachment for the actual cooking. There were cutters and grinders and blenders on which the dust lay thick, a double stainless steel sink ingeniously set into the antique stone sink, an enormous fridge-freezer. There was too much to take in as, led by Annie Mosscrop, they passed swiftly through.

Annie was still bringing them up to date on the life and works. 'He began with a nasal inhaler that would shift industrial strength catarrh. The Hardiman empire grew from that.'

'Herbal?'

'Of course. Everything's herbal – no nasty chemicals. People will buy anything these days if there are herbs involved. He'll be waiting for us in the office.'

She led them down a corridor lined with figures under dust sheets. 'As you can see, he doesn't use much of the house since Mrs Hardiman left.'

'What's under the dust sheets?'

'Armour mainly.'

The office had once been the library of the manor. Many of the books – *Mr Sponge's Sporting Tours* and the novels of Trollope, Dickens and Thackeray bound in leather – were still in place, but filing cabinets had been added, a telephone and fax, a computer, copier, a TV set with a video-recorder, and a large leather topped desk with a swivel chair. There was a darkish portrait in oils of

Oliver Cromwell above the desk. This had been brought in by
Mr Hardiman; it was not part of the original furnishings of the
house. He sat beneath it, looking masterful, as Hetty and Geoff
were introduced. All the other portraits were of hanging judges.

They were to begin by watching a video. A tape had been
made of the preliminary classes and from it Annie had made a
compilation of clips of the six remaining finalists, each lasting –
on Mr Hardiman's instruction – exactly fifteen seconds. He
pressed the Play button and an attractive young woman appeared
on screen, began to sing *I Know that My Redeemer Liveth* and
was cut off in the middle of a bar.

'Beverley Prendergast, soprano and single mother,' Mr
Hardiman said. 'Calls herself a student and works part-time in a
hairdressing salon.'

He pressed the Play button again for fifteen seconds' worth of
a dark and rather caddish looking man in his thirties singing part
of the chorus of *The Road to Mandalay*. 'Simon Letby, bass-
baritone. You don't have to worry about him.'

'Why not?'

'Gentleman farmer. Doesn't need the money. Anyway he's a
friend of mine.'

Hetty knew that it was always the best friend who had
committed the crime, and made a mental note of Mr Letby.
Meanwhile the next contestant was to be seen on screen, a rather
dumpy woman in her forties singing *Che Faro* from Gluck's
Orfeo.

'Glenda Jason, contralto. A furnace of passion with a husband
in a wheelchair.'

'That's not fair,' Annie said.

'Gossip never is.' Fifteen seconds of a boy treble singing *Pie
Jesu* from the Fauré Requiem, a very accomplished performance

from an eleven-year-old who gave the impression of being totally in control both of himself and his material. Mr Hardiman did not identify the boy at once. He had pressed the Pause button and was staring at the frozen picture. 'There's something about that boy worries me. I'll put my finger on it eventually. I always do.'

'Brian Borrowmere, boy treble,' Annie said to Hetty and Geoff. 'He not local – doesn't have to be for the Golden Voice. He travels about. Does a lot of competitions.'

Mr Hardiman pressed the Play button and gave them fifteen seconds of the *Habanera* from *Carmen* by a red-haired lady in her late twenties with a magnificent bosom which may have been a little assisted. 'Rita Locheed, mezzo. Single. Fashion buyer for a department store in Manchester.'

'There's your passionate furnace,' said Annie.

'No, she spreads it about too much. It's not banked up like Glenda.'

The last finalist was a gloomy middle-aged man singing *Oh, Ruddier Than the Cherry* with accuracy but not much conviction. This was Les Maynard who worked for a local estate agent. 'Prime suspect in my view.'

'Why?'

'No talent. Couldn't hope to win without nobbling the others.'

'If it *is* nobbling,' Annie said. 'It might actually be illness. A virus.'

'I do have some medical knowledge, Mrs Mosscrop. Just find me a virus which only strikes finalists.' He turned to Hetty. 'But it's not simple nobbling. Out of the four who've gone, two weren't much loss, one had an outside chance and one a good one. There's no pattern.'

'When was the list of finalists made public?' Hetty said to Annie.

'Three months ago, just after the heats.'

'And one week ago the trouble began,' Mr Hardiman said. 'That doesn't say virus to me.'

Geoff coughed. 'I suppose . . . they will all have been practising . . . rehearsal kind of thing. They'd all be anxious. They could have over strained.'

So far Mr Hardiman had ignored Geoff. Now he turned his full attention balefully upon Mrs Wainthropp's associate, who squirmed under it. Mr Hardiman let him squirm, then spoke, 'I like a lad who thinks for himself. If he keeps his mouth shut and doesn't interrupt his betters.'

Hetty stood to go. 'I won't have my associate insulted. We don't have to accept this job.'

'No, but you will. The Supergran Sleuth doesn't refuse a challenge. There's five days to go before the final. Shall we say two hundred a day plus reasonable expenses? Free board and lodging provided here at the Manor.'

'I've a home and a husband.'

'Get him over here if you think you need a chaperon. I'm hiring you as a detective, Mrs Wainthropp, not a call girl, and I want you here where the action is in case we have any more of these virus attacks before the final on Sunday.'

'How can anybody tamper with somebody's vocal chords without them knowing?'

'That's what I'm paying you to find out. And prevent.'

Two hundred a day for five days. She had seen Geoffrey's eyes light up, and certainly Robert would approve. Hetty decided they had better start at once at the Festival Office; she could phone Robert from there. 'Only may I ask you to fetch him, Mrs Mosscrop. Our transport won't take three. I'll give you a list of things for him to bring.'

155

Annie was intrigued. 'Fingerprint powder? Infra-red camera? Bugging devices?'

'Underwear. A nightie of course. And something for Geoffrey to change into.'

'Will I have to wear a tuxedo? For the evening like?'

'I doubt it.'

Hetty said, 'And there's some food in the fridge that'll only go off if it's not eaten.'

The Festival was being held during the Easter holidays at the Mary Arbuthnott High School for Girls, which somehow had over many years avoided becoming either comprehensive or a mixed-sex school. It was mentioned in guidebooks as a prime example of Victorian Gothic and the chapel had a stained glass window ascribed to Pugin. It was in the chapel that the Golden Voice Final would be held.

The Festival Office consisted of a desk, filing cabinet and telephone in one corner of a waiting area furnished with armchairs and coffee tables. Notices pointed to MAIN HALL, CHAPEL, and COMMUNITY STUDIES STUDIO, the three venues in which different classes were being held. A coin-operated machine serving black or white coffee, tea, chocolate or a nourishing soup, which seemed to consist of elements of the three other beverages mixed together, stood against one wall of the waiting area next to a table on which books about music were set out for sale with a notice asking purchasers to pay at the desk. The desk itself was covered with entry forms and lists of entrants for the various classes and there was also a roll of tickets, like old-fashioned cinema tickets, for members of the public (mainly mothers and friends) wishing to attend as audience at £1.50 per session, and a black metal money-box in which the ticket money was kept.

Next to the desk was a notice board covered with posters advertising local cultural events, including the Blainthorp Amateur Operatic Society's forthcoming production of *When Did You Last See Your Father* by Edward German and Arthur Wing Pinero, which was decorated by a reproduction of the famous painting of that name. And behind the desk sat the Assistant Festival Organiser, Freddy Slater, answering questions, issuing directions to those many contestants and members of the public who could not read the notices, selling tickets and doing all the work of a general dogsbody.

Hetty sat next to the desk, using the telephone to phone Robert. Since there were classes going on in all three venues, very few people were in the waiting area, but from a practice room just off it there could faintly be heard the sound of a pianoforte playing Erik Satie's *Gymnopédie*.

Hetty said to Robert, 'Try to be ready when Mrs Mosscrop arrives. I've given her a list of things to bring: they'll take no time to collect. She'll take you straight to the Manor. Just pick out a couple of rooms and wait for us there.'

Geoff said to Freddy, 'Is it a full-time job working for the Festival?'

'Three weeks of the year. My degree's in Media Studies so I can't expect much better. The rest of the time I live with my grandfather. He's a herbalist.'

'A herbalist? Like Mr Hardiman?'

'Most unlike. Grandad's a proper herbalist. People consult him and he prescribes. Hardiman's herbal humbug you can buy over the counter.'

'Well, it depends, Robert. It depends on what our investigations unearth.' It was clear to Geoff that Robert at the other end of the line was making difficulties. 'I can't say more at the moment. Please don't annoy me. There's nothing in the allotment that can't wait a week in this weather.' She put down the telephone and said to Freddy, 'I'd like the addresses of all the finalists, please.'

'Even the ones who've withdrawn?'

'Particularly the ones who've withdrawn. If I were knocking out the opposition by causing them to lose the power of speech, a lost voice would be my best disguise. Then at the last minute I'd find what was never really lost and sail through on wings of song.'

'But they've *withdrawn*, Mrs Wainthropp.'

'And what's to stop them withdrawing the withdrawal?'

'The rules of the competition.'

'Don't muddle me with facts.' One of the few people in the waiting area was an angelic eleven-year-old boy reading a horror comic. Hetty, hyper-energetic as ever at the start of a new job, noticed him. 'Isn't that one of the finalists over there?'

'Brian Borrowmere. He comes in most days – just sits in, listening to the classes, gets to know the judges' likes and dislikes. Competitions are his life.' Freddy raised his voice to speak to Brian who slowly lowered his horror comic, the front page of which, Geoff noticed, seemed to be devoted to the life and lusts of a piece of green algae emanating from Outer Space. 'Brian, this lady is a private detective. She wants to interview all the finalists. You being here has saved her a pillion ride to Rochdale.'

Hetty thought, *There goes my cover!*, but the annoyance she felt was much more at the public aspersion on the Agency's mode of transport. However, she covered her annoyance with an expression of extreme amiability and went over to Brian.

'I've just seen you on videotape, singing beautifully.'

'Thank you.'

'Rochdale's a long way. How do you get here?'

'Mother brings me in the Rover. Drops me off and picks me up again. It's not really inconvenient.'

The horror comic went up again. The conversation was over as far as Brian was concerned. Geoff said to Freddy, 'Is he always this friendly?'

'He has the natural reticence of a great artiste.'

Hetty persevered. 'Have you had any trouble with your voice lately, Brian? Runny nose? Itchy throat? Touch of laryngitis? Has anyone been offering you sweets with a funny taste?'

The horror comic was lowered again. Brian said, 'I never have trouble with my voice, I never eat sweets and I never accept gifts from strangers. I am always extremely careful: that is why I succeed.' He stood up, folded the horror comic and stowed it away in the back pocket of his beautifully pressed whipcord trousers. 'And now, if you'll excuse me, the Open Entry Traditional Ballads has just begun in the Community Studies Studio and I should like to hear it.'

He left the waiting area, saying 'Chin up, Doreen!' affably to a young competitor who had left her class in tears and was being fussed over by her mother. Hetty stared after him. 'How can he lose?'

She returned to the desk and said to Geoff, 'We might as well start with the closest. That's the hairdressing salon and the estate agent.'

At the Tidal Wave Hair & Beauty Salon, Beverley Prendergast was drying the hair of a senior citizen.

Hetty said, 'You're a student, I'm told. Where?'

'Open University. I can't go away to study, not with a three-year-old kid.'

'How can you study singing by correspondence?'

'I don't. It's pharmacology. To be a pharmacist. In a chemist's. My mum does it. It's secure. You're always in demand.'

'But I heard . . . Mrs Mosscrop was telling me, if you win the competition . . .'

'Oh, I'll turn professional if I win. That's where my heart is – singing. Pharmacology's something to fall back on.'

'You've heard what's happened to some of the others?'

'You don't have to hear. You just look at the poster down by the obelisk and see who's been crossed off.'

The senior citizen, who disliked being talked over, decided to enter the conversation. 'You what?'

Beverley switched off the hand-drier. 'She's asking me if I've lost me voice.'

'Why, what is she, deaf?'

'No, Edna, she's a private detective.'

'Well, it takes all sorts. You can go on with the drying, but I shall keep an ear open.'

Hetty said, 'Pharmacist – means people come to you asking about their ailments?'

'When I'm qualified. People all over town come to mum with all sorts when they don't want to bother the doctor.'

'If you wanted to . . . make people ill – I'll come right out and say it, make them lose their voices, what would do the trick, do you think?'

The question clearly worried Beverley, who switched off the hand-drier again. 'I don't really know.'

'Take a guess.'

Edna said, 'She's going to be the Golden Voice of Blainthorp. I've got a fiver on her. And she's studying to be a chemist. That's a damn sight more sense than poncing about with a camera, spying on folk who want to get divorced.'

Beverley said, 'I wouldn't know how to start. We try to help people get well, not make them ill.'

'Whom God has joined let no private detective put asunder.'

'Ignore her,' Beverley said. 'She gets notions. They wouldn't cancel the competition, would they? It's only four dropped out: there's still a good entry. It would mean so much to me to win, and I really have a chance.'

Hetty said to Edna, 'We don't do divorce.'

Geoff went to Spenlove & Pettigue, the estate agents in Sheep Street, and was told that Mr Maynard was showing a house to a prospective buyer. They were happy to let him know the address, and the young lady at reception drew him a rough map and told him not to interrupt if Les were on the point of making a sale though her own opinion was that these clients, who had been to view six desirable properties already, were congenital ditherers who would still be at it come next Christmas.

As Geoff arrived on the scooter, Les Maynard was standing outside the house under the 'For Sale' sign, a bunch of keys drooping from one hand, watching a car drive away.

'Mr Maynard.'

'Right.'

'Your office said you'd be here.'

'Have you come to view?' An eye well used to summing up the financial status of prospective clients took in the size of Geoff and the age of the scooter. 'You might find the house too big for you.'

'Come to see you. Should we go inside? It'd be more private.' He wheeled the scooter up the front path, Les at his side, and parked it in the porch. 'You didn't make the sale, then?'

'How do you know?'

'Body language.'

Les unlocked the front door for the second time in an hour and took Geoff into the hall. The doors of the downstairs room were still open and the whole ground floor was bare, empty, echoey, with no furniture, carpets or curtains.

'Here we have the light and airy entrance hall, leading to all downstairs rooms. You don't mind me doing the patter, do you? Got to keep my hand in. They call me Des Res Les, but truth to tell I haven't moved so much as a caravan in the last three months.'

'I've just come from watching you sing on a bit of videotape. Something about a ruddy cherry.'

'I'm not doing that in the final. It didn't really extend me.'

'These finalists who've been losing their voices . . . Mr Hardiman says you're the prime suspect.'

'Meaning?'

'He thinks you're nobbling the others.'

'Does he? Well, he's putting up the prize: he can say what he likes. Though if I'd gone from rags to riches on the back of a little herbal doodah for sticking up noses, I might have a few more charitable thoughts towards them still struggling. Why does he say that?'

'Because you need the money and you've no talent. That's just his opinion, mind; I wouldn't know meself.'

'He's right in one respect. I do need the money. I'm working out three months' notice at the moment. As for talent, I wouldn't have got to the final if I was no good, but it's true I'm not the best.'

'Four pulled out. And no other cases of laryngitis in the district under the age of sixty-five. Can't be coincidence.'

'Tell Oliver Hardiman to prove it. Now if you'd like to see the rest of the house I'll show you, but if not you might as well piss off.'

It was not a rewarding afternoon. They interviewed Eileen Hargreaves, Osbert Edrington, Ken Badgett and Harry Hope, but since the first three were still in some vocal discomfort and Harry Hope couldn't talk at all, discovered very little. The four had been given nothing out of the ordinary to eat or drink, nothing they had not already eaten or drunk for years, and what they had consumed had been prepared by their nearest and dearest or by themselves or in some public canteen or restaurant where other people had also been eating and had been unaffected. They had not, as far as they knew, been stabbed with the ferrules of poisoned umbrellas, salivated upon by bactrian camels, or subjected to any other alien influence. As finalists they had avoided people with colds, that being only common sense in their position, and anyway they didn't *have* colds; losing one's voice was entirely different. And yes, they had been practising, of course they had, but had been careful not to overdo it; they knew the risks.

So much for the nobbled. No clue to the nobbler. 'I feel as if I'm being manipulated,' Hetty said.

She, Robert and Geoff were sitting at the enormous table of scrubbed elm in the kitchen of the Manor. Mr Hardiman, who did not do cooking, had gone out for food. They had assumed that a man of his wealth would be able to pay someone to come in and cook, but Mr Hardiman did not like people intruding on his space, certainly not in the evenings: there was a woman came in three afternoons a week to clean and that was enough. In Hetty's opinion this was quite clearly not enough, since most of the surfaces of the Manor were by no means clean, but she kept her opinion to herself. No sense in stirring things up.

'Will he be long, d'you think, with the food?' Robert said.

'Pushed one way to stop me looking another.'

'There was a place outside town I noticed, coming in with Mrs Mosscrop. Gourmet Continental Cuisine.'

'If one of them nobbled all the others, and then won for want of any competition, you'd know at once that he or she must be the nobbler.'

Geoff said, 'Self-defeating that. They'd have to scratch the event. You might get the cheque if you made a fuss, but not the gold cup and certainly not the countrywide career.'

'Select Dinner Parties a Speciality. I expect he's gone there, being it's our first night.'

'How's it done, that's the problem. Find that out and we'll know who's doing it. Eileen Hargreaves still looks like a boiled beetroot.'

Geoff said, 'Could be a different motive altogether. Someone out to spoil the Festival.'

'Why? It's been going on for fifty years.'

'Not the prize and the promotions.'

Robert said, 'Y'right. Could be some business rival trying to scupper the sponsorship.'

'He hasn't got any business rivals. It says on the label, "Hardiman's Herbal Healing is Unique".'

'Some enemy then. Someone doesn't like him.'

Mr Hardiman's Jaguar could be heard arriving outside. The door was opened and slammed. Geoff said, 'If it's just people who don't like him, we'll never get through them all before Sunday.'

The kitchen door was thrust open, letting in a blast of April air and letting out the fug. Mr Hardiman was carrying four packets wrapped in newspaper which he dumped unceremoniously on the table. 'Pie and chips. Northern food for northern folk.'

They took it in that this was their dinner. Geoff said, 'No bread? No afters? Wine from your capacious cellar? Château Laffy something? Three Star Special Offer?'

Robert said to Hetty, 'I brought some lettuce if you want a salad.'

'Men don't eat salad. Only women and poofs eat salad. My wife ate salad. You don't need plates,' said Mr Hardiman.

Robert and Geoff took a packet of food each and began to unwrap. Hetty got up and fetched plates, knives and forks for all four of them. She said, 'When did she leave? Your wife?'

'What's that to you? I'm not one of your suspects.'

'You learn never to rule anyone out in my job.' She sat, unwrapped the packet, and subjected the pie within to a preliminary scrutiny before placing it on her plate.

'Must have been ten years ago. She was never right after the boy was born – some post-natal rubbish: nothing pleased her. A year of that and off she went. Good riddance to them both.'

'She took your son with her?'

'Why not? Sickly little devil, just as well to let him go. He could never have run a business like mine. You're not eating.'

She could challenge him and score a point by refusing the pie, but she was hungry and there was nothing else on offer. She put the pie on her plate with a few chips and picked up her knife and fork.

Geoff said, 'I think I'd like some salad.'

Glenda Jason, Mr Hardiman's 'furnace of passion' was in the kitchen with her husband Bill. She was clearing the table, already dressed to go out. He watched her from his wheelchair.

A door from the kitchen opened directly into the garage. Bill said, 'You going out again tonight?' She gave him half a look but no reply. 'That car's done eighty miles since Monday.'

'Checking up on me, are you?'

'You bet your miserable stunted life I am, woman.'

'Worried I'll find myself a toy-boy or something?'

'More likely to be the or something.'

The table was clear. 'You'll be washing up, then?' He would. The height of the sink had been adapted for the wheelchair. 'Putting on your pinny and rubber gloves?'

'Even toy-boys have their pride. Finding a man without pride or self-respect is bound to wear the tyres out and put a few thousand miles on the clock.'

She went over to the garage door and opened it. 'I might be late again tonight. Don't wait up.'

In the kitchen of the Manor the meal had progressed. Hetty had discovered that she was not as hungry as she had thought, and a bought pie from a takeaway was no substitute for real food so she had left most of it. Both Geoffrey and Robert had helped themselves liberally to salad. Mr Hardiman ate heartily from his newspaper packet and was not a pretty sight.

'My hope is that whoever's doing it will stop the moment they know we've a detective on the case.'

He clearly had no great opinion of her investigative ability. Did the man even realise how insulting he was for most of the time? Probably not. Nobody in this town answered him back. 'Mrs Mosscrop told us you were quite a whiz at these competitions yourself.'

'I was a Boy Wonder. At eighteen I was all set for a music school in London. Then I started getting more colds than were good for me, and I realised the potential in the North West for nose and throat remedies. Winter and summer there are more blocked snouts in Lancashire than there are pie and chip dinners.'

She looked at him, head in the trough, eating like a pig. 'And you stayed with the pie and chip dinners.'

Albert Slater, the herbalist, Freddy's grandfather, sat in an armchair by the fire in his front room, sipping from a steaming mug. He received patients in this room, so it was as much consulting room as sitting room, with a whole wall covered with books and a lectern on which a leather-bound copy of Culpepper's *Herbal* stood open. There was a shelf full of flasks filled with coloured liquids (mostly for show as he would readily admit) and another of brass containers filled with dried herbs.

Freddy sat with him. This was a learning period. Freddy had a notebook and pen but most learning with this sharp old man was on a question-and-answer basis – the Socratic Method.

'This is good,' Albert said. 'What's the extra taste?'

'Berberis and aquilegia.'

'Aquilegia – "in which the lion doth delight." A cure for the plague which never worked.' He grunted. 'No valerian?'

'Why? Do you want to be put to sleep, grandad?'

'Why not? Provided I can ever teach you enough to take over the practice, I'd go to sleep happily and never wake up.' He sipped. 'Who is this Betty Maincrop?'

'Hetty Wainthropp. She's a private detective. Could we start? I may have to go out.'

'Everybody goes out in the evenings these days; I don't know why. We never did when I was a boy.'

'Grandad!'

'Oh! . . . Right! First question. I'm sixty-five, female, with asthma and arthritis. My voice has started to go because of the beclomethasone I've been taking for the asthma. What will you prescribe?'

'Hardiman's Herbal Linctus to lubricate the throat.'

'Don't wind me up, boy.'

'It's all herbs, isn't it?'

'Herbs, what herbs? Two drops of menthol, a tincture of comfrey and let the problem solve itself.'

'But that's what *you* always say — "help the disease to cure itself."'

'If I say that it's out of knowledge. With Oliver Hardiman it's pig ignorance. The man's a public menace to health. Something should be done about him.'

Freddy wrote carefully in his notebook, speaking the words as he wrote. 'Something . . . done . . . about . . . Oliver . . . Hardiman.' He looked up and made what Annie Mosscrop called his endearing face. 'Grandad, I really do have to go out soon.'

Les Maynard was cleaning his teeth. The red leather presentation case of Hardiman's Herbal Preparations in gold-topped bottles rested on top of the bathroom cabinet. Next to it was a glass containing Mrs Maynard's false teeth in a light solution of bleach.

Les finished with a flourish on the canines, swilled his mouth out with Total Care Antiplaque Coolmint, ran water from the tap over the head of the toothbrush and put the brush back in its holder, looked at himself in the mirror, then la-la-ed a scale up and down, holding the last low note. 'Down! . . . Down! . . . Down! . . . Down!' he sang. 'Down among the dead men, shall . . . I . . . lie .'

Then he took down the presentation case, removed from it a cut-glass bottle of green linctus, opened it, gulped down a swig of linctus from the bottle, returned the stopper to the bottle, the bottle to the case, and the case to the top of the cabinet.

He left the bathroom. His wife Dagmar was already in bed, reading a magazine. She put it away and turned out the bedside light as Les climbed in to join her.

He began to sneeze. He sneezed again and again, seemed to be unable to stop.

'No, Leslie, no!' Dagmar Maynard said. 'You can't get a cold now when we need the money so bad.'

Robert had gone up to bed already. Hetty climbed the grand central staircase with Oliver Hardiman. The staircase was said to be by Grinling Gibbons but was already looking the worse for a cheap aerosol polish bought at a supermarket.

'Geoffrey was asking, who's this mystery celebrity judge?'

'I wish I knew. From Dame Joan Sutherland down they keep refusing.'

She went on to the bedroom Robert had picked out for them, and found him waiting in his pyjamas. The bedroom was approximately the size of a small town hall and contained an enormous four-poster bed with a canopy.

'Don't blame me,' he said.

'I don't.'

'It was the smallest bedroom I could find on this floor. Geoffrey's is larger and he's only a lad. I don't think we have to draw the curtains of the four-poster unless you want the privacy.'

Hetty ran her fingers down one of the bevelled posts and looked at it. 'Dust.'

'I haven't found out where the bathroom is yet,' Robert said.

Rita Locheed's bathroom cabinet was much bigger than Les Maynard's and the red leather presentation case fitted into it comfortably. The bath was deep with a shower attachment and a curtain. Enormous fluffy towels hung over heated railings. There were essences and oils and a huge bar of soap with oatmeal stuck into it. There was mirror glass set into the ceiling above the bath and a mirror covering the whole of the wall opposite. There were indoor plants of the kind which enjoy a humid atmosphere. Even the neon lights were of that delicate rose tint said to have been favoured by Marlene Dietrich in later life because they conceal wrinkles.

The bathroom was in darkness but there was somebody in it who had chosen not to use the rose-tinted lights. The somebody moved cautiously, then switched on one of those torches much favoured by motorists, matt black and covered in rubber. The beam played first over the shower curtain, then moved to the bathroom cabinet and drew closer.

A gloved hand touched the mirrored door of the cabinet and began to ease it open.

Suddenly the bathroom door was opened from the outside. Rita Locheed stood in the entrance. She was wearing a silk robe and nothing underneath and the landing behind her was dark because, coming from the bedroom, she had not bothered to switch on the light.

The beam of the torch swung round sharply to illuminate Rita, standing in the doorway. Time stopped. Rita stood there as if in a still picture, her mouth open in a frozen scream.

Rita could see a dark figure but it was behind the beam of light which dazzled her. It had a bulky shape with some sort of plumage and the face . . . the beam of the torch swivelled to show her the face. It was a cat-face. Now the frozen scream emerged from Rita's throat, but it came out more like a whimper.

The cat-creature grabbed a tooth glass and smashed it in the wash-basin. Then it charged straight through the bathroom door, past Rita, across the dark landing, down the stairs and through the open front door. Rita screamed again, this time longer and louder, and managed to switch on the bathroom lights. Hyperventilating, she pushed her back up against the wall and tried to regain control.

Simon Letby came from the bedroom, naked and bewildered. He looked at Rita, alone with a broken tooth glass, panting in rose-tinted light.

'Don't the neighbours ever complain about the way you react to spiders in the bath?'

Rita, still speechless with shock and holding her throat, could only point in the direction of the dark staircase and the open front door.

So now there was an episode for Hetty Wainthropp to investigate, with all the clues still fresh.

Hetty was in the bathroom with Rita, now fully dressed in country casuals, but with a man's college scarf wound round her throat to protect it. Simon Letby, also by now fully dressed, remained on the landing with Geoff and Oliver Hardiman, ready to enter the proceedings if summoned.

Hetty stood by the open bathroom door. 'I'm you. Right?' Rita was sitting on the bath, one hand to the famous bosom, which was still heaving a little to indicate distress. 'Now, would you please stand exactly where the burglar stood?'

Rita took up position by the bathroom cabinet, an imaginary torch in her left hand, her right extended towards the mirrored door. On the landing Oliver Hardiman's mobile phone rang and he answered it. 'Hardiman!'

'Thank you,' Hetty said to Rita. 'Now – standing where I am, what did you see?'

If Rita had been asked that question immediately after the episode she would have said, 'Nothing.' It was dark and she had been dazzled by the light. But during a night spent in discussion with Simon scraps of memory had come back to her. The beam of the torch with which it had illuminated its face had also illuminated the back of the creature's head in the bathroom mirror and the creature itself, when it had rushed past her, had run like a man not an animal and had been wearing some sort of jacket and breeches.

'I see. Right. Thank you for letting me know,' Mr Hardiman said, and put away his mobile phone.

'Ringlets,' Rita said. 'Long ringlets. The sort little girls make by wrapping rags round their hair. And a hat with a feather. Big, like a plume of smoke twirling round. And a huge lace collar.'

'Sounds like Prince Rupert of the Rhine without his horse,' Simon Letby said to Oliver Hardiman.

'How did the fellow get in?'

'The front door's a Philips lock. Anyone can open a Philips with a piece of plastic. She hadn't locked up properly because . . .'

'Because you hadn't gone yet.' Mr Hardiman was sour. He did not approve of casual sex, even for the upper classes. Or any sex, come to that. Sex was an unnecessary complication in the business world.

Geoff, who had watched and listened to this exchange, made a note.

'Right!' Hetty said. 'We'll change places.'

Hetty moved to the bathroom cabinet and Rita to the door. Oliver Hardiman said to Simon, 'Mrs Mosscrop phoned just now. Les Maynard's lost his voice.' And Simon Letby grinned and said, 'I may win yet, then.' And Geoff made a note.

Now Hetty was standing before the cabinet, one hand in front of her as if holding a torch, the other out to the mirrored door. She said to Rita, 'Close your eyes.' As Rita did so, Hetty turned quickly, her left hand holding out the torch, the other . . . what was the other doing? had it opened the door of the cabinet?

'Open. Describe the face you saw.'

'Catlike. Smiling. It was horrible.'

'You saw that immediately?'

'No. It shone the torch on its own face before it ran.'

'I find that interesting. How tall?'

'Can't be sure. About your height. Maybe a bit taller.'

'And one hand out towards the door of the bathroom cabinet. Try to see that hand.'

'It broke a glass. Smashed it. Deliberate. To make a distraction, I suppose.'

'Where did it get the glass?'

'Shelf below the cabinet.'

Hetty turned back to the cabinet and opened it. 'There's nothing here of any value.'

'Eh?' Mr Hardiman came from the landing. 'Isn't the presentation case there? That's valuable.' He took the case out of the cabinet and opened it to show Hetty the contents. 'Cut-glass with 18-carat gold trimmings. I wouldn't insult my finalists with throwaway prizes. These bottles are meant to be handed down from one generation to the next, topped up when they're empty from plastic refills.'

Hetty said to Rita, 'Have you used any of these yet?'

'No. I'd no reason.'

'Then you can take that scarf off. You're not losing your voice: it's just shock. And don't touch any of these remedies.'

'You what?' said Mr Hardiman.

Hetty moved past him onto the landing and on down the stairs, ignoring his indignation. She was in full flood now, the little grey cells all sparking. 'Geoffrey, get me the presentation case of a finalist who's lost his voice.'

'Les Maynard. Just withdrawn.'

'Don't touch the contents.' She turned to Simon, 'And you can make yourself useful by phoning the rest of the finalists and warning them not to use any of the Hardiman's Herbals they've been given.'

'Hang on!' said Oliver Hardiman.

She was already halfway downstairs and spoke to him over her shoulder. 'I assume you have a lab somewhere in your factory that can make a chemical analysis of the contents of Les Maynard's presentation case?'

There was a conservatory extension at the back of Bill Jason's house which had been adapted to the making of wine. Demijohns of variously coloured liquids, each with an airlock at the top, were producing yeasty bubbles at intervals like an old man farting in the bath, and there was a shelf of bottles of chemicals, all labelled, which Robert was examining with interest.

'Ammonium phosphate . . . ammonium sulphate . . . that's a lot of ammonium you've got there. Is it that choking stuff they put in smelling salts? Potassium metabisulphite . . . bentonite . . . citric acid. Isn't science wonderful?'

'I told you. She's at work.'

'Who'd have believed you could make wine from tinned peaches, marigolds, peeled bananas and – what's this one again?'

'Birch sap. It's a hobby.'

'It'd have to be; I can see that. But who drinks it?'

'Me and Glenda. In front of the fire. On cold winter nights.'
An odd expression had come into his eyes, a hint of moisture.
Was it remembrance of things past or anticipation of things to
come?

Robert said, 'And she's had no trouble at all with her
voice?'

'It's top class. She'll walk away with the cup. Then she'll be
singing for our supper. All those radio jingles for chest rubs!
Hardiman's Herbals proudly presents Glenda Jason, the
Blainthorp Nightingale.'

But Robert knew that Glenda was not the favourite to win the
competition. He had stopped off at the betting shop in Market
Square and checked on the odds. Even in a depleted field, you
could get twelve to one on Glenda Jason. Was her husband
whistling in the wind like some British heavyweight preparing
for a world title in Madison Square Garden, or was it a cover to
conceal the fact that they were somehow nobbling the competition
with banana wine richly spiced with ammonia?

Too many questions, but they were for Hetty to solve. All he
had to do was to report back. 'Isn't it rather anti-Green though,'
he said. 'Sapping the strength of birch trees to brew homemade
plonk?'

Annie and Freddy were sorting through schedules at the desk in
the festival office.

Annie said, 'Some man in a cavalier's costume broke into her
bathroom and scared the daylights out of her.' She looked at one
of the bits of paper in front of her. 'Do you realise that this
unfortunate adjudicator has to listen to eight different women
singing *Summer Time*?'

'Did she say it was a man? I thought . . .'

175

'What?'

'I heard she hadn't been able to remember much detail.'

'I think that when it comes to remembering the difference between a man and a woman that's the kind of detail Rita will always get right.'

There was another cross on the poster. Les Maynard's face had been defaced.

Albert Slater, well wrapped up against the weather, stood looking at it. Beverley, with her three-year-old daughter in a pushchair, joined him.

They stood together in silence for a while considering what had been done. Then Albert said, 'Down to five?'

'Seems so.'

'My grandson tells me you need the money.'

'I do.'

'Good luck, then.' He tipped his hat to her and walked on.

Case conference in the kitchen of the Manor. Hetty sat at the head of the huge table, at the other end of which Geoff was laying places for lunch. Since Mr Hardiman was not with them, they had raided the fridge and found sausages and bacon and sliced bread. Robert was frying all three – bacon first, then sausages, then bread – in a cast-iron pan on the ceramic hob of the electric oven. If he had read the instructions he would have known that he was using the wrong pan.

Geoff said, 'Someone in fancy dress is spiking the Hardiman's Herbal Preparations in the finalists' presentation cases with a substance guaranteed to leave them speechless. And with only five finalists left, and two of them actually present when the mysterious cavalier made his nefarious attempt—'

'Leaves three,' said Hetty. 'Beverley Prendergast, Glenda Jason and Brian Borrowmere. And since Brian is an eleven-year-old boy, staying with his mother at a hotel in Rochdale, practically speaking we're down to two. Beverley's training to be a pharmacist, which means she knows all about medicines, and Glenda's conservatory is chockful of chemicals. Both highly suspicious. And I don't like any of it.'

'Interesting that the cat-burglar dresses as a cavalier and Mr Hardiman's name is Oliver.'

Robert turned over sausages satisfactorily brown on one side. 'Maybe Oliver beat this cavalier in a singing contest when they were both young. At Marston Moor.'

'Concentrate on the fry-up, Robert. Every man is worthy of his hire. No, the cavalier costume is easy – floppy clothes, long hair in a wig, feather on the hat to make you look taller – much better than a polo-neck pullover and a balaclava if you want to hide any feminine bits and pieces. All the costume does is make the criminal unisex. Means, motive and opportunity. Means – the chemicals in the linctus. Opportunity – well, I don't suppose any of them keep their bathrooms locked, and if the cavalier could break into Rita's house he—'

'—Or she.'

'—could break into any of the others'. It's motive we're still hung up on.'

Geoff said, 'I think we need to delve into Mr Hardiman's past. There were scrapbooks in his bookcase.'

'And there'll be Yellow Pages by the phone. Let's find out where a body would go to hire a theatrical costume around here. We'll have our lunch first and adjourn this meeting to the office before he gets back.'

* * *

Oliver Hardiman had left the boffins to analyse the contents of the presentation case and told them he would be back at two o'clock for a detailed report. Everything was going wrong and it seemed to him that all this bloody Wainthropp woman was doing was to complicate matters. He drove over to Simon Letby's place, where he kept a hunter, and rode out over the rather denuded Letby acres to cool down. Simon rode with him.

Simon said, 'I wanted to talk to you about Rita.'

'What about her?'

'She wants to back out of the competition. Says what's happened was a warning, and if she goes on with it she'll be punished.'

'Down to four! Can't have that. Talk her round.'

'You know the whole thing's on local radio?'

'Couldn't be. I'm a major shareholder.'

'Was. They had a lot of fun with it.'

Mr Hardiman's mobile buzzed. His horse went sharply sideways. Simon said, 'I wish you wouldn't take that bloody thing with you wherever you go. It makes the horses uncomfortable.'

'Hardiman!' Oliver barked.

It was Annie Mosscrop to tell him about the feature on local radio.

'Who gave them the information?'

'I don't know. They wouldn't say.'

'Don't tell me you don't know; you're paid to know. Somebody must have released that information without my sanction.'

'It's not a question of releasing it, Mr Hardiman; it's not a secret. Everyone in Blainthorp knows. There's that poster where someone keeps crossing off the faces.'

He cut her off. Annie looked at Freddy and raised her eyes to heaven at the unreasonableness of it. He grinned and shrugged. So much for Oliver Hardiman.

Simon said, 'Which way do you want to go?'

'No way. I've had enough. I'll go back to the factory and wait for the result of the tests.'

He turned his horse and headed back towards the stables. *Just as well that mare has a mouth like vulcanised rubber*, Simon Letby thought: *he'd be the ruin of a decent animal*. Enjoying the memory of Oliver's fury, Simon Letby smiled and rode on alone.

Glenda and Bill had finished their lunch and were listening critically to a tape-recording of Glenda singing *Blow the Wind Southerly* to a piano accompaniment. It came to an end and Glenda switched it off. Bill said, 'Watch it. Those sibilant esses are creeping in again.'

'You know I'll be late again tonight, don't you?'

He looked at her, his face expressionless. Then he said, 'You'll be the death of me; you really will.'

Lunch was over and the whole staff of the Wainthropp Detective Agency were pursuing their enquiries in Mr Hardiman's study. While Robert kept watch at the window, Geoff consulted the Yellow Pages covering Blainthorp and adjacent districts, four volumes altogether, and Hetty had collected three folio volumes of scrapbooks, leather-bound and with gold lettering, from the bookcase.

'The moment we hear the tiny patter of the Jaguar's hooves, it's out of here and back to the kitchen as if butter wouldn't melt in our mouths.'

'Men don't eat butter. Only poofs and women eat butter.'

Robert said, 'That's not true: he was wolfing it down this morning. And most of the marmalade.'

Hetty turned pages. 'He's got everything here from the age of eight. And it's not just Blainthorp. He went all over like young Brian. Remind me what I'm looking for.'

'The ones he won.'

'He won them all. If he didn't win he didn't keep the programme.'

Theatrical costumes were under Fancy Dress. Geoff was appalled to discover how many sources there were. 'There's hundreds . . . Manchester . . . Preston . . . all over. Medieval mantles from Macclesfield with genuine fake fur. Vampires' teeth from Oldham.'

'He had a restricted repertoire, I'll tell you that,' said Hetty.

'I don't know where to start.'

'The nearest.' Programmes, photographs, certificates, some turning yellow but all neatly aligned with photo-corners at the edges to keep them in place without the use of glue which might show through. '*Pie Jesu . . . Pie Jesu . . . Panis Angelicus* – makes a change – *Pie Jesu* again. There's something tickling my memory buds.'

'Out!'

They had not needed Robert to watch. They could all hear the roar of an angry Jaguar. Hastily they put back the books and hurried down the corridor through shrouded suits of armour to be back round the kitchen table digesting their lunch in post-prandial languor.

It was wasted on Mr Hardiman. Like March, he came in like a lion. 'I've had the report from the lab. No alien substance whatever has been added to the herbal preparations in Les Maynard's presentation case. They are all exactly as they left the factory.'

'Could they have done the analysis too quick and made a mistake?'

'My full technical team has been working flat out, Mrs Wainthropp. They've checked and double-checked. There is no mistake. So, since *your* team is now back at first base, perhaps you'd like to stop lounging about in my kitchen and get on with your work.'

And he went on out like a lion.

'I took Tanya over to mother's this morning and I'll go round myself when I've finished here. I'm not going back to my place until the competition's over.'

In the salon Beverley was washing a client's hair. Most of Beverley's clients were old age pensioners because she was soft-hearted and took the clients the other stylists didn't want. Her professional life was high on social concern and low on tips. However, it would all change when she won.

There was someone tugging at her sleeve. It was Edna with a sprig of white heather.

'Bring you luck.'

'Oh . . . thank you.'

'Don't let the buggers get you down.'

'Edna!'

'If a Member of Parliament can say it, then I can say it.' She was on her way out. She had shown the other stuck-up lasses in the salon that old Edna knew where her loyalties lay. 'Don't forget: I'll be there on Sunday, rooting for you, baby.'

A little way down the street she passed Robert, loitering in a doorway. He was on protection duty this afternoon, looking after Beverley, though she did not know it. He was to keep her safe and report any suspicious occurrence. Geoff was similarly employed at the supermarket where Glenda worked part-time. Geoff knew the ways of supermarkets; he had worked on a check out himself.

Hetty had gone back to the Festival Office. She knew she had to do something, but not what that something should be. A person like Oliver Hardiman did not realise that, after a disappointment, one needed time to bounce back. She had been so sure the stuff – whatever it was – had been in those presentation cases. She had even wondered whether someone in the factory might be doing it.

Annie said, 'If only we had enough singers left to make a show of it, the publicity would be wonderful for getting bums on seats.'

'What's the position about your celebrity judge? Nobody's tried to nobble *him*, I trust.'

'Her. We had a bit of trouble finding someone and ended up with the resident contralto at the Winter Gardens, Siltsea. Now she's cancelled because of the bad publicity. It puts us in rather a spot.'

'I'd better get out of your hair. You've got so much to do.'

She would wander for a while, look in on some of the classes, get the feel of things. Her singing days were long over, but she remembered the choir, the organist who had told her she ought to turn professional and Mr Dabney who had got his comeuppance at the Three Choirs Festival. She remembered her appearance at the Floral Hall, Fleetwood, as Chuckles Chinchilla. This was still an atmosphere in which she could feel at home, get an idea, see the way clear.

She stopped to inspect the poster advertising the Blainthorp Amateur Operatic's forthcoming production of *When Did You*

Last See Your Father. She had never heard of the opera, but remembered the picture well.

Freddy arrived at the desk in a rush and began to remove outer garments. 'Sorry I'm late. Errands for grandad.'

Annie was looking at Hetty examining the poster. 'She's talking about protection for the remaining finalists. I don't know how she's going to manage it with just the one scooter.'

Hetty wandered on. A group of children, one dressed as a cowgirl another as a gypsy, were waiting outside the main hall, and from inside could be heard the voice of a teenage girl singing *Tonight* from *West Side Story* not at all well. 'What class is this?'

The gypsy answered, 'Twelve to sixteen – *Songs from the Shows*.'

'You all waiting to perform?' They nodded. 'Nervous?' They nodded. 'Just think as you go through that door, *I'll enjoy it, even if they don't*.' Young Brian Borrowmere stood apart from the other children, and seemed to be disassociating himself from them. Little snob! But she must be pleasant. 'What are you going to sing, Brian?'

'I'm not. I'm just waiting to go in. It wouldn't be fair on the others to enter when I'm a Golden Voice finalist. Also my mother doesn't like me doing *Songs from the Shows*. She says adult emotions sung by children are sick making.'

'What about your dad? Does he throw up easily as well?'

'I don't know. He hasn't lived with us for years.'

When Did You Last See Your Father? 'Do you know how many years?'

'I'm afraid not. He doesn't often come up in conversation.'

One of the boys was teasing the cowgirl, pulling her cowboy hat down over her eyes. She was beginning to be tearful. If she was intending to perform that song about being as corny as Kansas in August from *Oklahoma!*, tears would not be appropriate. Brian moved forward. 'Stop that, Colin!'

'Stop what?'

'Winding Georgina up just before she has to go on and face her public. It's not professional. In fact, it's almost cheating.'

'Pardon me for living.'

But he moved away from the cowgirl. Hetty said to Brian, 'There's a picture on a poster in the waiting area, *When Did You Last See Your Father.* My son used to have the jigsaw. I've been wondering exactly when you last saw yours.'

The song in the main hall had finished, and the door was opened to allow latecomers into the audience. Brian said, 'I'm never rude to older people, Mrs Wainthropp, because one never knows when one might need them. So I'll just say *au revoir* for the present. I'm sure I'll see you around,' and followed the other children in.

Just the same, the little grey cells were beginning to stir.

Robert spent the whole afternoon doing nothing in particular outside the salon, and when Beverley emerged at five-thirty, he followed her, keeping his head down and trying to look as unremarkable as he could. He had been told to see that she reached home safely and then take a taxi back to the Manor, but quite soon it appeared that Beverley was not going home. He quickened his pace. If she were not homeward bound where was she bound and was it important to the enquiry? He would have to be careful to keep her in sight.

Beverley, as she had told her client, was going to spend the night at her mum's place. She very soon noticed that there was an old man in a dirty raincoat who seemed to be following her. Beverley had been warned as a girl about dirty old men in raincoats and what they were likely to do unless severely discouraged. She stopped suddenly and turned round. The dirty old man stopped also and stared into the window of a shop selling discount furniture. No way was that old man interested in a three-piece floral suite with matching curtains.

She looked around. When did you ever see a policeman in Blainthorp High Street? But there was one and she had better grab him while she had the chance. She walked towards him. The old man, she knew, was still following. She stopped when she reached the policeman and spoke to him.

Robert saw Beverley talking to the policeman but could not hear what was said. He saw the policeman nod gravely, and then begin to walk towards him. The policeman drew nearer and nearer. Robert broke and ran.

He did not run far. A woman pedestrian, seeing the old pickpocket running and a constable in chase, put out her umbrella and tripped Robert up. He fell sideways on the pavement, skinning his elbow and bruising his face. Then the police constable arrived, sat on his chest, and phoned for back-up to bring the criminal in.

Glenda only worked two and a half hours on Thursday afternoons and then went home again. Geoff followed her, then had a word with the neighbours and discovered that Glenda quite often went out at night on her own, sometimes two nights a week; they were not sure where.

'What about yesterday night?'

'Y'right. Yesterday she went out. Don't know when she came back, but it would have been late because we were in bed.'

Yesterday night the cavalier had paid a visit to Rita's bathroom. Geoff took the scooter to the Festival Office to collect Hetty and found her in better spirits than she had been after lunch. 'I think we may have a lead, Mrs Wainthropp.'

'Then lead me to it.' Good spirits made for bad jokes.

They would question Glenda under the pretext of having come to protect her. They took the scooter back to the Jasons' home and Glenda swooshed by them in the car on her way out. She waved as she passed them.

Bill was closing the front gate. Even in a wheelchair he seemed to get about. Hetty said, 'Where's she gone?'

'She helps out behind the bar at the Green Bay Tree on Singles' Nights and does a cabaret for the dinner guests.'

'We've come to protect her.'

'It's not necessary. They're all friends there.' She was dithering, looking for an excuse to stay. 'Would you and the lad like to come in for a glass of homemade wine?'

At just about this time the police were phoning Mr Hardiman to ask him to vouch for the dirty old man who claimed to be a private detective in his employment.

'Not for Geoffrey,' Hetty said. 'He's driving.' Bill poured a glass of the birch sap for the two of them. 'Thank you.' She sipped. 'Delicious!' And it was, tasting a little like the winter mixture boiled sweets she used to get sometimes as a child, but with a lingering comforting aftertaste. 'It must get lonely in the evenings with Glenda out.'

'I know where she is.'

'What time does she leave the Green Bay Tree?'

'About eleven.'

'And sometimes . . . she's a bit late getting back, I dare say.' He was looking at her, amazed. 'Much later than you'd expect.' It had been a shot almost in the dark with only neighbours' gossip to go on, but it had hit home. 'She was late last night.'

'How the hell did you know that?' Hetty smiled, a wise smile,

186

indicating infinite reserves of knowledge. 'Has someone been talking?' She smiled again. 'That Mavis at the Bay Tree?' Another smile. She could keep it up for ever. 'Well, it's no business of anyone else.'

'So you want to keep it quiet?'

'I don't want people talking about it. Who would?'

'Trust me.'

A silence. He was wondering whether she really could be trusted. He looked at Geoff. 'Not in front of the lad.'

'Oh! . . . Very well.' This was clearly not the time to get on her high horse about Geoffrey being her associate. 'Geoffrey, would you wait outside, please?'

Geoffrey left to wait outside. It seemed to him that rather too much of the Agency's work involved the junior partner waiting out in the cold while the senior partner drank homemade wine or communed with the Spirit World in the warm by the living room fire, but he bore no malice. No doubt Mrs Wainthropp would tell him all about it in her own good time back at the Manor.

Meanwhile Bill Jason was explaining why his wife was sometimes late getting home at night.

'She'd been to a Cultural Evening in Manchester with the Townswomen's Guild. Some play at the Library Theatre – there was a whole lot of them went, with wine and cheese in the foyer and you meet the actors after. Herbert Sprinter or some such wrote it; he must have a funny imagination. It was about husbands and wives pretending to be other people – lovers, toy-boys, scuba divers, the postman even or yoghurt delivery – it was all pretence but it raised the temperature like. She and me were going through a bad patch at the time. We gave it a whirl, and ever since . . .'

'She comes back late and pretends you're her lover?'

'It goes all through the day. I look at the mileage on the car and accuse her of deceiving me. It's a game. Keeps things fresh between us. Being a married woman yourself, you'd understand.'

'Well . . .' said Hetty. Since taking up the detective business, there was no doubt she'd learned a lot.

'What I can't get into my head is how you could have known. Who told you?'

'Nobody. I was just fishing. Thank you so much for the wine. We've had a very interesting chat. And I don't think Glenda's in any danger of losing her voice at the Green Bay Tree.'

Nevertheless she and Geoff went out there, had a meal at the bar and listened to Glenda's sensuous rendering of *I've Got You Under My Skin*. It made a change from *Blow the Wind Southerly* but as far as Geoff was concerned it was a change for the better.

Means. Motive. Opportunity. The words went round and round in Hetty's head as they took the scooter back to the Manor. Geoff was worried. With her head full of speculation Mrs Wainthropp sometimes forgot to adjust her body-weight on the corners.

They breezed into the kitchen to find Mr Hardiman and Robert eating fish and chips. 'You're late,' Mr Hardiman said.

'We had ours in town. I've got work to do. May I use your office? I'd like to have a look at those scrapbooks of yours if you don't mind.'

'I had to rescue your husband from a police cell.'

'You what?'

Hetty's head was so full, she had hardly looked at her husband. Now she took in his condition. Robert had a black eye, his face was bruised and his shirt torn, the collar in particular almost torn off.

'He's rather the worse for wear as you can see.'

Robert said, 'I'm all right, love. Just a misunderstanding. You get on with what you've got to do.'

She was in two minds. Should she stay and try to tend Robert's wounds, comfort him, reassure him that he had done well when clearly he had done very badly? Oliver Hardiman would think her a callous bitch if she did not, not that she gave tuppence for his opinion.

Robert said, 'Please! I'd rather.' There was a note of steel in his voice. She had heard that note seldom, but never ignored it when she did. She went on to the office.

Geoff sat next to Robert and picked up one of his chips. 'Beat you up, did they?'

'I should never have tried to run.'

It was tedious work. Earlier Hetty had not known what she was looking for in the scrapbooks. Now she did.

At eleven o'clock Mr Hardiman appeared with cocoa. Hetty said, 'What's the North West Young Singer of the Year Competition? It doesn't seem to have been a festival as such.'

'More important. Preliminary heats, then the finalists sang against each other. And the best man won. Or woman. Not that it ever was a woman when I was around.'

'Sounds like the Golden Voice of Blainthorp.'

'No Gold Cup. No cheque. No countrywide exposure on radio and TV. You did it for the honour.' He looked over her shoulder at the programme. 'That was when everyone decided I had a career in music.'

'Oliver Hardiman . . . *Pie Jesu* – yet again. Do you ever see any of the other finalists? Eric Leavesden? Mary-Anne Winterbottom? Ethel Warders? Michael Moroney?'

'Too long ago. So much has happened since.'

'Thank you,' said Hetty. She closed the book. It was over.

Next morning at breakfast, finding him at the kitchen table, tucking into boiled eggs and mounds of buttered toast she told him she, Robert and Geoff were going home.

'Giving up on the job? It's only Friday. You won't be paid.'

'Who said anything about giving up? My professional opinion is that there'll be no more trouble before the final. I'll be at that, of course, just to make sure it all goes off safely, and I'd like you to invite some people around here afterwards.'

'Why?'

'That's how it's done in the Poirot books. He gets all his suspects together, sitting about on gilt chairs, and puts his finger on the murderer. I've not had the opportunity in any of my cases up to now.' She poured herself a cup of coffee. 'Now I'll have a quick bite of breakfast, then pop round to Les Maynard's house and pick up a tube of toothpaste.'

He was looking at her. She could see the admiration growing in his face. It was a pleasing sight for Hetty. 'You're not so green as you're cabbage-looking, Mrs Wainthropp.'

'Nothing like, Mr Hardiman.' She tapped the top of her boiled egg briskly. 'I'd take it kindly if you'd give Robert a lift.'

'Pleased to. And there's just one thing I'd like you to do for me, if you'd be so kind.'

That one thing – since she would be at the final anyway – was to be the mystery judge. An appropriate costume would be supplied.

For Hetty, who, when disguise was necessary, was used to getting her costumes from Oxfam, Sue Ryder or some other charity shop, it was something of a revelation. A lady came from Manchester with two cardboard boxes, one large, one small, acres of tissue paper and a seamstress for the final adjustments. Nothing like it had happened to her since her wedding.

She sat next to Oliver Hardiman in the front row of the Chapel.

Her long dress was mostly gold lamé, she wore a half-mask of black silk with a diamanté trim, and she wore a magnificent red wig. She looked every inch a diva and even Dame Joan Sutherland herself could not have carried it off better.

The chapel was full. Every music-lover from Blainthorp and the surrounding area was there, and a bus-load of the Friends of Radio Three had been bussed in from Chorley. Edna had brought a banner reading, 'BEVERLEY PRENDERGAST SUPPORTERS CLUB' but it had been taken away from her at the door. The five finalists sat in the choir stalls until each came forward in turn to sing under the Pugin window. The order in which they sang had been decided by lot, and this was it:

Beverley Prendergast sang Reynaldo Hahn's *If My Songs Were only Winged*. The whole chapel was still. More folk than Edna wanted Beverley to win. Hetty listened intently.

Simon Letby sang *For the Mountains Shall Depart* from Mendelssohn's *Elijah* and hit a wrong note. Hetty flinched.

Glenda Jason's *Blow the Wind Southerly* was received with more respect than appreciation. Geoff thought she would have done better to stick with *I've Got You Under My Skin*.

Rita Locheed had stayed with the *Habanera* from *Carmen* but you could tell her heart was not in it and anyway the acoustics of the chapel were not suited to it.

Brian Borrowmere sang the *Pie Jesu*. Hetty lifted her half-mask to wipe away a tear. She had never heard a purer voice before and probably never would again. She looked sideways at Oliver Hardiman. Tears were raining down his face.

She said to him quietly, 'You're looking at yourself at his age?' He nodded. 'He's your son, Mr Hardiman.'

He could not face the knowledge as it came crowding in, and turned his head away. Hetty said, 'That being so, I don't think I should give him the prize, even though he is the best.'

He nodded again. *Pull yourself together, Oliver*. Even joy must not be allowed to discompose a public man. He turned to look at the audience. At the back of the chapel, sitting in an aisle seat, was his wife, Beata. She wore that look of patient self-approval which he had grown to dislike so intensely during their life together, but he supposed that, if he were to get the boy back, he would have to take the mother as well.

'And the Gold Cup goes to . . . Miss Beverley Prendergast.'

Cup and cheque were presented to tumultuous applause. It was for the best. It would be easier to make successful radio and TV commercials with a nubile soprano than a boy treble. 'Don't worry, lad,' Oliver Hardiman said to his stiffly resentful son, 'You don't need a Gold Cup. You've got the whole of the Hardiman Herbal Empire to inherit.'

So they all went back to the Manor, where the cleaning lady had swept and dusted all day. Freddy Slater and his grandfather, Annie Mosscrop, the finalists, even the ones who had scratched, they walked through suits of armour, no longer swathed in dust-sheets, to the Great Drawing Room to sit in gilt chairs brought in for the occasion and to be given champagne, poured by Geoffrey. And when they were all comfortably seated, Hetty Wainthropp, still in her gold lamé dress but without the half-mask and wig, took centre stage.

'Mostly,' she said, 'it was to do with wrong trails. I never really believed that one of the finalists was nobbling the others, but I did swallow the idea that it was the bottles in the presentation cases being spiked.'

'Why?' Mr Hardiman was not sure that he enjoyed playing second fiddle in his own house.

'Some business competitor trying to damage your firm.'

'We *have* no competitors in the North West.'

'Someone trying to show you up, then. Damage what should be damaged because it wasn't worth having in the first place. Someone who doesn't believe Hardiman's Herbal Healing actually heals. What caused them to lose their voices, Mr Hardiman. That's the nub. What was actually used to do the job?'

He was uneasy. 'How should I know?'

'Aren't you an expert on herbs?'

They were all looking at him. Showing him up! He should never have allowed the woman to play this game. He knew what it was, of course. Tease, shift focus, set up somebody else before making the pounce. But he had not expected her to play with *him*. 'I'm a businessman. I don't need to know the details of what goes into the product these days. I pay other people to look after that.'

'So you're no expert, Mr Hardiman, in spite of your know-all attitude?' He closed his eyes. He must be patient, he would be patient. This woman had forgotten that a service industry like hers can only flourish on goodwill, and she had just lost his. Hetty went on with her game. No wonder Poirot enjoyed this kind of thing; it was fun. 'But we do have an expert on herbs amongst us,' she said. 'Mr Slater, what do you think was used?'

'Has to be something like Tsnchai leaf. A Chinese herb. In substantial amounts, used over a period, it causes inflammation of the mouth or throat.'

'How long a period?'

'Regularly over a week or so. I give it to my patients homeopathically in tiny doses to stimulate the body's own defences against hay fever.'

'How would you give it in substantial amounts without anybody knowing?'

'Add it to something with a strong taste where it wouldn't be noticed. Tea caddy. Instant coffee.'

'Homemade wine?'

'If you like. Not the leaves, of course. Make a tincture.'

'Anything taken by mouth?'

'Right. You don't even need to swallow it.'

'This tincture of yours – you could inject it into toothpaste?'

'I could. So could anyone.'

'Les Maynard's wife wears dentures so she doesn't use paste.' She turned towards Freddy, who became uneasy under her gaze. 'Does your grandson Freddy have access to this herb and know its properties?' Mr Hardiman grunted.

Albert Slater said, 'It's me, Mrs Wainthropp, that has no manner of use for that quack, Oliver Hardiman, not my grandson.'

'Are you saying you did it?'

'I'm not saying I didn't.'

Mr Hardiman was out of his chair. 'I'll have you. A tinpot herbalist in a country town! I'll ruin you.'

'That'll do from you, Oliver Cromwell,' Hetty said. 'Sit down and hold your peace. You can bully your way around Blainthorp, but I'm in charge of this meeting.' Mr Hardiman lost the battle of wills and sat down again. 'Anyway Mr Slater was never the cavalier. Breaking and entering? Bolting downstairs? At his age?'

'You're enjoying this,' Simon Letby said.

'I own I am,' said Hetty.

Geoff said, 'Shall I go round with the champagne for refills?'

'Not yet. I've reached the best bit. Step forward the wardrobe mistress of the Blainthorp Amateur Operatic Society aka Mary-Anne Winterbottom.'

There was a silence. They were looking at each other, not knowing what she meant. All but Annie.

Annie said, 'Is this the bit in the Poirot stories when the criminal makes a run for it? If so, I have to tell you I've no clear way to the door.'

Oliver Hardiman said, 'You?'

'Me.'

'*When Did You Last See Your Father*?' Hetty said. 'What it put into my mind at first was that Oliver Hardiman had lost a son, but that was another false trail I made for myself. The real trail was much clearer. Cavaliers and Roundheads. She didn't have to look in the Yellow Pages. The costume was already to hand.'

'Why?'

'Revenge. Robert was right; the cavalier was getting her own back on Oliver.'

Mr Hardiman said to Mrs Mosscrop, 'I've never harmed you.'

Hetty said, 'I think you have. Mary-Anne – Annie. Married name Mosscrop, but born Winterbottom. In every one of Mr Hardiman's scrapbooks you were among the contestants. Until suddenly – you weren't.'

Annie said, 'North West Young Singer of the Year Competition, 1960.' She spoke directly to Oliver. 'You were twelve; I was fourteen. You winked and smiled at me and whispered that it was a two-horse race.'

'You sang *She Moved Through the Fair* in the heats. It was beautiful.'

'And it moved me through to the final. You teased me about the obsessive way I wiped and blew my nose just before going on stage. And while I was in the loo, you opened my purse and put sneezing-powder on my hanky. You must have planned it or you wouldn't have had the sneezing powder with you.'

Young Brian said, 'Oh, dad! It's not professional.'

'Right,' said Hetty. 'More like cheating.'

Annie continued. 'I had to walk off in the middle of my second verse. They couldn't even give me a merit mark. After that Aunt Amy changed her mind about paying for my musical education. It seemed to me my life had stopped but of course it went on. Second-rate A Levels, third-rate university, fourth-rate advertising agency, fifth-rate marriage and two first-rate kids. Divorce. The kids grow up. I return to my roots. Finally revenge. I'm proud of what I did. I'd have pulled it off completely if Mrs Wainthropp hadn't come a bit too close. Even so, a final with only five golden voices can't have done Hardiman's Herbal Healing much good.'

'You won't get away with it. I'll sue you for every penny you've got.'

'No, dad,' said the heir to the Hardiman empire. 'We don't want the publicity.'

'Five finalists nobbled! Robbed of the chance of fame! They'll do the suing and I'll pay the lawyers.'

'Will you?' Hetty spoke to each of the scratched finalists in turn. 'Eileen? Osbert? Ken? Harry? Les? Even if he pays . . . will you sue?'

Each slowly shook his head. Les said, 'We'd look stupid. We all knew we hadn't a real chance: it was always going to be Beverley or Brian. I wouldn't give you the satisfaction, Mr Hardiman.'

Again Annie Mosscrop aka Mary-Anne Winterbottom spoke directly to Oliver Hardiman. 'What really hurt was that, after you'd ruined my chance of fame, you threw your own away simply to make money. I could have gone on, just as you could, and for me it mattered. I would have liked . . . just once . . . to sing in a really big hall with a full orchestra.'

He could not meet her eyes or even, he discovered, remain in the room. If the villain was going to make a run for it, he, it seemed, was the person most appropriate. He did not run, but walked to the door, head down, opened it (no police were waiting outside as they would have been in a Poirot story), turned and said to his guests, 'Enjoy yourselves. I shall be in my study. I have work to do.'

Annie said, 'Geoff, I'll have that refill now.' She raised her glass to Hetty who drank to her in return. And they did enjoy themselves. They had plenty to talk about.

Hetty left the party with Robert and Geoff; they would not be staying the night at the Manor. As they walked past the suits of armour, Hetty said, 'A good job well done.'

Robert said, 'Mr Hardiman's found a son.'

Geoff said, 'Young Brian's got the dad he probably deserves.'

'Beverley's won the prize.'

'Annie's got her own back.'

'And nobody hurt at the end,' Hetty said. 'That's the way I like it. The one thing I don't care for in the Poirot books is that someone always ends up getting hanged.'

Woman of the Year

Ackersley High Street on a fine spring morning. Market day.

Myra and Trudi, two of the women from the Refuge, had come shopping together. Myra was in her early forties, dumpy with a bad complexion and greasy hair, Trudi twenty years younger in a thin coat, pale, her hair scraped back; she still had that frightened look, like a hare, which newcomers to a Refuge have and take some time to lose.

Myra carried the old leather shopping bag which was always used, whoever did the shopping. It had only her purse in it at that moment; they had not been to the market yet. Their first stop was at Braithwaite's, the chemist's. 'Want me to go in for you?' Myra said.

Trudi shook her head and they went in together.

Further down the street, near the entrance to the market, a motorbike was parked. Loitering nearby, watching and waiting, was a young man in a leather jacket and jeans. He was not a biker – no studs, tattoos and short hair – just a young layabout, presumably unemployed since he was not at work on a weekday morning. The bike was expensive, though. He saw the women, saw where they went and moved closer so as to be near when they came out of the shop.

The traffic lights at the corner changed from red to green. Traffic moved forward. A bus with the driver under instruction was at the front.

Myra and Trudi came out of the chemist's shop. Trudi handed a small package to Myra, who put it away in her pocket. The young man in jeans moved swiftly forward towards the two women and called, 'Trudi!'

Her head jerked up. She saw him. Her mouth opened wide but no sound emerged. She ran blindly away out into the middle of the road in front of the bus. The driver was only under instruction; he had no experience of this kind of happening. He did his best, stamping on the brake. Maybe he was not as quick as a more experienced driver would have been, but he had no real chance of stopping in time, and anyway, it has to be said in his defence, that the bus did not run over Trudi. It just hit her. Which was enough.

Myra had not moved, had not been able to move, had not had time to move. It all happened so suddenly, almost at once, only seconds between Trudi's seeing the young man and lying in the road in front of the bus: it was as if the whole incident took place inside a bubble within real time and the real world of the High Street. Then the bubble burst and real time started again. Myra screamed.

She screamed once, twice, then turned to face the young man in jeans whom she now knew must be Trudi's husband, Gary. He had not moved either, but was standing where they had first seen him, stock still and horrified. Myra ran at him, hitting him in the face with the leather bag.

'Beast! Animal!'

He pushed her away against a shop window, and she fell over. He shouted at her, 'Piss off, you stupid bitch. It's not my fault.' Then he ran back up the street to his motorbike, started it and drove away at speed.

Myra picked herself up and walked slowly back to where Trudi lay. Traffic was at a standstill and a small crowd had already gathered round the body, so that she could no longer see it. She could hear the distant sound of an ambulance approaching – or was it the police? Would an ambulance come so quick? She tapped on the shoulder of a woman in the crowd.

'Will you let me through, please? I'm her friend.'

Mrs Hetty Wainthropp, Supergran Sleuth, had been invited to the Woman of the Year Luncheon.

This was not the national function at the Savoy Hotel in London but it was still a considerable honour – the Mid Lancs Woman of the Year Luncheon. And Hetty was not to be just one of those paying for a place in the banqueting room; she was to be at the top table with five other Women of the Year, a Lady Mayor, an Olympic medallist (bronze for netball), a professor of medieval history, a television newsreader and the daughter of a duke who had done great work for charity. She was not to make a speech – the Lady Mayor would do that for them all – but she would be seen and envied by all the other women, and no doubt written up yet again in the *Record*.

She stood giving herself a critical once-over in the full-length wardrobe mirror. She had taken an hour to dress and make up, to say nothing of the time spent in the bath; she had lashed out the day before on a manicure and facial with hot towels as well as having her hair styled; the dress was her best, five years old and she could still get into it. She looked every inch the successful professional woman.

'Will I pass?'

Robert said, 'Just don't get gravy on the collar.' He made a discovery. 'Them shoes are new.'

'Bought in the market yesterday.'

'Cheap shoes from the market! When you'll be up on the platform with a duke's daughter! What can you be thinking of?'

'It wasn't the price. They match the dress. Aubergine! I knew at once I had to have them. Perhaps the heels are slightly higher than I'm used to.' She turned back to Robert. 'Come on, tell me how nice I look. The taxi'll be here soon. There was a time when praise wasn't altogether foreign to your nature.'

'You look wonderful. You always do in my eyes. You'll do us credit.'

Hetty blushed. 'Don't over-egg the pudding, Robert.'

Robert went to the door and called downstairs. 'Geoffrey! She's ready. Stand by to burst into spontaneous applause as the Woman of the Year descends the staircase.'

Hetty took a last look, then moved to the bedroom door. 'One of the Women of the Year. There are others.'

He stepped out of her way and bowed. 'After you, my lady.' How silly he was sometimes! Well, she would probably have to walk downstairs in an elegant and graceful manner at the four-star hotel where the function was to take place. It would do no harm to practice. She hoped there would not be too much walking. The heels were, now she gave her mind to it, just a tiny bit uncomfortable.

Geoff was at the bottom of the stairs looking up. As she took the first step, Robert nodded. He burst into spontaneous applause on cue and Robert joined in from the bedroom door. The front doorbell rang. It would be the taxi.

On the third step the heel of the right shoe twisted sideways and broke. Hetty cried out and began to fall. Geoff, who was opening the door to the taxi driver, heard the cry and came running back, but was too late to break her fall. She fell all the way down the remaining stairs and landed at the bottom all of a heap.

'Are you all right?' Robert was dithering at the top of the stairs.

'No. I'm not.'

Geoff was kneeling by her. 'She's hurt, Mr Wainthropp. She came down like a sack of coals.'

'I'll phone the doctor. And the Lunch people to tell them she can't come.'

Hetty struggled into a sitting position. There was blood on her face and one eye was closed. 'You'll do no such thing. It's an honour, this lunch is, and I don't intend to miss it.' She turned indignantly to Geoff. 'Sack of coals!'

The Lady Mayor wore her chain of office, the professor the robes of a Doctor of Philosophy; the duke's daughter wore cashmere and pearls, the TV newsreader was dressed by Chanel, the Olympic medallist wore her Olympic medal. Hetty wore a black eye and an old pair of flat-heeled shoes which did not go with her dress.

All the same, she attracted interest and admiration. 'These life and death struggles with desperate criminals, Mrs Wainthropp!' the Lady Mayor said graciously, as they stood side by side at the washbasins in the Ladies Room, freshening up after the Lunch, 'We all do so admire your courage.'

She patted Hetty's shoulder. The pain was excruciating. Then the Lady Mayor adjusted her chain of office and swept out, passing in the doorway a rather more down-to-earth lady coming in. This was Helen Rance, once a senior social worker, now retired.

'I've a job for you if you want it, Mrs Wainthropp,' she said.

They were not alone. All the cubicles were occupied, hot water swirled in washbasins, light perspiration was removed from and face powder applied to the faces of the ladies in the Ladies. 'It's hardly the place,' Hetty said.

'DCI Adams told me to look out for you.' That made a difference. 'Though he didn't warn me about . . .' Mrs Rance's gesture took in the black eye and bruised face.

'It only happened this morning. It was the shoes. Pride is painful.'

'Well, I'm bound to say it's all to the good for our purposes. I'll wait for you outside. The DCI will join us.'

And she went with no further explanation, leaving Hetty with her mouth open and the word, 'Why?' still hardly on its way out.

The explanation came from DCI Adams. He, Mrs Rance and Hetty sat together over coffee in comfortable armchairs in the lounge of the hotel, and from time to time women who had been paying guests at the Lunch would approach timidly to pay their respects to the Supergran Sleuth and tell her how much her example illuminated their own drab lives. This was very gratifying to Hetty, and particularly gratifying that it should happen in front of the DCI.

What was worrying Mrs Rance and the DCI was the death of Trudi Hawes in Ackersley High Street.

'There's no doubt it was an accidental death. She came out of the chemist's and heard her husband call her name. She looked up, saw him, panicked and ran straight out into the road. The driver of the bus never had a chance of stopping in time.'

'What was her husband doing there?'

The DCI was careful. 'He says he was looking for her.'

'In Ackersley?'

'They lived – he lives – in a tower block in Blackburn. Since she took the child and left, he's been going out every day checking all the towns within twenty miles or so – Accrington, Clitheroe,

Barnoldswick, Colne, Bacup – all over. He'd park his motorbike
and hang around the shopping streets and the markets, the Social
Services and the DSS, hoping to see her. He says.'

'Every *day*?'

'He's unemployed. Nothing better to do, he says.'

It did not need the use of the words 'he says' three times to tell
Hetty that the DCI did not believe a word of this story. 'I don't
like it,' she said. 'It doesn't feel right. Why should he pick
Ackersley on the very same morning his wife goes in to collect
her Child Benefit?'

Helen Rance said, 'It doesn't feel right to me either. That's
why I've come to you. He must have known where to find her.'

'You think someone told him?'

The DCI said, 'Right. Who?'

Mrs Rance had started the Refuge, got a committee of women
together, raised money, found premises, joined the Women's Aid
Federation and they were in business. The difference between
their Refuge and most others was that theirs was in the country.

'Mostly the women need to get away where the men can't find
them. They need time and space to sort themselves out. Even so
most Refuges are in towns. Means they're hard to hide. The other
people living in the street soon know. We've gone further. Ours
is six miles outside Ackersley.'

'Easier to hide, harder to protect.'

The DCI said to Mrs Rance, 'I told you she was sharp.'

Hetty said, 'How do the women know where to go?'

'They ask. Desperate women ask for help.'

'Ask who?'

'Reference library, Citizen's Advice Bureau, Social Services.
All they get is the number of a Help Line to phone. Where they
go depends on where there's a vacancy. They're directed to a

particular town – Ackersley in our case. They come with their
kids by bus or train, phone the Help Line again when they arrive
and we pick them up from the station.'

'But everybody knows now, don't they, where your Refuge is?
It'd all have come out at the inquest.'

'The coroner decided no purpose would be served by
revealing the address. Trudi's own address was the flat in
Blackburn.'

'What you're saying . . . You go to such trouble to keep the
location secret that it has to be someone at the Refuge told Gary
Hawes where to find his wife?'

The DCI said, 'Well, it certainly wasn't Trudi herself or she
wouldn't have panicked when she saw him.'

'A member of staff?'

'There's only two. I want you to understand . . . We don't
nanny the women who come to the Refuge. We try to help. Help
with forms, with getting the money they're entitled to, most of
all help in finding somewhere to live and start again. But only
what *they* want. There's a child worker and a manager, but the
women run the Refuge.'

'Just the same it won't be the women who'd be employing
me.'

'No, it'd be the committee. The women move on as and when
they feel ready. The committee has to keep the Refuge going from
year to year.'

'What do you want me to do?'

The DCI said, 'Go under cover. Find out what's going on. I
can't put anyone of my own in because it's the old problem: no
crime has been committed. Anyway, looking the way you do at
the moment, you'd be more convincing. It's a job worth doing.
Are you on?'

Mrs Rance said, 'I'm afraid the money's not good. Can you do it for two hundred a week?'

'Ow!' she had a momentary vision of a reproachful Robert shaking his head, and banished it. 'Plus reasonable expenses?'

'Done.'

The DCI said, 'I'm afraid you can't go in one of your famous disguises because of all the paperwork – Social Security and so on: you have to be the person you say you are. Mrs Hetty Wainthropp running away from her brutal husband.'

'Robert? Who'd believe it?'

'Him they won't meet. I'd start as soon as possible if I were you. That black eye won't last for ever.'

Hetty decided that she had better go that very day before Robert had time to build up objections.

She arrived home to find him in an apron cleaning the oven. This was by way of being a tribute to her as Woman of the Year because he knew it was a job she particularly disliked doing.

'I'm leaving,' she said. 'Going to a Refuge for Battered Women.'

'Why?'

'You've been knocking me about, haven't you? I'd better pack a suitcase and get out of this posh gear into something a bit more downtrodden.'

And she went on upstairs to do it. 'I've never laid a finger on her,' Robert said to Geoff. 'Though God knows she can be irritating at times.'

She changed her clothes, packed the holdall she had last used to take her gear to Mrs Lola Hattersley's house, and they sat down together for a cup of tea. Hetty said, 'Trudi had a little girl, two years old. The Social Services took her into care. She doesn't understand, of course. I don't know what they tell them at that age.'

'You don't have to go so sudden. Do some background work first. Send Geoffrey to the Reference Library.'

'When *they* go it's often sudden.'

'It'll be night when you get there.'

'It's often night.'

It seemed to Robert that a certain amount of self-dramatisation was going on. It was a sad story, no doubt of that, but you had to keep a level head in this world if you were to see things clear. He himself had never even mentioned the size of the fee, which was below the national average weekly wage. 'I tell you straight, Hetty,' he said. 'I don't like you going into this alone.'

'I've no alternative. I can't take Geoffrey in a pushchair now his beard's beginning to sprout. Anyway I've got other work for him. It wasn't just chance her husband finding her in Ackersley that morning.' She gave Geoff a piece of card from her handbag. 'He lives in Blackburn. Here's the address.'

Geoff was alarmed. 'But he's violent.'

'You're my associate.'

'I'm only eighteen. And getting younger.'

'Remember what you said to me on our very first case? We're not quitters. Well, this is no time to change your spots. Use cunning.' She looked at her watch. 'I must go if I'm to catch the bus.'

She was on her way, going out into the unknown like somebody in *Star Trek*. It was too soon, Robert did not know what he felt about it except that he did not feel comfortable. 'How can we reach you?'

'You can't. I don't know myself where the Refuge is. They'll pick me up at Ackersley station. It has to be secret, Robert. As soon as I can get out, I'll phone.' She opened the front door. 'My cover starts here. Try to persuade me not to go.'

'It'll come to no good,' Robert said to Geoff, then called down the street after the straight-backed woman who was walking out of his life, 'Don't leave me. I'll never hit you again. I promise.'

Two of the village women who were coming up the street the other way turned to stare after Hetty. It would be all round the houses by nightfall and no matter how convincingly it was denied afterwards when the case was over, there would always be people who believed it.

'She'll be okay,' Geoff said. 'She's pretended to be other people before. And enjoyed it.'

'She won't enjoy this. She's going to have to live among women who know what it's really like to be battered and abused day after day. They'll see right through her. And when they do—'

'And when they do, she'll leave.'

She had been picked up at the Ackersley Bus Station by a woman in an old Volvo estate who did not introduce herself, and driven out along country roads already dark, through one village and then another until at last they reached the gates of a large house in its own grounds. Hetty had been left with her luggage outside the imposing front door and told to ring the bell.

The estate went back down the drive, never to be seen by Hetty again, and she waited, listening to the noise of the bell reverberating inside the house, until the door was opened by a small black boy.

'I'm Mrs Wainthropp. You're expecting me.'

He nodded, held the door for her to come in, and Hetty picked up her holdall and did so. The small boy closed the door behind her and went away. From a room not far away the sound of a television programme could be heard.

Hetty looked about. There were notices on the inside of the front door.

'DON'T OPEN THE DOOR
IF YOU DON'T KNOW WHO'S OUTSIDE'
'NEVER LET A MAN IN'
'PROTECT THE OTHER WOMEN
YOU'RE LIVING WITH'

and by the side of the door was a press button with a sign 'ALARM' and the alarm itself on the wall above it. There was a large staircase with a battered balustrade and a haircord stair-carpet directly in front of her with a brightly coloured mural of bunny rabbits and a spaceship on a wall to one side of it. This place looked as if it had once been a manor house, and had suffered several changes of owner and use, getting steadily worse for wear with each change of ownership. 'I'm out of my depth here,' she said.

'We all are when we arrive.' The small black boy had returned with a black woman in her early thirties, presumably his mother, who came forward to greet Hetty. 'I'm Ruth.'

'Hetty. They said I'd be expected.'

'You are. Would you like to see where you'll be sleeping and then maybe get a bite to eat?'

'I would.'

Ruth spoke to her son. 'Zeb, nip down to the kitchen and see if there's any food left.' He was off at a run. Ruth led Hetty upstairs. 'I'm afraid you'll be sharing just for tonight, but we'll work something out in the morning.'

Half past eight. Her husband and her associate would also be

watching television, probably the football. The room Hetty was
to share for one night only with somebody called Myra had four
bunk-beds in it, but that was because children had to be allowed
for: the Refuge always tried to ensure that each woman had a
place of her own, with or without kids. Hetty dumped her holdall
on one of the beds and was told where she could wash and how
to find the kitchen.

There was food, as Ruth must have known there would be –
bacon from a large communal pack, beans from a communal tin,
sliced bread, tea from a communal pot, milk from a two-litre
plastic container. Hetty would not be obliged to shop communally,
Ruth explained, but it worked out cheaper. She remembered that
Trudi had been shopping in Ackersley for the Refuge when she
had been found by her husband. Shopping *with* someone. It came
to her that the someone had been Myra Sopwith. Unless there
were two Myras at the Refuge this would be the woman with
whom she would be sharing the room tonight.

She fried bacon in a pan, turned the rashers over, added a
couple of dollops of baked beans from the tin. There were already
three woman and two children in the kitchen. One of the women,
Karen, was clearly middle-class and therefore the children also,
Lucy and Josh; the girl looked about twelve, the boy about eight.
Ruth sat with Noreen, a woman in her early twenties, and was
teaching her to read. Since Lucy and Josh were doing homework
under their mother's supervision, the atmosphere was generally
studious. From outside in the hall some of the other children in
the Refuge could be heard playing merry hell.

Noreen read with difficulty. 'We . . . will . . . go . . . to . . . the
. . . mar . . . ket . . . to . . .' She hesitated, unsure. 'Boy?'

'Buy.'

Josh looked in the direction of the sound of the roistering

children. 'I don't see why we have to do homework. Nobody else is.'

'Harry is.'

Since Harry was thirteen, the oldest child in the Refuge, this did not seem to Josh to be comparing like with like. 'Harry's clever and I'm not.'

Noreen was having difficulty with the word after 'buy'. 'Ah . . . ah . . .'

'Good. Try it like this.' Ruth gave a short 'a' instead of the long 'a' Noreen had been pronouncing.

'A . . . pless?'

'Apples. Very good.'

The sound outside reached a yet higher level. It seemed possible that some of the children had found a toboggan and were using it on the haircord stair-carpet. Hetty said, 'Is it always as noisy as this?'

'Worse,' said Karen.

'You forget, don't you? Children grow up and you forget what it was like when they were young.'

A grown woman being taught to read! But Hetty knew well enough that there were teenagers leaving the local comprehensive school without being able to read and write and it was unlikely that they would get better at it as they grew older. And in her own village Bert Ramsden's wife read the newspaper to him every evening and did all the figuring and Sally Harbottle had difficulties with forms and such. No, on consideration, she was not surprised that Noreen could not read. What was surprising was that there was someone at the Refuge teaching her. She finished her meal and went early and thoughtfully to bed.

Myra was there already. Hetty had brought a clean nightie but Myra wore her undies in bed. Although Myra had been at the

Refuge for a couple of months, she had left no impression of her own on the room – no photographs, nothing pinned to the walls, no knick-knacks bought at Ackersley Market and brought back to make the place look homey.

Hetty watched her taking a couple of tablets with a glass of water. 'I'm terrible with me nerves,' Myra said. 'I wouldn't get a wink of sleep without me little moggies.'

'Have your nerves always been bad?'

'Oh, no. When I was a young girl I never had a nerve in me body. Even at the beginning – because it showed up early, you see, with Tom; he was always ready with his hands if you displeased him – but even then I thought, Well, you get through these things. And time went on, and it got no better, and the doctors don't know what to do with you but give you tablets; they can't stop him battering you. And since Trudi was killed, me nerves have been real bad.'

A way straight in without having to ask. 'Trudi?' Hetty said.

'We were friends. I don't make friends easy, even at a place like this. I was with her. We'd been to Ackersley to shop – groceries and such.'

'How did it happen?'

'We went to the post office to pick up the Benefit – she had a little girl, but the social took her away after. When we came out, her husband was there. She ran into the road and a bus hit her.'

'But I thought . . .'

'What, love?'

The post office? But they'd been coming out of the chemist's when they saw Gary. Myra did not know that the woman with the black eye and bruised face to whom she was telling the story already knew the details, so she had felt able to lie. But why? What was there about the visit to the chemist's? 'Never mind,'

Hetty said. 'I'm a bit confused, to tell you the truth.'

'We all are, first off. You'll settle down. You're not on tablets yourself, I don't suppose?'

Late into the night, as Myra lay in the bunk opposite, deep in a moggie induced sleep, Hetty lay awake in the narrow bunk-bed with the bunk above her forming an uncomfortably close false ceiling. She was unused to sleeping alone, and her ribs were paining her from the fall, but she tried to get her mind clear, putting what she knew so far and what she felt into some sort of order. At some time well past midnight she heard Noreen's baby crying in the room next door, and after Noreen had succeeded in quietening it, Myra, who had been doing no more than snore gently, began to whimper in her sleep.

Robert was also unused to sleeping alone. He sat up in the double bed, propped against pillows, trying to concentrate on a paperback, *Death Comes to a Problem Solver* by Carol Crane.

There was a knock at the door. It was Geoff with two mugs of cocoa. Robert said, 'Can't you sleep?'

'Not a lot. Would you like some cocoa?'

'Thank you. Cocoa'll do well. Worried about this feller in Blackburn? The husband?'

'I'm worried about Mrs Wainthropp.'

'Makes two of us.' Robert blew on the cocoa to cool it. 'I'll go if you like. Might be easier. Talk to him man to man. You can look after the phone in case she rings.'

'No, I've got to do it.'

'Suit yourself.'

Both of them took a serious sip of cocoa. Geoff said, 'Man must endure his going hence even as his coming hither. The readiness is all.'

'You sound like our Derek. He were a bit of a self-dramatiser when the mood took him. He even wanted to go to one of them acting schools for a bit: the English teacher gave him notions. But it were computer studies got him in the end.'

'I've been thinking I might take a leaf from Mrs Wainthropp's book. Go in disguise like. Do you think the budget would run to one of them clipboards – just a cheap one? It does look more professional. And I wondered if I could borrow your reading glasses? Something to give me a studious look.'

'When you're lying it's best to stick as close to the truth as you can.'

'I shan't lie much. Just ask questions.'

'I was thinking of Hetty. I keep sending her these thought-messages of encouragement and support, but of course there's no telling if she receives them.'

Begwyn House was certainly isolated. The nearest village was a couple of miles away though the daily bus to Ackersley passed the main gates.

These, like the rest of the establishment, were run down with peeling paint and rusty hinges. The drive was metalled, but weeds were pushing through the tarmac, and on either side was tussocky grass with a few overgrown shrubs in what might once have been beds. There were three wide stone steps up to the front door and a wooden ramp at one side, because Begwyn House had been an old people's home in one of its more recent incarnations. In the grass near enough to the door for mothers to watch their children while sitting on the steps was a small play area with a swing, roundabout and climbing frame.

Hetty stood on the steps with Karen, watching the school run. Six children were crowding into the back of a Land-Rover – Zeb,

215

Lucy and Josh whom she had met the night before, Sinead (6), Shere (7) and Meryl (8). A pale, thin lad, Harry, sat up front with the driver, Jean, the part-time child worker. Hetty would have to keep the names of these children in her head and also remember to whom they belonged. Probably she would have to try to find a way of questioning them, since the source of the leak might be no more sinister than a Refuge child talking to an Ackersley child at school. Though Trudi's little girl had not been of school age.

'Shere, come *on*. We'll be late.' The likelihood of being late was probably all part of the excitement. The Land-Rover moved away to a chorus of *You'll Never Walk Alone* from the kids at the back. Harry did not sing.

Karen said, 'Peace, perfect peace for the rest of the day.' Odd to find somebody middle class at the Refuge; you wouldn't expect it. Hetty had now met all the other women, and none of them was middle-class, though Ruth had been a teacher.

'I'm to talk to someone called Angie.'

'She's the co-ordinator. She'll want you to sign a Licence Agreement; it's just a promise to obey the rules and pay the rent.'

'What rules? What rent?'

'Very few rules and very little rent. Come on, I'll introduce you.'

Angie had a tiny office just off the hall, but – since the policy was that there should be no managerial secrets and the women ran the Refuge – business was usually conducted in the common room. This, in the days when Begwyn House was home to the gentry, had been a large sunny sitting room. Now it was still spacious and sunny but everything in it, from the TV set, bookcase of paperbacks, carpets, curtains, armchairs and sofa, had been given by kindly people who no longer had a need for it or bought second-hand and very cheaply.

Angie sat with Hetty and Karen at a table to one side of the room. Noreen's baby, Kirsty, was in a cot, watched by her mother. Ruth was in an armchair, feet stretched out, eyes closed, resting. Delia, a woman in her mid thirties, mother to Harry and Sinead was hoovering. Delia liked to have something to do; she could not keep still. But since she was also insatiably curious and generally suspicious of anyone new, she kept switching the Hoover off and drifting over to linger behind Angie's chair. Sharon, mother of Meryl and Shere, was with Myra in the kitchen, cleaning up.

So far Hetty had been asked very few questions. The women at the Refuge respected each others' privacy. A newcomer would talk when she was ready to do so and usually those who had been most hurt took longest before they were able to talk. Hetty had to make a decision. She could keep quiet and nobody would press her, but they might wonder why she herself asked questions. Or she could encourage questions from them in order to establish her right to ask questions in return.

The danger was that, however close she tried to stick to the truth, she would have to tell some lies, and might be tripped up. She decided that the safest lies – if she could bring herself to tell them – would be about her relationship with Robert. They would be expecting the worst of him. And she had better put it on a bit, go a bit downmarket, make herself seem to be more old-fashioned than she was.

Angie said, 'Do you need money? We'll arrange for your Social Security to be paid to you here but it will take time to get it through. Until then we can lend you ten pounds if you think you can manage.'

'I've got some money. Took it from the tobacco tin under the mattress before I left.'

'You're a pensioner?'

'My husband was made redundant. We live on that.'

'He's hurt you badly this time.'

'Threw me downstairs.'

'Do you need a doctor?' Hetty shook her head. 'How long have you been married?'

'Must be forty year. You lose count.'

'And all that time . . . ?'

Hetty remembered what Myra had told her about her husband, Tom. That had been bad from the beginning, but Myra was only in her forties, and Hetty was sixty. It might be easier for them to believe that Robert's ill-treatment of her had shown up early in the marriage (because people start as they mean to go on) but only got really bad in the middle years. 'No, no, when we were married he hardly ever touched me,' she said. 'And when we had Derek – that's our son: he's in Australia now – well, Robert were a bit mixed up in his mind about the new responsibility and such . . . you know like . . .'

'Not being cock of the walk any more?'

'If you like. But even then he only hit me occasionally when he had a drink in him. It were after the redundancy he got bad. He'd brood a lot and get these rages. It were to do wi' negative equity. He kept adding up all we'd got and what we could expect and it was never enough. He said it were my fault because it was me wanted to buy the house in the first place. And he said I wasted money.' She indicated her bruised face. 'If you think this is bad you should have seen me the time I left me purse on the bus.'

Was that enough? She hoped so.

It seemed to be enough for the time being anyway. Angie said, 'We've an Agreement – bit of paper for you to sign – about how we live here. There's a little rent to pay, not much. We usually share on food, but you can buy you're own if you'd rather.'

'I'll share.'

'There's not many rules – no loud music at night, never go into anyone's room without asking, and no men ever to be allowed in, whatever the excuse. I've known them stand at the door and cry where I was before, but for everyone's sake you must never weaken.'

And Robert, the wife-batterer?

Geoff had gone out to visit Gary Hawes. Robert stayed indoors where he could hear the phone if it rang. He tried to keep himself busy, but could not concentrate.

He decided to iron a shirt, put out the ironing-board in the kitchen, heated the iron. The shirt collar resisted him and he gave up.

He set out the Agency's account book and files on the kitchen table in order to bring the accounts up to date, but the figures kept turning into a jumble, and he entered the same invoice three times.

He made himself a mug of coffee and forgot it. He scrubbed out the bath and put bleach in the toilet bowl. He walked about in every room. The allotment, where there was always work to be done, would have been the best place to pass the hours, but he could not leave the house.

He sat on the bottom step of the staircase staring at the silent telephone.

'Ring, damn you!' he said. But it didn't.

Gary Hawes' flat was fourteen floors up with an outside walkway. Geoff was wearing Robert's reading glasses with the heavy frames and carried a clipboard in which there was a pad of yellow lined paper. He had also equipped himself with a file containing photostats (which he had made at the Reference Library on his way) of newspaper reports of the accident and the coroner's inquest. The scooter had been left chained up at the multi-storey car park at the town centre, which Geoff considered likely to be safer than the area outside a tower block.

'It's a project we're doing at school.'

'Oh, aye?'

Gary had answered the door in T-shirt and boxer shorts which might indicate a relaxed and non-threatening attitude. Geoff himself looked about fourteen. There was no reason, given the ordinary courtesies of social intercourse, why the whole visit should not be conducted in a friendly way.

'I've been looking it up in the local papers.' Geoff showed his file. 'Making photostats and such.'

'Looking what up?'

'That accident at Ackersley when your wife was killed.'

Silence. Gary seemed to be trying to commit Geoff's appearance to memory in case he were ever asked to identify Geoff's body in some mortuary after an unfortunate accident probably involving physical violence. The motorbike could be seen in the hallway behind him. Suddenly his right hand shot out, grabbed Geoff by the collar and lifted him into the air. Geoff tried to keep a tight grip on his props, but the clipboard fell onto the floor of the walkway.

'Just think yourself lucky I don't chuck you over.'

Fourteen floors onto concrete. 'Please don't. I may not bounce.' Gary put him down again, and Geoff stooped to recover the clipboard. 'I wanted your side of things. I don't think they've been fair.'

Gary stepped back in his hallway and slammed the front door.

That was it, then? Geoff looked at the closed front door. Not
what could be called a successful investigation – Mrs Wainthropp
would not be pleased – but at least the investigator was still all
in one piece. He turned, and began to walk back down the
walkway. He heard the front door open again behind him.

'Come back here!'

Geoff returned to Gary, who was standing at his front door
again.

'You what?'

'The boys in my class at school . . . there's some of us think
there's been an injustice done. The men aren't always to blame
in these cases. Not entirely.' Gary was staring at him again. Non-
threatening? What a hope! To be non-threatening was not in this
man's nature. 'Sometimes not at all,' Geoff said.

'You'd better come in.'

Hetty and Karen walked together beside the river which ran behind
the house. Karen said, 'I love the sound of water. I often walk
here.' Hetty noticed that she walked with a slight limp. Karen
said it was a broken bone badly set. She had fallen against a
cupboard door.

'Was that true or what you told people?'

'It's odd. You don't think of wife-beating as a middle-class
thing. My friends would never have believed it; even mummy
didn't *really* believe it. "You must have done something to upset
him," she'd say. Peter's such a lovely man, you see, outside the
home. He's kind and considerate, takes enormous pains to be
liked, collects good opinions as if they were little glass animals.'

'Street angel, house devil.'

'Same with your Robert?'

'Up to a point.'

'I tried to hide it from Lucy and Josh. Kitchen cupboard doors! They must have thought those cupboards had a life of their own. Then one day Lucy said, "We know" so I packed a couple of suitcases and we left.'

'Why a refuge? Why not your mother?'

'He'd have followed. I was afraid he'd manage to get custody of the kids – still am. I mean, he is a solicitor; he knows the law.'

Gary had put on a pair of jeans and was lounging with his feet up on the sofa. No refreshment had been offered. There was a phone. That meant quarterly bills. Was that usual for an unemployed person on Supplementary Benefit? The furniture was minimal and Gary clearly did not bother to keep it clean. Perhaps that was why he had gone to Ackersley to get his wife back.

'Okay, I thumped her. Nowt wrong with that. Everyone does it. My dad took his belt to our mam regular. You have to show who's master.'

Geoff leafed through the photostats. 'It says here that you broke Trudi's jaw in two places because she didn't have your tea ready. And when the baby cried—'

'Watch it!'

'Right. Sorry. Right.'

'That's what *she* did. All mouth. Giving me the needle. They don't realise that when they make their bloody judgements. Listen to this: I wrote it down so's to remember it. "Talking clever is the woman's weapon against which a good man has to defend himself." You don't know what it's like till you have to live with it.'

Geoff made a note on his pad. 'Faults on both sides, you'd say?'

'Six GCSEs and couldn't keep the house clean or get the meals on time.'

'It's very true that, in't it, about them talking clever. You wrote it down, you say? Can you remember who said it?'

'A wise man. An educated man. He gave me a bit of paper from his pocket and I wrote it down.'

Would that bit of paper be a clue if Gary still had it? Impossible to ask for it. Unwise even to press him any further for now on the name of the man. Maybe Geoff could work back to it.

Hetty said to Ruth, 'You're teaching Noreen to read.'

'Reading's important.'

'Yes, it is.'

'My dad – he was on the buses then so we didn't have much money – he and mum were so shocked by the schools over here, they sent me back to Jamaica to get an education. At least I can teach Zeb myself.'

'Getting an education didn't stop you being beaten up later.'

'Oh no. I think it made it worse. My husband used my education against me as an excuse. He said I had contempt for him, and needed thrashing to teach me better manners. But Noreen's husband battered her because she was good for nothing and dragged him down.'

'That's what you got to get clear. She'd only herself to blame.'

'Running into a busy road when all you did was call her name?'

'Right.'

'Lack of consideration. She exposed you to public hostility. It said in the *Record* the coroner spoke out very sharp.'

'I'd be a public outcast if I didn't have good friends of me own.'

'I was wondering what you were doing in Ackersley that morning.'

'You know what I was doing. It was in the paper. I went out every day looking for her. Different places.'

'I was wondering why Ackersley *that* day.'

'Had to be somewhere.'

'Like where was it the day before and the day before that?'

'You trying to make something of it?'

'No! Just getting things straight.' Slow down, Geoff. Back-pedal. But the thoughts had started buzzing and he could not slow down. 'Like . . . I couldn't help noticing the motorbike in the hall. Very impressive, state of the art you might say, but since you're unemployed at the moment . . .'

'I've always been unemployed.'

'And the phone. I mean, the rental . . .'

'You have to have a phone if you've got a little kid. Social Services made us put that in.'

'But you've still got it. And it says in the *Record* the little girl's been taken into care.' He hoped it did say so in the *Record*: Geoff himself knew because Hetty had said so. 'Why didn't you object to that?'

Too far. Too far too quickly. Gary swung his feet off the sofa and stood up. He had clearly had enough; the danger signals were all flashing.

'Look! I need a phone; I don't need a kid; it wasn't me forgot to take the bloody pill. You come worming your way in here like some bloody detective!'

'Most unlike. An over-enthusiastic schoolboy merely.'

'Out!'

'Mr Hawes, believe me—'

'I'll count to five.'

'I'm going.'

He was already on his way as Gary began to count, had

squeezed past the motorbike by 'Two' and reached the front door and opened it by 'Four'.

'Goodbye, Mr Hawes. Thank you for your time from all us boys in 6A.'

'Five.'

The door closed behind him and he leaned against the wall with his eyes closed, recovering. When he opened them he saw, further along the walkway, a stout middle-aged lady in a floral blouse standing outside her own open door. This was Doris Dyford, Gary's next-door neighbour. She put her finger to her lips and led him along the walkway to the point at which a junction made a turn off which would take them out of Gary's sight if he were to reappear.

'The walls in these flats is like cardboard,' she said. 'Living next door I could hear everything that went on. She never tried to defend herself, you know. I'd hammer with me fists sometimes and shout, but he never took no notice. It's lies what he said in the coroner's court. He never went looking for her. He'd lie in bed most days and go out in the evenings.'

'Why didn't you tell the police?'

'We don't talk to the police; you'd get a reputation. Any road he didn't kill her: it was an accident.'

'Somebody told him where to look. Who?'

'That's for me to have not the faintest idea and the boys of 6A to find out.'

'There are no boys of 6A. Only me, and I need help.'

'There's a man comes to see him sometimes. In a suit with a posh car.' *An educated man*, Geoff thought. *Gave Gary a bit of paper from his pocket to write down the wise words that fell from his lips.* 'He never comes up. I suppose he thinks the car'd be vandalised.'

'Well, it would.'

'Gary goes down and they sit in the car to talk, Up to no good, I'd say.'

'What kind of car is it?'

'I don't know, love: I've no experience.' His disappointment was pitiful to see and would have melted harder hearts than hers. 'But I took a note of the number just in case it might come in useful.'

Middle-of-the-day dinner was not a meal taken by the women of the Refuge. The children had school dinners and the main family meal – staggered according to the children's ages – was tea. But the women did get together in the kitchen at about twelve-thirty for mugs of instant coffee and a plate of sandwiches.

Hetty said, 'Angie told me I should talk to the Housing Department, but I don't know where I want to live.'

'Nobody's rushing you,' Ruth said. 'It takes us all time to sort ourselves out.'

Myra had filled a mug of coffee and balanced it on a plate with a couple of sandwiches. 'I'll take these to Noreen. The baby's playing her up.'

Hetty supposed that Noreen had replaced Trudi as Myra's particular friend. Why? Was there a special attraction? She had, she thought, begun to suss out what it might be. 'Trudi had a baby too, didn't she? A little girl.'

She could feel the increase in tension. The reference to Trudi had worried the other woman. Sharon said, 'What do you know about Trudi?' Sharon had lost teeth before coming to the Refuge and often covered her mouth when she was speaking.

Time to be innocent. 'Myra was telling me about her last night. About the accident and such. I lay awake thinking about it.'

226

'Thinking what?' This was Delia to whom suspicion came easily.

'Why she died.'

'She ran in front of a bus.'

'I was wondering how did her husband know where to find her.'

The other women looked to Ruth for a lead. Ruth said, 'That's what scares all of us.'

'I was wondering did anyone leave the Refuge after the accident.' A note of apology would not come amiss. 'You're bound to have these thoughts when you can't sleep.'

Sharon said, 'Kath left. Yesterday morning. With her kids. That's why there was room for you.'

'Went into a B&B,' said Delia. 'What kind of life is that?'

'Seems odd she chose to go so sudden.'

Karen, the middle-class one, was angry. 'It's not odd at all. If you're thinking Kath had anything to do with it, you're way off-beam.'

'I don't mean to offend you. I speak as I find.'

Delia said, 'We know why Kath went. She said herself she daren't stay here waiting for a flat. If Gary found Trudi, her Ken could have found her, and if he had he'd have killed her, and it wouldn't have been an accident and it wouldn't have been quick.'

Ruth said, 'Kath would have been the last person to break security. This place works on trust. We're all jumpy about Trudi's death – scared – don't know what to think – but if we don't trust each other we've got nothing at all.'

Time to go. Hetty said, 'I'm sorry if I spoke out of turn. I won't have a sandwich if you don't mind. I'll just go and sit for a bit.' She left the kitchen, the picture of an elderly woman put out by the hostility of the young. Sharon said, 'She asks a lot of questions.'

'Too many,' said Delia.

Ruth said, 'Well, she's new.'

'If you was going to hire someone . . .'

'*Hire* someone? To do what?'

'Worm her way in. Find out about us. About the Refuge. It'd have to be a woman.'

'No woman would do it.'

'Want to bet?'

Four faces, taking in the meaning, trying to assess the risk. Sharon said, 'Somebody told Gary where to look. You can't get away from that.'

Ruth said, 'Those bruises are genuine. She wouldn't have made them herself.'

Karen said, 'I'll take her shopping with me tomorrow morning. If she phones out, we'll know.'

Doris had said that the man who came to see Gary drove a posh car and she had made a note of the number. That information was of little direct use to Robert, but it was DCI Adams who had put Hetty on to this case (at a very low fee) so it seemed to Robert that the DCI ought to help.

And it began well in an atmosphere of cordiality. 'Robert, come in! I hope I may call you Robert. I always think of you as Robert.'

But it was no good: he could not be comfortable in a police station. 'I always think of you as Detective Chief Inspector.'

He explained the situation, what had been learned and how, the vague description of the car and exact note of the number.

The DCI was embarrassed. 'Robert, there are private detectives all over the North West who have their own ways of getting access to the computer at Swansea.'

'We're not that kind of firm.'

'And I'm not a bent copper. I can find out whose car this is, but I can't pass the information on to a member of the public.'

Robert was bitter. 'You got Hetty into this. Placed her in danger. Now you won't help.' Even as he said the words he knew that he had made a mistake. This was not the way Hetty and the DCI communicated; they had made a sort of friendship which depended on give-and-take not reproach. Across the desk he watched DCI Adams experience a moment of anger, control it and then go cold.

'She was offered a job and accepted it,' the DCI said. 'She's in no danger of anything more serious than being thrown out of the Refuge. However, I take note of what you say.'

Robert went home disconsolate. There had been no telephone call from Hetty or anyone else in his absence. He sat hunched in front of the living room fire like a broody parrot staring into it.

'You feel so helpless.'

Geoff said, 'We need a camera.'

'Why?'

'That man with the posh car who comes to see Gary is the only lead we have, without Mrs Wainthropp's already solved the case on her own. We'll have to keep watch. Get pictures. And that camera you took to Italy that got sat on in the bus from Pisa won't do. We need a real surveillance camera with a zoom lens. Like bird-watchers have.'

Robert lifted his head.

'And we know one.'

Robert nodded. They did.

'And he owes us.'

'That deaf and dumb lad you saved from the kidnap?'

'Profoundly deaf and without speech. And he's not a lad. And it wasn't really a kidnap. But he'd be glad to help.'

Hetty had been back to see Angie in her little cubbyhole of an office.

'You asked me this morning did I want to see a doctor? Is there one comes in regular?'

'Whenever we ask. She's very understanding.'

'There's some tablets I've been taking to make me sleep. I forgot to bring them.'

'I'll make an appointment for you with the doctor. If she thinks you need them, she'll prescribe.'

'You don't keep any here? In case of emergencies like?'

'No.'

'Thank you.' She left the office, leaving Angie clearly puzzled. Well, puzzlement was a pity; Hetty had no desire to arouse it or any other condition of mind which might lead to questions, but her request had been reasonable. If she had really been on tablets and forgotten to bring them, she would need to get more and whom else could she ask? There was something odd about Myra's little moggies, something odd about her visit with Trudi to the chemist's which had somehow turned into the post office.

The truth – or part of it – was in the tablets; she was sure of that. And anyway she had nothing else to go on for the moment. There had been a poster on the wall just above Angie's head – A WOMAN NEEDS A MAN LIKE A FISH NEEDS A BICYCLE. The things they put on posters these days! Hetty's own taste would have been for a picture of Ripon cathedral, but it takes all sorts.

Later she sat side by side with Noreen on a bench by the front steps of Begwyn House and watched the school bus return.

'Baby asleep?'

'Took a bit 'a time. She'll wake up now. Allus does when the kids come back.'

'Did Myra find you? She was taking you a sandwich.' Noreen nodded. 'You and Myra are good friends?'

'Maybe. She used to be Trudi's friend but it seems like now she's mine.'

The children piled out of the back of the Land-Rover and scampered indoors shouting for their teas. Harry followed from the passenger seat of the cab, pale-faced, slow, head down. Hetty said, 'That boy's not happy.'

'Who is?' Noreen got to her feet and gave Hetty a hand up. 'I better go in.'

'Are you getting enough sleep?'

'No. Can't be helped, though. The doctor gave me tablets, but I daren't take them. If Kirsty woke up in the middle of the night, I'd be dead to the world.'

'Wouldn't any of the others help?'

'Ruth would, but I don't like to ask. Her own kid still has nightmares;it wouldn't be right. And Myra's offered.'

'Does Myra know you've got tablets?'

''Spec so. You coming?'

As they went indoors Myra, who had come round the side of the building from the back, watched them go and bit her lip.

It was a funny sort of investigation, not like anything Hetty had tackled so far.

In a normal case you went around asking questions – sometimes in disguise maybe, but you never had to keep it up for long – and in between you went home, discussed the day's developments with Robert and Geoff and decided what to do next. You did not live among the suspects as one of them and you did not have the problem of filling in time between asking questions, because to do nothing else but ask questions would make the other women suspicious.

Hetty had been allotted a room of her own now, which had been Kath's; she was no longer required to share with Myra. She could always go there and lie down or just sit, and nobody would disturb her, but she was an active woman, not given to prolonged sitting or lying down.

She sat for a while and told herself she was thinking, but nothing much came of it. She went down to the kitchen and got herself a bite to eat and passed the time of day with Sharon and her kids. Then the kids went off to the play room for an hour's structured creative play under the supervision of Jean, the part-time child worker (as opposed to the unstructured uncreative unsupervised play on the stairs the night before) and the women went into the Common Room to watch television. If Hetty had really been battered this would have been a healing time but as matters were she found this amount of leisure hard to bear.

Harry was sitting at the table at some distance from the TV set, his fingers in his ears, trying to read a book and make notes. It would be homework which he could not do in the kitchen while Noreen was having a reading lesson with Ruth. *When in doubt*, Hetty said to herself, *question the unhappy ones, because there's a reason they're unhappy and it may help you get an insight.* She went to sit opposite him.

He took a finger out of one ear to make a note in his exercise book. Now she was close to him she could see that he was weeping silently.

'Can't you use your mum's room?'

He shook his head. 'Full of stuff.'

232

'I only came in last night but I've got a room of me own now. It's quiet. There's no table but the light's good. I'll let you in and you can have it for an hour.'

'Don't bother. The play room'll be empty when the little 'uns go to bed.' It was cold – a put-down, what they used to call a snub. An ignorant interfering nosey-parker had been rebuffed by a lad trying to get on with his study under difficulties. And she had only been trying to help.

She might have been affronted, but in fact she was hurt and it showed. She got up to leave him alone, since that was what he wanted, but he looked up at her, and there was so much misery in his eyes. 'But . . . thank you,' he said. 'Very much. Just the same.'

Hetty came to a decision. 'Can I come and see you in the play room later? For a talk?' He nodded.

She let an hour and a bit pass and then went to the play room, where the table was covered with finger-paintings and the floor with Lego. Harry had made an island for himself at one end of the table and sat on a folding chair behind it. He shut the textbook he had been reading. 'I'm sorry I cut you off a bit short. It gets to you, this place. I don't know why I bother with homework. Nobody's interested.'

'It's a new school?'

'And there'll be another when we get rehoused. I've never made friends easy.'

'Couldn't bring anyone home?'

'Right. You have to keep pretending there's nothing wrong, but everyone knows. I've thought . . . if I work hard . . . get away to college . . . get right away. Five more years, I'll be eighteen.'

'Your sister'll be only eleven.'

'Kids like us grow up quickly. I've had enough. Stopping mum drinking. Talking her out of suicide. I miss having a dad, you know. Not the one who beat mum up – just a dad. Someone to take a bit of weight.'

'Did he beat you up too?'

'That's when we left.'

The door was opened abruptly. His sister, Sinead, was in the doorway. Harry said, 'Out!'

'I want to show mum my painting.'

'In the morning.'

She did not dignify this with a reply, but marched in, picked up her finger-painting and took it out with her, banging the door.

'Your mother's not drinking here in the Refuge?'

'No, she's got support. Sinead too – kids her own age. I've got nobody – the women too old and the little 'uns too young. I don't belong here.' He was looking up at her directly, challenging. 'Nor do you.'

How did he know? She must be wary. 'I don't follow you.'

'You've not been battered.'

Easy to counter. 'Look at this face!'

'Doesn't fool me.'

'My body aches. I'm bruised in places it's not for you to think of.'

'It's all put on. You're strong. You've not been beaten down.'

'Ruth's strong.'

'She's been here nine months. You're a new arrival, and you're stronger than Ruth. And you're interested in other people. The women who come here – mum included – aren't interested in anyone else when they arrive.'

She knew he was right. But she had to be interested in the others. That was her job. He said, 'How long do you think you've got before they find out?'

234

If he was to be an ally, she had better trust him. 'I don't know. Not long it seems.'

'Don't worry. I shan't betray you.'

'Are there any other outsiders among the women here? In your expert opinion?'

'You're thinking of Myra. *She's* not strong.'

'No, but she's interested in other people. Always trying to make friends.'

'It's not the same. Myra clings to other people because she can't bear to be on her own.'

She looked at him. He was only thirteen and his insight into the folk around him was keener than her own. 'You'll do well at college,' she said.

Outside Sharon could be heard gently chiding her loved ones at play. 'Go to bloody bed or I'll clip your earhole.' Harry grinned at Hetty who raised an eyebrow and wrinkled her nose. Thus was their alliance sealed.

She waited until near midnight and went to visit Myra in her room. Gary had known Trudi would be in Ackersley that day and it was Myra who had gone with her. Myra had lied about the visit to the chemist. The truth had to be in the tablets. What did the kids call them? – uppers and downers: the 'little moggies' would be downers – mogadon to help you sleep. Valium, she supposed, which had been prescribed, as Hetty remembered, to several of the women in her own village during the eighties by Doctor Fox who had since moved on, would keep Myra going during the day. Somehow the tablets must be the connection between Myra and Gary.

She knocked, said, 'It's me, Hetty,' and entered without waiting to be told to come in, thus breaking one of the rules of the Refuge. Might as well be hanged for a sheep as well as a lamb.

Myra was sitting up in bed, one hand behind her stowing something beneath the pillow. Hetty said, 'I hope you don't mind me disturbing you. I'm not used to being on me own. It's difficult to settle.'

'Don't worry, love. Everyone needs a friend.'

'I thought last night . . . watching you take them tablets . . . I used to be on tablets meself. I lay awake. Noreen's baby was crying. I thought, "How shall I manage?"'

'They took you off?'

'Doctor said I mustn't persist or I might become addicted.'

'They all say that.'

'I suppose I could ask the doctor that comes here.'

Myra was scornful. 'She's worse than any. Say what you like she won't prescribe unless you're mental.'

'But she's prescribed for you. Hasn't she?'

Sometimes the detective business was so easy. Myra had already given herself away and now knew it. Hetty watched the thoughts chasing across the woman's face. Then Myra said, 'There's a doctor in Ackersley you can go to private.'

Turn the screw a little. 'Did Trudi go to him?' No reply. 'You told me last night she'd been collecting her Child Allowance from the post office when Gary called her name. But I read about that accident in the paper. You'd been to the chemist's.'

'Who are you?'

'Just someone like yourself.' Give her a moment, then press home. 'Who told Trudi's husband she'd be in Ackersley that morning?'

'Not me.'

'Who knew, besides you? You'd sell your mother to get tablets, let alone Trudi.'

'How could I get them from Gary Hawes?'

'Drugs. He could be supplying.'

'Moggies? Valium? Librium? The kids don't take those drugs now. Just people like me when the doctors won't prescribe. You're on the wrong track.'

A beautifully crafted house of cards shivered and then collapsed. Hetty realised that Myra was right. *The kids don't take those drugs now.* Crack cocaine, heroin, ecstasy, cannabis – for all she knew Gary might be able to supply any of those, but not the tablets Myra thought she needed.

'I believe you.' Nevertheless Myra had begged tablets from Trudi and was already courting Noreen as a possible replacement. She would do more than beg if she had to; she would steal. She did not belong here with the other women. 'Just the same, don't you think it's time you moved on? Started a new life?'

'I don't move on.'

'You can't stay here for ever.'

'I go back.'

Hetty stared at her, unable to believe what she was being told. 'Back to the man who battered you?'

'Back to what I know. You don't begin to understand someone like me, do you? "Start a new life"! I can't live by meself; I'm frightened; I've no experience. So I stay as long as I can and then go back to Tom. He's allus glad to see me – for a while. And when he goes too far or I'm afraid he'll kill me, I run off again and some Refuge takes me in.'

'And is that how it will be? Always?'

'Maybe he'll change as he gets older.'

'Maybe.' Hetty left the room. The truth was not in the tablets after all. She would have to start again.

* * *

The phone rang early in the Wainthropp house next morning.
Robert raced to get it. 'Hetty!'

'Too early,' Geoff said.

It was DCI Adams. 'Robert?' Robert's gesture to Geoff was
intended to let him know who was calling without interrupting
the caller, but his gesture was more uncontrolled than
informational and only caused him to knock over the tray of pens
and the notebook which were kept by the phone.

'There's been an interesting development,' the DCI said. 'After
you left me yesterday I sent someone to lean on Gary Hawes, just
to see if anything fell out. Something has. A call from a solicitor
instructing us to cease harassing his client.'

Robert said to Geoff, 'Notes. Take notes as I speak.' And to
the DCI, 'I don't understand.' Geoff picked up the notebook and
pens and stood at the ready.

'Robert, use your loaf. What is a man like Hawes doing with
any solicitor at all, let alone one with a middle-class practice and
a brass plate in Whalley?'

'Oh!'

'Are you with me?'

'I think so. It's the man who comes to see him, isn't it?'

'Could be.'

'Does he drive a posh car, by any chance?'

'A BMW.'

'I suppose I know better than to ask what the number is?'

'I suppose you do, but I can't prevent your jumping to
conclusions. And I *can* tell you the name of the firm. After all,
you might want a solicitor yourself one day.'

Peter Parmenter & Partners. Geoff wrote it down. 'I'll see
about that camera. If they've been in contact so quick they'll be
in contact again. Either he'll come to Gary Hawes or Gary goes

to Whalley. Either way, we should be there.'

Meanwhile Gary was on the phone himself, calling one of his mates. 'Are you free? May be a job for us. I'll know later this morning. Stay by the phone. Tell Wayne and Ray.'

Hetty had been taken shopping by Karen. When they reached the post office in Ackersley, Karen said, 'I just have to go in here for a moment. I shan't be long.'

There was a phone box close by. It was Hetty's opportunity to phone home, reassure her husband, and catch up on developments. She took it.

Geoff had already gone for the camera, but Robert was by the phone. He told her quickly about the connection between Gary Hawes and the posh solicitor from Peter Parmenter & Partners. Not quickly enough. Karen had set up the opportunity for Hetty to phone, came out of the post office very soon after going in and saw Hetty replacing the receiver.

'Phoning home?'

Hetty almost blanked out. She had to come up with something convincing and it had to be fast. There was a greengrocer on the corner with a display of daffodils for sale outside. 'The Chapel.'

'Sorry?'

'In the village where I come from. I'm famous for me flower arrangements. You don't think about that kind of thing when you run away from home. I had to arrange a substitute for Sunday.'

It had been a close-run thing. Luckily middle-class people would believe anything.

Robert and Geoff arrived at the tower block by scooter. 'Better find somewhere safe for it,' Robert said.

'I think I know a place.'

They took the scooter up in the lift to Doris Dyford's flat.

Luckily she was in, at her most conspiratorial and delighted to
let them leave it in her hall. 'And if you've a clothes-horse and
some washing that needs airing, they'd come in very handy.'

'And a black plastic bag,' Robert said. 'Suitable for litter.'

They did not have long to wait in their improvised hide before
the BMW arrived below and Gary went down to it and sat next
to the driver. They would be able to get pictures of the two men
together, but that would prove nothing and would not tell them
what, if anything, was being planned. They needed some sort of
listening device and had no way of getting one.

'That's where the black plastic bag comes in,' Robert said.

He left the hide and went down to the litter-strewn area in
front of the tower block. Then, tacking from side to side, picking
up paper, bottles and empty beer cans as he went, he made his
way towards the BMW. But however close he drew to the car,
would he be able to hear anything that was said inside it when
the windows were closed on this chilly April day?

Gary said to the solicitor, 'How did you find the place?'

'Easy. I knew it was somewhere near Ackersley. The children
had to be at school nearby, and there aren't many in that area. I
provided someone with a photograph of my kids, and once he
spotted them, he followed the Land-Rover.'

Gary was hurt. 'I could have done that.'

The solicitor smiled and shook his head. 'Horses for courses,
Gary. Debt-collecting, putting on the frighteners, I couldn't ask
for better. Covert surveillance needs someone less colourful.'

Malcolm Stone's telescopic lens showed everything clearly.
Geoff took a photograph of the solicitor handing a bundle of
banknotes to Gary. Should be useful. Hard to explain away. Robert
drew closer.

'And another two hundred when the job's done,' the solicitor said. 'Once they know they've been found, the place is useless. Then we move on to the next. So soon as you can, please.'

'I've got the lads on alert.' Gary got out of the BMW, still holding the notes. 'You've really got it in for Refuges.' Robert was within earshot now.

The passenger door of the BMW was still open. The solicitor spoke from the driving seat and Robert could hear clearly what he said. 'A man's wife and children should be under his control. That's what holds society together. It's time the men fought back. Beginning with Begwyn House.'

'Right!' Gary closed the door, then noticed Robert standing near him holding the black plastic rubbish sack. 'What do *you* want?' The BMW moved away.

'If that's waste paper you're holding, don't make litter. Give it to me now.'

'Piss off,' Gary said, put the money carefully away in his pocket and went back to his flat.

Robert spent five more minutes picking up litter and then went back to Geoff in the hide. 'A solicitor!' he said. 'You wouldn't expect it.'

Doris said, 'I never listen but you can't help hearing with the phone being on the dividing wall. Before the car came he was phoning his mates and now he's on the phone again. They'll meet in Clitheroe, he says, and go on together.'

Geoff said, 'It means trouble, Mr Wainthropp. No doubt about it.'

'Then you and me had better be there to stop it.'

Begwyn House. Somewhere not far from Ackersley. No time to go home for weapons even if they'd had any beyond a few gardening tools, a kitchen knife and the catapult and steel ball bearings with which the ten-year-old Robert had intended to sell his life dearly if the Nazis had ever landed near Oswaldtwistle. The scooter was not a quarter as fast as Gary's motorbike but he would have to rendezvous with his mates. Robert and Geoff decided to go immediately to Ackersley buy a map there and hope to reach the Refuge before them.

Hetty was in Angie's office. She had opened the filing cabinet in which personal records were kept and was reading a file. What she saw was what she had hoped to see. She nodded, put the file back, and left the room.

Outside Ruth was standing by the open door to the Common Room. She said, 'Would you mind coming in for a moment? We're having a meeting.' She stood aside to let Hetty precede her into the room, then followed her in, locked the door, took out the key and gave it to Delia who put it in her pocket.

All the women of the Refuge were there – Delia, Sharon, Karen, Myra, Noreen, Ruth. Hetty said warily, 'Where's Angie?'

'Don't you know she's out? You should since you've just been poking about in her office.'

Hetty looked at the faces, every one hostile. Karen said, 'We've been wondering about the phone call you made this morning.'

'I told you.'

'Flowers, you said.'

'Just the arrangement. I don't supply.'

'Why did you have to go to Ackersley to make the call? There's a phone here. Nobody would have objected. It's only men we don't phone.'

'I'm sorry. I never thought.'

Ruth said, 'And in Angie's office just now?'

'Checking the details in my file.'

Delia said, 'You've been sent here to spy on us, haven't you? You're not one of us.'

'Every woman is one of you or could be. I've been here long enough to learn that.'

Myra said, 'That's words. That's just words. She was asking me questions last night. Making accusations. About the tablets.'

Ruth said to Hetty, 'We know about Myra and the tablets.'

'And you don't mind?'

'I said we know, not that we don't mind.'

Myra said, 'Why are you here? You've not been battered. You don't need the Refuge.'

Karen said, 'Why *are* you here?'

No point in trying to bluff it out any longer. They were onto her. What would they do, what *could* they do? A locked room. Six to one. They could hurt her. Part of her knew that she should be afraid. They were more afraid than she was, but fear can drive out finer feelings; they could hurt her badly. She discovered that she herself was not afraid. But no more lies. 'Wainthropp Detective Agency.'

'I told you she'd been sent to suss us out. The kids said there was someone following the Land-Rover a couple of days ago, but Jean didn't believe them.'

Jean was the child worker. Dereliction of duty, Jean! But Hetty supposed that the kids often reported oddities during the school run; it was all part of the excitement. She said, 'This place works on trust, you told me. And I've betrayed it. I don't feel good about that, but you've not trusted me either.'

Ruth said, 'No. We haven't. Who's employing you?'

'Your management committee. Mrs Rance.' It might be a time for first names. 'Helen.'

The first name was the clincher. They knew she was telling the truth. 'Without warning us?'

'How could they? I'm employed to find out why Gary Hawes knew Trudi would be in Ackersley that morning. When Trudi died, trust flew out of the window.'

Karen said, 'They think one of us may be responsible?'

'That's what you think yourselves, isn't it? That's why you were all in such a tizz-wozz yesterday dinner time in the kitchen.'

Myra said, 'Not me. I never told nobody.' And to Hetty, 'You said you believed me.'

They were looking at Myra, looking at Hetty, did not know what had passed between the two of them, did not know what to think or whom to trust.

Hetty said, 'I do. It wasn't Myra.' She turned to Karen, 'As I think you well know, Mrs Parmenter.'

Now the focus of attention altered. 'Karen?' Karen blinked and raised her chin.

Hetty said, 'We only use first names amongst ourselves. That's why I had to look in Angie's records.' She said to Karen, 'My husband's a solicitor, you told me. Peter Parmenter & Partners. And now I discover there's a connection between Peter Parmenter and Gary Hawes.'

'I never knew that. There can't be.'

Ruth said to Karen, 'He knows where you are?'

'He knows it's near Ackersley. No more than that.'

'You'd better explain.'

'I had to sign a form to give my mother Power of Attorney. I told her to send it to Ackersley and I'd collect it.'

'And your husband wormed it out of her?'

'Told her he'd take the kids unless she co-operated.'

Ruth said, 'She believed that?'

'He's a lawyer. He knows the law. He says the Children's Act gives him access. And there are judges who've ruled that Refuges aren't suitable places for kids and ordered them returned to the family home.'

'You should have talked to us.'

'I was frightened.'

Hetty thought, *All those precautions. But there's always someone slips up.* Her job was done, but she could not call it a success when the end was only anti-climax and fear.

Delia said, 'If the kids were right . . . if somebody was following the Land-Rover . . .'

'He'll have found this place by now.'

Noreen raised her head. 'Listen.'

Motorbikes, more than one. Stopping at the gate. The women moved together to the window and looked out. Four men on motorbikes were at the end of the drive.

The women cracked into activity. Ruth said, 'Call the police.' Delia unlocked the door of the Common Room and ran to do so. 'Close the shutters. Noreen, see if the baby's okay and lock your door.'

Hetty said, 'Anything that's both heavy and portable up to the first floor and stand by to repel boarders.'

Geoff and Robert arrived at the gates to Begwyn House. The scooter had been complaining for a while; Robert had not yet mastered the art of cornering and was also unused to unfolding a map while in motion. They looked up the drive and saw Gary and his mates outside the house taking from the paniers of their motorbikes what they had brought with them to use – rocks big enough to cause damage but small enough to throw.

Robert said, 'Leave the scooter, bring the camera. We'll have to get close enough to influence events.' Beyond the neglected lawn at one side of the drive there were neglected shrubs which had grown into small trees. Unnoticed by the four men, the rescue party scuttled into shelter.

Gary strode up to the big front door and banged on it. 'Out! Out! Out!'

The casement window above the door opened and Hetty appeared. The other men joined in the chant. 'Out! Out!'

Hetty raised one hand like the Queen of Carthage quelling a rabble of unruly Phoenicians. 'Go away! We're not at home to callers.'

Gary looked up at her. From behind, Myra handed Hetty the jumbo can of communal baked beans. Hetty emptied the baked beans over him and followed it with the can, which cut his forehead. Then she dodged back quickly as the first rock came in her direction.

All the other windows of the house were shuttered from the inside but the casement above the door was needed for defence. Inside it were stacked sacks of smokeless fuel and potatoes, giant jars of instant coffee, iron pans and an electric iron, the TV set (though that would be the last to go), calor gas cylinders. Two more rocks shattered the glass of the casement, but nobody was hurt and the women's own field of fire was not obstructed. They heard the glass outside the shutters on the ground floor go.

The men had used most of the rocks they had brought with them, and had smashed the glass of most of the windows without breaking the shutters. Gary looked around him and saw the bench on which the women used to sit to watch the school run. It was bound with metal around the edges at both ends. 'Use that to batter the door down.'

Four husky young men with a wooden bench as a battering ram. They picked it up and ran at the front door. There was an almighty bang which resounded throughout the house. A sack of smokeless fuel hit the shoulder of one of the men at the front, but his leather jacket protected him and all four were wearing skid-lids. The calor gas cylinders would make an impact but there were only two and Hetty was reluctant to use them yet.

Bang! And again! The missiles from above were just bouncing off the four men. There was a rending sound. Ruth and Sharon were in the hall. The women had not anticipated a battering ram and anyway there had been no time to pile furniture against the inside of the door. Ruth remembered a poem she had learned at school in Jamaica – not because she had to but because it had taken her fancy:

> *Last night the queen had four Marys.*
> *Tonight she'll hae but three,*
> *Mary Beaton, Mary Seaton,*
> *Mary Carmichael and me.*

Women defending the door. Things run together in your mind. The men who had come to kill the King of Scots had removed the wooden bar from inside the door earlier so that it could not be locked against them. One of the waiting women had put her arm through the iron staples in place of the missing bar while the king cowered in the loo with his trousers down – the 'close stool' they called it then. It had done no good. The murderers had cut through the woman's arm and killed the king anyway.

Bang! The door knob fell off. No time for furniture. Ruth and Sharon flung themselves against the inside of the door with their backs to it. On the first floor Hetty and Karen manoeuvred a calor gas cylinder over shattered glass to the casement.

The four men, making another run, saw something above, and

247

checked. The calor gas cylinder fell just in front of the door and cracked a step before being pushed out of the way. Gary, who was directing operations from the Number Four position, looked up, grinned, gave a two-fingers sign and they were ready to go again.

Noreen came up behind Hetty with a bucket of soiled nappies: she did not use disposables because of the expense. As the battering ram hit the front door again and it began to split, she emptied the bucket. It was particularly fortunate that the two men at the front looked up in contempt and triumph as she did so.

Filthy and foul-smelling, the attackers were rattled. It was time for the second cylinder. Bingo! This time no leather jacket could protect a shoulder. 'I've had enough,' the injured man said to Gary, and his mate was in agreement. 'Teach 'em a lesson, your bloke said – well, we have. I'm going.' All four returned to their motorbikes.

Safely in shelter, Geoff said to Robert, 'I don't think we're needed.' The women at the casement stood watching and cheered, and Ruth and Sharon heard them downstairs and joined in.

Four motorbikes in retreat. 'They're going! they're going!' But one of them was not going.

Gary made a wide turn and headed back towards the house, gathering speed. Robert stepped out of cover, 'Where's he going?' and he and Geoff began to run towards the house. Gary was making straight for the battered front door. The steps were shallow: they did not impede him. He rode into and through the door, the Angel of Death in black leather and a skid-lid.

An iron frying pan swung through the air and struck the revenging angel on the side of his helmet. Gary Hawes lay on the floor, not knowing what had hit him, with Hetty and Karen, each with a frying pan ready to strike again, stood over him. The siren of an approaching police car could be heard by all.

Robert stood at the smashed entrance, not in tears but certainly anxious, with Geoff behind him. Hetty said, 'You can't come in. No men allowed.'

The Battle of Begwyn House was over. Peter Parmenter, with or without his partners, would have a lot of explaining to do to the police and although, given the necessity for secrecy, it was unlikely that he would be charged, his claws were pulled.

Hetty sat in her own armchair in her own front room, sipping a glass of Dubonnet with her own husband gazing at her from the armchair opposite and her associate, Geoffrey Shawcross, hovering at the door unsure whether this was one of those moments when two's company and an associate makes a crowd.

Robert said, 'Are you sure you're all right, love?'

Hetty considered the question. Was she? She'd been through a lot, learned a lot, shared a tiny bit of her life with some unhappy and desperate people, been (she supposed) in some danger towards the end.

The truthful answer to her husband's question floated to the top of her mind. 'I've never enjoyed meself so much in all my life.' She began to laugh.

Hetty's laughter grew and went out of her control. Robert caught it. When it had subsided into no more than manageable chuckles, he got out of his chair, went to his wife, gave a half bow and said, 'Would the Woman of the Year care to dance?'

She put down her glass, stood and moved into his arms which were held ready. 'It's not just for a year as far as you're concerned, Robert Wainthropp. It's for ever.'

He began to 'la la' but she shook her head; she knew the tune.

It was inside both their heads, locked in by memory; they danced to the music they had both first heard long ago, before they ever come to the village, before they were even wed, by a lake in a park with a bandstand and the bandsmen in red and gold improbably playing a waltz. They had eaten their sandwiches by the lake and then stood up and waltzed together to the music of the brass band by the lake. They had been courting, and that evening he had popped the question.

Geoff knew none of this. He could just see two people, whom he knew by now he loved, happy together and locked in total privacy, excluding him. Wet eyed he left the room, closing the door softly behind him.